WHAT WE

REMEMBER

WHAT WE

FORGET

THE BEST YOUNG WRITERS
AND ARTISTS IN AMERICA

A **PUSH** ANTHOLOGY

WHAT WE
REMEMBER
WHAT WE
FORGET

THE BEST YOUNG WRITERS AND ARTISTS IN AMERICA

A **PUSH** ANTHOLOGY
EDITED BY DAVID LEVITHAN

SCHOLASTIC INC.

NEW YORK   TORONTO   LONDON   AUCKLAND

SYDNEY   MEXICO CITY   NEW DELHI   HONG KONG

No part of this publication may be reproduced, stored in a retrieval system, or transmitted in any form or by any means, electronic, mechanical, photocopying, recording, or otherwise, without written permission of the publisher. For information regarding permission, write to Scholastic Inc., Attention: Permissions Department, 557 Broadway, New York, NY 10012.

ISBN 978-0-545-39714-8

12 11 10 9 8 7 6 5 4 3 2 1   12 13 14 15 16 17/0

Printed in the U.S.A.   40
First printing, June 2012

The text type was set in Electra LH.
Book design by Natalie Sousa

Editor's Note

This book marks the fourth PUSH anthology of the best young writers and artists in America. As with previous editions, the selections you are about to read and view have been chosen from the winners of the Scholastic Art & Writing Awards. This time, the writing and art were chosen from a four-year period, 2008 through 2011. It was by no means an easy task to cull the thousands of pages of winners from those years into the collection here. I am grateful to Erin Black, Justin Beltz, Zakary Grimshaw, and Rebecca Leach for their help in evaluating and compiling the work.

What struck me about the works in this anthology is the clear-eyed consideration that the authors and artists give to the world around them. It is a common criticism of teenage work that its gaze only falls internally, that teenage writers and artists can rarely see much further than themselves. The art created here, however, is reflective in much more than a mirror sense. The physical world around the artists comes alive. The people around them are given the dimension of human beings. The greater world looms large, while the details of everyday life fall into·

haphazard place. There is plenty of first person here, but these are *I*'s that are engaged by the *you* and the *us*.

It is heartening to me that a culture that pushes us further and further into disconnectedness, that diminishes the value of the actual and the articulate, can still produce writers and artists like this. I am grateful that for a couple hundred pages, we can see what they see and hear what they hear. It's the saving grace of any generation, to unleash the observers into the world, and partake in what they share.

— David Levithan

Table of Contents

Our City Undressing

I'm thinking about my last visit to Memphis,
the night I paused to watch a hungry wren
peck a cigarette stub beneath the overpass.

Its slow burn etched itself into the trembling branches
of an oak tree and the privacy held with each
stirring leaf in autumn took with it the only
childhood I could afford,

the whistling of a night train quieted on Quince:
which might have, for this poem, carried my father
into Yazoo City for the first time,
for the next nineteen years.

I could say I was alone then,
barefoot and blameless like the black kids
from Nicholtown —

who in those days buried themselves under
the chipped treasures of cedar mulch
in search of a dead girl's bones behind our schoolyard —

and I could say their flight from this town was seasonal,
like the tides scratching against a river's shore
in Yaoundé, Cameroon,

where you wish for a father who can hold you & hold you.
Iris, I'm worried about these absences.

Any day now my father could circle a field in Mississippi
and depending on the direction of the wind, decide
once he reaches the prison's boundary line
he'll cross it.

I can imagine the bullet, rushing through the sky
like a speck, entering him. And for a moment,
just for a time, he would rise.

Then explode. Falling first on his knees,
his opened palms caving:
a slow, stunning wreck.

Before this night ends,
to our fathers:
We were lonesome for you.

After the train rolled away from fifth station
and the living was not easy. After a daughter woke

alone, the night before lost in her memory
when someone danced her all the way to his bed,
spread the ripples out of black sheets
and undressed, no. Stripped her.

Often, we hold each sorrowing
like the sky keeps smoke in its bassinet.

Long after the wind has blown,
and someone finds a missing girl's shoes,
her dress beneath the roots of this land.

We knew you would and yet,
still asked you not to hurt us.

Marionettes

Reason being, the first time I visited my mother in prison,
I couldn't help thinking things would be easier if they'd kept
    her there.

The officers, who had nothing better to do but walk in
    circles —
always, fingers on their pieces — thought our linked hands

were for prayer, as if we could possibly remember any God.
It's only that I've tried everything but giving in.

Past those green fields of bowing buffalo, the lake
where geese argued like homeless men over dimes,

that Texas Longhorn — one solid, brown fixture
of pure animal — let barbed wire dig into her nose,

because she suffered like the rest of us.
Not that you deserve it but I'll tell you —

I've been selfish. Those March nights
my mother was pregnant, I watched her

standing alone in the darkness of our kitchen,
holding her belly so tight as if the baby were about to fall out,

and I cried because I knew she didn't want to fail this one.
Maybe that spring, she thought those water tupelos,

the baby turtles who had yet to see this fractured world,
wanted to keep her dusty vodka bottles, the red
Versace symbol tattooed along her spine.

But we were both children, who for the first time
took one step into Earth and liked the way

it felt against our feet. Once in a dream
she told me if we were a family of birds

we'd be hawks, our heads stuffing into our backs,
our shoulders lifting like marionettes.

We'll live, she said, *in a letter*. A *b* or a *g*.
Leaving the past behind like shadows,

like the footsteps we take after church when God
gets to see how ugly we can be to one another.

Sometimes, I wish I had the courage to love her,
despite the way, when I was seven, she took my face

in her hands and slapped me like an animal.
In that moment I could have snatched her,

shaken her shoulders until the strings
connecting us fell from my fingers,

and wrapped my arms around her waist,
even though we both knew she didn't deserve it.

Last time we'd been to that lake
my mother leaned over the dock's edge

so she could look into her own eyes
and see how the world had its way with her.

I know my own story. My mother made a rose
from cardboard and toilet paper in her cell,

scribbled over it with broken pieces of crayons,
and somewhere on the stem, in a place I can't find,

she's written our names. It's not what I've wanted
to protect her from the image of what's left:

the black specks stained to her lips,
the few eyelashes she has yet to pull.

Rather, I'm trying to protect myself from fearing
that the day she dies I won't be sorry.

Maybe hours after the storm she'll ask me if I can whistle,
if I know how to roll my tongue in the language

of pigeons, and nothing will have mattered.
You would have lied too.

Because who am I to tell her that last night's lightning,
the skeletal interruption of her sky, wasn't beautiful?

For a Missing Mother

That afternoon we found you crazed and crumpled on third in
    the baseball field,
its diamond dust a swirl embracing the three of us, someone
    flowered
your face in bruises, wrecked your nose and left it hanging.

A girl I knew lost her entire left side in a wildfire and the day
    she promised
I would not suffer from anything weathered or smoldering,
was not the night she pictured in our garden.

We lit every bittercress and watched the white petals double
into themselves like napkins, spread every ash over the bird bath.
Mama, each star above shined for us:

The tender accidents we've made. I know it was the aching
you did not mean to hold me so close & still don't.

                                             – Victoria Ford

Noise

A boy asks me why I'm so quiet.
His words are loud and smiling; he
asks me why those
Chinese girls never talk.

And I tell him:

Boy
when I walk I
don't just move upon the earth but
with each step I
make the world

Spin.

Sweetie
when I dance the
soft padding of my feet
makes the ground

Tremor.

Baby
when I sing, my heart throbs
against my voice and I
make the air

Quiver.

And honey
I may not be
the loudest girl you know
and I may not be
one to scream my words
and I may not be
someone who
fills the air with useless babble —
but when I speak, yes,
when I whisper I
make men

Listen.

– Vivian Truong

All Lights Coming at Us from the Sound

And there is the wedding tonight on the beach, all the guests dressed up and it rains and I'm there to film, given a camera older than myself to hold and thank God it's a short ceremony because I almost drop it it's so heavy. Everyone looks up and the bride comes down from the big winding stairs in the reception hall, where the ceremony relocates during the storm. And she walks to where her husband stands, where I stand with my arms shaking under that heavy thing, recording this moment in sharp black and white. The camera drifts to Erin, her standing in the corner, pinned up, her blue dress, her face soft in all the light coming in through the windows — it's still sunny even though outside it thunders. The bride begins to speak and I focus back on her, and she says "I do" and she's kissed, and she and the groom have their first dance and they eat; Erin and I sneak out to the beach when we notice it stops raining. Now it's dark, two hours of wedding gone by the same way all weddings do. We take off our shoes and run out to the water, the sound lit up with the skyline of the city and all those apartments on the water.

A wedding arch is in the sand, this one cheap plastic, made to stay outside and get wet, and we walk over to it, cautious of the instinctive kiss these things provoke. But there isn't any tension, us three years apart, friends since elementary, Erin going off to college soon while I'm starting sophomore year.

This is what we share before she leaves for college: the simple beach, the same loud wedding songs drowned out by the tiny waves lapping at our feet, the bell buoys.

Your mom said there's a lesbian wedding upstairs, she says.

Really? I say.

Yeah, she says. We should check it out.

So we walk to a gazebo and pluck the sand from our feet, carefully putting on our shoes. And we slip back in unnoticed, making for the doors to the hallway when my mom spots us. You! she says. We need you.

Us?

Yes, Mom says. The DJ won't let anyone dance till someone swing-dances first. And you're the only ones who know how.

Oh. We don't know that much, Erin says. Only a few steps. And we know different styles.

I'm Lindy Hop, I say.

I don't even know the name of mine, Erin says.

Well . . . practice for a few minutes, Mom says. And then go to the dance floor. Because I want to dance, goddammit.

So we slip out into the hall, standing there for a moment, laughing, thinking about summer. This is the first time we've seen each other in months, but here we are, we're making jokes, we're acting like we did when we were young. This is what we do, climb deep into the nostalgia of our roots. And now we teach each other our respective styles, humming what few swing songs we know to catch the beat. Rock-step, back, forward, and kick. You got it. Alright. You ready? Let's do this.

12

And the doors open and we walk onto the floor, all giddy with everyone watching, with everyone waiting to be dazzled with our flips and spins and jump-kicks, but we do none of those. We only know the simple stuff, the stuff they teach old married couples who go to dancing classes to add excitement to their lives. But here we are, look at us, alternating jumps and steps; I spin her out and in, her hair flying up like a second dress, and we just keep on, smiling, and it's good and simple and beautiful and I'm laughing, and she's laughing and people start to clap along. And we become a blur of brown and blue, we're improvising, making up moves. We're like marionettes with our clumsy feet, but it's good, and it's simple and beautiful and it's frustrating. And the song ends and we leave the floor with applause, sitting down, exhausted, us red in the face. I excuse myself for the bathroom, the door to the men's room slams when I walk in, checking under all the dirty stalls for shitting feet, and I curse.

This time last night it was just me and a phone and I lie on my bed in the dark, Elliott on the other end, us making small talk to keep from doing homework. What's the assignment again, for English? Uh . . . well, you had to read those two books over the summer. Well, yeah, I read those, of course. Oh . . . well, you have to write an essay about your best friend or something. Oh, yeah, right, who did you do? I did Erin . . . did you do yours yet?

No, Elliott says. I'm not sure who I should write about. Maybe I'll combine a few friends into one.

I did that a bit for my essay about Erin, I say. Just to be able to write more. I feel like a part of us was lost. She's been at summer camp so I haven't seen her in months. But we're going to a wedding tomorrow night, I say. And I can't wait.

Erin's the one who's old enough to be your mom, right? says Elliott.

Hah, no, I say. She's three years older. But we've known each other since we were kids.

A silence comes and then I can only hear his exhales coming in, distorted through the phone. I've only known this Elliott a year, but now every night there's always us on the phone, always us finding something to talk about: our friends and all the countries we'll never visit, all the places we'll never see.

A man walks into the bathroom while I stand so close to the mirror scowling and it fogs up from all that swearing. I see him and pretend to blow my nose, and I walk back out, walking back into the wedding room, and Erin comes up. Alright, let's check out that *other* wedding, she says.

So we're sneaking out again, down the hall into the elevator, feeling once more like we're young, making faces in the slick black of the reflective walls all around us, and we stick out our tongues and cross our eyes and laugh, and it's good, and Erin fixes her hair.

I'm still not sure if I should write about you or Mary or Greg, Elliott says. Too many to choose from.

I don't know what you'd be able to say about me, I say. I mean all we do is talk on the phone.

Yeah. You're boring, Elliott says, and he laughs. Maybe I'll write my essay about a friend of mine who's secretly gay, he says, and no one suspects but me.

Awesome, I say. Good luck with that.

*   *   *

14

The elevator opens and Erin and I step off and start down the hall, the music from the upstairs wedding room low and droning. Erin bites her lip, expecting strobe lights and erotic dancing. We turn the corner; outside the wedding room, two people sit on the floor, their heads hung, bored enough to look dead. But Erin walks right by, peeking into the room from the doorway to find everyone sitting, all those people quiet around round tables, conversation already exhausted. Drat, she says. This sucks.

Honestly, I'm surprised no one suspects, I say.

Because it's true? Elliott says.

No, I say.

Well, you *do* find a new girlfriend every two days, he says.

Yeah. I guess I'm just good like that, I say. But . . . I can't tell when girls flirt.

Yeah, same here, he says.

When they flirt I just think they're being nice, I say. And then, bam, they're my girlfriend. I don't know how it happens.

Yeah, he says. I mean, I like girls . . . pretty girls, but they do nothing for me.

So what does that mean? I say.

I don't know. What do you think it means?

I guess we're asexual.

Yes, he says. We're asexual.

And we laugh at this; we laugh at all the girlfriends we've had and their faces, and the way they kiss and the way we look at them with their eyes closed, leaning in.

But in all seriousness, he says. Are you?

Back down we take the stairs, Erin exaggerating disappointment to entertain me, to make me laugh. The stairs, big and winding, are almost too grand for this place on the beach; a chandelier hangs and it's so close it sways when we walk by, through the lobby, and we can hear music from our wedding hall again, all those same party songs muffled by big doors. That was so disappointing, Erin says. I wanted girls popping out of cakes.

Is that really what you want? I say. Because, you know, I can arrange that.

Well, I feel like we're both avoiding the question . . . , I say, now biting my lip in the dark. So are you, or are you not?

Am I asking or telling? Elliott says.

What?

I asked you first, he says.

No fun, I say.

I asked you first.

Well, I say, I mean it seems like we're both trying to say it without actually saying it here. I feel like we're both too afraid, or something, like if we —

I'M FUCKING GAY.

And I stop. Elliott's words bring a silence and I'm sitting up now in my bed, breathing fast, hunched over, and he's breathing hard into the phone, I can feel it.

And he says, You don't have to respond to that.

No, it's okay, I say. Me too.

And Erin and I sit back down at our table, and it feels like it's the first time we've sat all night, so we pick up our forks and eat, and I'm thinking about her and the wedding and how — fuck — I want this, this is bullshit, I fucking want this. I want a wedding with a woman, with dancing, with swing dancing, and cake, and hair flying up, and I want a house and a kid and a yard and I want to build a tree house. And Erin chews her food, and I'm just sitting there, staring at all those dancing people.

I want to introduce you to Erin, my mom says, coming up from behind with some woman she knows. Erin's my future daughter-in-law, she says, and Erin smiles and laughs and I'm just staring at all those dancing people. And Erin gets up and goes to the bar to get some virgin drink and she asks if I want any, and I say no, barely audible over all the music. And she goes up to the bar and gets a drink for me anyway, me at the table just staring at all those dancing people, all together; they've all got their own rhythm, all smiling and they're all pretending that this is their wedding day, too, and for a moment all that young love is alive like it was twenty years ago inside them, and I'm watching them. I wish I had that old camera now, that ancient thing on my shoulder. I wish I could film this, could film everyone's faces and feet, stepping in and out, each couple synchronized. And Erin comes back with a drink she got for me, and she raises her glass and says, Let's make a toast, just us. To not losing touch when I go to college. And to never change or keep secrets. And to get married and adopt a bunch of babies. And I'll be an actress and you'll write all the movies I'm in, she says, and we'll be happy. And our glasses clink, and she smiles so I smile and we drink, and we take in big sips of whatever it is we're drinking and she puts her drink down and wipes her mouth and I just keep staring at all those people dancing.

– *Domenic D'Andrea*

17

Speedbird

The first time I took Adderall, I whacked a boy over the head with *Allez, viens!* Our real French teacher was pregnant, and under the care of a substitute who spoke halting Spanish, we were not doing our crossword puzzles. Instead, an eighth-grade boy stood over a sixth grader, his hands wrapped around her neck. My muscles twitched. "Stop!" I screamed, but not loudly enough for the sub to hear over his acid jazz. But he heard when I wonked the book down.

My mother picked me up from Northeast Junior High in her Buick.

"What's wrong, honey?" my mother said, rubbing my shoulder.

I explained the story, sobbing. And I continued crying, clutching my heart all week, smearing the ink on the Peanuts strip that I read during Saturday detention.

Finally, as we drove to Domino's, my mother called the HMO. "Hello," she said. "My daughter's member number is 03-174-584. She started taking Adderall last week and now she can't stop crying."

She dropped me off outside Walgreens. I sat on the curb of Lowry Avenue, pizza box on my lap, sobbing. "Here," my mother said, sitting down next to me. She offered me a diet cream soda and half a Xanax. I dug my face into the faded floral shirt covering her belly.

When I rubbed my eyes again, everything was calm and drenched in light.

Two years later, writing a paper on "Harrison Bergeron" at 11 P.M., I should have considered why I stopped taking Adderall in seventh grade and switched to Prozac. I did not. Instead, I remembered an article in the Strib about the speed market in Dinkytown. University kids took it to study.

I remembered briefly the *Allez, viens!* incident, but I wrote it off, thinking: I was eleven, and now I'm almost fourteen. I'm practically a university kid. I can handle this.

After forty-five minutes, it didn't seem to work, so I took another. And another three hours later when the first seemed to wear off. Then one after Popular Song Writing at the water fountain in front of Algebra II.

For the next month, I continued in this fashion.

I loved my life on Adderall. I constantly felt blessed: at lunch, as I drank a plastic bottle of Coke Zero and ate pickles and carrots with mustard from the salad bar and joyously read about Mesopotamia; during the night, as I shot pictures of myself in my underwear and found those pictures on thinspiration sites; after school, when I sat in the glass library downtown. Every moment save for those on Thursday mornings when I had to abstain. My mother drove me out to the Eating Disorders

19

Institute in St. Louis Park. They would draw blood and I had to come up clear for amphetamines.

"God, Mom," I said, "this is ridiculous. I do not have an eating disorder." I took the swig that finished my Diet Coke and cracked open another.

"Yeah, well, tell that to Dr. Reeve," she said, taking a bite of her peanut butter sandwich. We drove opposite rush hour.

"Even so, why do we have to go all the way out to *St. Louis Park*? They're a bunch of suburban bourgeoisies."

Unlike the Regions Hospital, where my psychiatrist worked, Methodist Hospital smelled like salmon. I strolled through the automatic doors, drinking my third can of Diet Coke, and into a purple box. On the floor, purple carpet; on the walls, purple wallpaper; on the elevator door, a purple sign asking in Helvetica "Do you binge eat?"

We rode to the fourth floor, where only the wallpaper was purple. I crushed my can and stuck it in a potted palm.

"Oh, Emi," my mother said. "Take it out."

"I'm just storing it there, Ma."

I sat in the reception area of the Eating Disorders Institute. The EDI is a place of tapping feet, sagging pants, and Citizen watches swinging loose on thin arms. It hadn't occurred to me that having an "eating disorder" would allow me to schmooze with the rich. Instead, I — wearing a skullcap to hide my greasy hair — resented them and resented the fact that I was there. While I may have been losing seven pounds a week, the impulse definitely seemed different between the girls in Juicy sweats and myself. I had never started out on a diet. I had set out on a mission to destroy myself. I probably would have managed without the Adderall, but I blame it anyway.

"Margaret Nietfeld?" a nursing assistant in kitty-printed scrubs called from the doorway. "Can we get your weight today?"

"Hell no," I said.

Nights, I wrote. I tried to analyze "The Rime of the Ancient Mariner." At 3 A.M. I gave up and began writing my "true work": namely, horrible poems. I titled each of them "Ode to Speed."

And I paint my body (in the metaphysic actions)
I am a canvas, and it hurts,
but I am a sail.
And speed, speed, my albatross.

For my mood at the time, "albatross" was grossly inaccurate. I loved Adderall. I had done nothing wrong; I was not ashamed. In fact, I felt pretty badass: As I lost weight, my Levi's hung off my ass. Every day I wore the same pair of 504s and the same XXL black cashmere sweater. Strands of blond hair clumped to it and hung from my shoulders in alarming clumps. I didn't wash my hair, save for the evenings when I ate cookies at readings at the library and then threw up in the shower.

The albatross image never occurred to me as an omen, despite my weekly appointments at Methodist. Now it seems painfully ironic and I seem painfully ignorant. I just liked the way "albatross" sounded, the way it rolled off my tongue after flicking all day the word "speed, speed, speed, speed."

"Wow, Emi," Dr. Reeve — my real psychiatrist — said as she opened her office door, "you look like shit today."

"Thank you," I said, sitting down, in my black parka.

21

"You're not supposed to be happy about that," she said, standing up. "Take off your coat." She cleared plastic dinosaurs from underneath the other padded chair and pulled out a scale.

She worked at Regions, not the eating disorder hospital. I stood in my black sweater and Levi's 504s. "Take off your sweater, too."

"But I'm cold," I said.

"Do I look like I give a shit?" Reeve said, aiming her dark eyes at me. "You come in here, skinnier than last week, with greasy hair. You obviously don't care that I get any sleep at night, so why should I care if you're cold? Take off your other sweaters, too."

So I pulled them all off, threw them on the chair. "I washed my hair last night, Reeve," I said.

"Wash it in the mornings from now on. One hundred and nine." She plopped into her swivel chair, her bob and the venetian blinds casting shadows over her face. "One hundred and nine. Do you still think you're fat?"

I pulled my sweaters back on. "I never thought I was all that fat. I just started losing weight." I sat down and wriggled my arms into my parka. I wanted to tell her about the anorexic I met with a bloated stomach and thin legs, how I thought — delusional — that starvation would be a beautiful way to die.

Dr. Reeve stood up and brushed a lock of her blond bob behind her head. "Well, we can get all Freudian and shit about the deep issues behind your eating disorder once you stop losing weight. But for now I'm going to tell you the opposite of what I tell my obese patients." She drew a pyramid on her white board with "Fruits and Veggies" at the top, "Hungry Man, etc."

22

in the middle, and "Häagen-Dazs" at the bottom. She'd been a French poetry major as an undergrad.

"Do you think you can do this?" she said.

"I already do eat cookies," I said. Although I wanted to, I didn't mention that I only ate the chocolate chips, to supplement my diet of Coke Zero and Adderall. I picked my nails and pretended that I didn't understand how sick I had made myself. My heart jerked and thrashed, my head throbbed despite ibuprofen and Imitrex. I had reduced my personality to sweat-stained T-shirts, coffee, and silence.

She was the only person who seemed to care about me as a person. I trusted her but I wouldn't tell her anything. She would lock me up and put a note in my chart: "Do NOT prescribe stimulants."

"So, Dr. Reeve," I said, looking up at her, "I'm having a hard time concentrating."

"It's because you're *starving*," she said.

"No, I don't think so. I think Adderall would help."

Her face hardened into a grimace.

"There's no way in hell I'm giving you amphetamines." She stood up and walked to the door. "I hope you know that I go home at night and cry because you won't gain weight," she smiled. "And now you think I'm joking. Schedule an hour again next week."

I wanted to tell her that I wasn't losing weight to hurt her. That was merely incidental.

One afternoon in the beginning of November, I found myself with two dollars — bus fare or coffee. I was at Patrick Henry in north Minneapolis, three miles from home, five miles from

23

downtown. I walked downtown. Snow blew. It was minus-4 outside. I felt blessed, chosen by God. I stopped next to 94 at a SuperAmerica and bought a giant Styrofoam cup of coffee and an M&M cookie. My hands were so cold; they didn't want to grip the cup. I stood in the doorway of the bar. Trying to drink, back to the street, snow whipping in my hair. By the time I reached the library the streets were dark. I stood in the bathroom and rubbed my purple hands under the heater.

The next day, I went to Methodist Hospital drinking a can of Diet Coke, with my feet up on the dashboard. I rode the elevator up to the fourth floor, where — for the first time — I did as I was told. I put on the gauze gown, I peed in a cup, I offered my vein.

I sat down on the exam table. A fat nursing assistant took my pulse (42), my reclining blood pressure (90/60), my standing blood pressure (90/40).

The doctor came in. "So, Margaret," she said, "are you still going to deny that you have an eating disorder?"

I looked out the window. Outside, the sun shone on the parking lots and haze draped the office parks and skyscrapers far, far out in Minneapolis. "Yeah," I said finally, "I don't really know what happened." I wanted, suddenly, to tell her about the Adderall, to throw my hands up and say, *"It wasn't my fault!"* And maybe, if I had, I would have followed the twelve steps and not a meal plan. But probably not.

"Well, Margaret, at this point it doesn't really matter. We're admitting you."

I pulled my sweaters on over my furry back. I went back outside. I told my mother. I went to see Dr. Reeve in St. Paul.

"You asked for it." She folded her arms over her chest. "I told you to gain weight and you wouldn't. Do you think I'm going to advocate for you at this point? Get on the scale."

I kicked the dinosaurs away with my sneakers. Sweaters and all, she read off, "Ninety-four pounds. Look, Emi, you have two options at this point. You're smart; you can do whatever you want. Either you can go to Methodist among the prissy suburban girls, wanting to get better, and stay for six to eight weeks. Or you can go, wanting to be sick, and get locked up for a nice long time."

I folded my arms over my chest and briefly considered crying. "I'm sorry," I said. "I didn't do this to hurt you."

"Of course not, you're sick," she said, her face softening. "Don't apologize."

I wanted to explain what happened with metaphoric significance. *I found a golden feather,* I wanted to say, *I followed it to the Firebird and my whole life lit.* But I knew that would have just sounded psychotic.

"Anyway," she stood, "it's up to you now. I'm triple-booked." She led me to the door. "Congratulations, you're my sickest patient."

Wearing a white wool sweater with the left sleeve blackened, burnt from sitting too close to the heater, I rode with my overnight bag back to the Eating Disorders Institute. Tired and cold, I watched nightfall over 94E at 4:00 in the afternoon and drank my last Diet Coke. It began to drizzle and I listened to the windshield wipers.

With ketones in my blood, urine with a specific gravity of 1.04, low blood pressure, with bradycardia and arrhythmia, and a BMI of 14.7, I walked through the automatic doors into the lobby of Methodist. I surrendered myself to reality, to chicken noodle soup, to blind weights and vitals at 5:00 A.M., to shut curtains at 5:00 P.M. We were not allowed to look out after dusk because we could see ourselves in the reflections.

After a week, fourteen viewings of *Elf*, and a tripled dose of Abilify, an atypical antipsychotic, I knit in the dark box of the dayroom. A giant TV lit the room. Our faces glowed green and red in the colors of Christmas.

Around me, the girls of Edina, Lakeville, Eden Prairie, and Minnetonka wore sweatpants printed "Pink" or "Juicy" down the left leg. They tapped their feet as they knit tight rows of afghans. I wore my Levi's and my black cashmere sweater. My hair hung limp over my face. The only person from Minneapolis, I would have fit in better in rehab.

But during the day, through the fog outside the window, I could see Minneapolis. At night, I snuck out of bed and pushed my head under the curtain. All I could see were lights and I clung to them, the last reminders of the life I had left, burning.

Scrambled Eggs

Jaundiced and coated in amniotic fluid, I was born female. I weighed 9 pounds, 8 ounces, stretched to 24 inches, and had an ovarian cyst the size of a chicken egg. As one obstetrician stitched up my mother's episiotomy, the doctors on call filed in to poke my belly in awe. By the time I could walk, the cyst would dissolve, along with its simple declaration of biological sex. Already I was trying to nurse through my father's shirt.

My mother, quickly approaching forty, had wanted a blond daughter to name Honey. She met my father, a blond RN without a place to stay. They married a month later. When she told him she was pregnant, he didn't believe her. And then he said, "I think I'll move back in with my mother." Before he could leave, he pushed a patient in a wheelchair down a flight of stairs, killing him. He lost his nursing-home job and, with it, his patient's drugs. But when my father held me, "he fell in love," my mother said. I slept on his shoulder as he dissected motherboards, watched *Jeopardy!* and shopped Best Buy. My mother couldn't stand being at home with him, so after six weeks of a six-month maternity leave, she went back to work, processing film at the state crime lab.

For all the importance my father placed on having a daughter and not a son (my father abhorred Grason, my mother's son from her first marriage), I was not distinctly feminine. I wore my brother's "ideally unisex" sweatpants and flannel pajamas and a purple and yellow Barney pullover. My brother, who is twelve years older than me, taught me how to do karate and build Lego rockets. He took me by my ankles and swung while I giggled and screamed, spinning. I ate Chunky Beef Sirloin and staged fire-rescue crime scenes. I have a picture of myself at thirteen months, blond-haired in my Barney sweater, inserting a CD into my computer. Instead of ballet or gymnastics, I played kickball in the street and soccer in the alley with a group of kids from the block, their heads swarming with lice.

I hadn't realized any distinction between the sexes until I was pulling on the mandatory skirt for my first day of school. I had known, theoretically, that I had "girl parts" and that my brother had "boy parts," and that's why he was a boy and I was a girl. At Fourth Baptist Christian School, wearing a skirt was necessary to qualify as a girl. I had imagined "school" as a warehouse with a kidney-shaped pool surrounded by desks, where I would learn how to be a firefighter. Or a medical missionary, or a Christian comedian, or a defense attorney. Instead, I learned that instead of saving lives, I should save myself for marriage and follow the gender roles inscribed on the back of the Ten Commandments.

My teachers, concerned with my "unfeminine behavior," called my parents almost daily about my uncombed hair, dirty or mismatched socks, and skirt that flew up on the jungle gym. And by second grade, my floral skirt was too short. Every few weeks, I knelt on the floor in front of the class to test whether my skirt was long enough. The hem never touched the ground; I was tall.

One day, my teacher sent me to have a heart-to-heart with the principal. "Knees," he said, "are fundamentally sexy. We can't allow you to have them show." When I figured out what sexy meant, I didn't understand how legs could fit the bill. But I hadn't watched professional volleyball, either.

My norms for marriage and relationships didn't come from my parents, but from *Leave It to Beaver*, which I watched with my mother while eating Moose Tracks ice cream. Unlike June Cleaver, neither of my parents cooked besides my father's occasional bratwurst on the propane grill or my mother's Pillsbury brownies.

"Mom," I asked, "why don't you cook?"

"I don't have time," she said, sighing. "I work. Why don't you ask your father why he doesn't cook? He's here all day."

"Women cook," my father said. We ate rotisserie chicken and bagged salad on the bed, again.

In front of the television, my mother explained chromosomes and, with them, sex. I was surprised but unshaken. "Sperm cells are tiny," she said. "They don't contain much and they don't have any mitochondrial DNA. The X chromosome is so powerful that only one is activated." The strength of the egg compared to the slithering sperm was clear. "More boys are conceived than girls," she explained. "But more girls are born. The boys die off before they're born."

I pitied boys. Their testosterone-severed corpus callosum made mental math excruciating, their Y chromosomes made reading herculean. I adored my father but knew he had to compensate. Unlike my mom, he lacked a job, biceps, and two X

29

chromosomes. I believed him when he said, "Nail polish is too sexy" and "The Girl Scouts are filled with lesbians." Even more than I was missing out, he was too.

When I was in fourth grade, riding home to watch *ER* at 4:00, he told me, "I'm changing my name to Theresa." His thin blond hair hung down to his shoulders and nubs of breasts stuck out from his shirt because he was so fat. "I was thinking about just changing it to Terry, but I thought I'd just be direct."

"Oh, that's cool," I said.

At Northern Sun, a leftist store downtown, we chose a purple embroidered purse. He bought Birkenstocks. I picked out "Siren" 10-Hour Lipcolor that painted his thin lips orange in our bathroom.

"What do you think?"

"It looks pretty good," I said. I smeared some decade-old lilac eye shadow on his lids. Then he rubbed it off with peach cold cream.

Finally, my father, who had been ordering estrogen online from India, got an estinyl prescription and a lesbian therapist whose parrots imitated the answering machine.

"Ring, ring, ring," one parrot said. I looked up from Stephen King.

"Hello, you've reached the private, confidential line of Karol Jenson," the other parrot cooed. "If this is an emergency, please call 911. Please leave a message after the tone." Sometimes it was not the parrots and a client would begin to speak. So much for "private, confidential."

Karol was the first lesbian I met. She was tall with short hair, although not as tall as Ellen, my father's 6-foot-5 role model. Ellen was curator of the electricity museum in Minneapolis.

30

She transitioned into a woman at fifty. Her wife, Mary (who writes Embroidery murder mysteries), stayed with her even after the surgery. At dinner at Olive Garden she explained, "The trick is to find the ending first." My father smiled.

"Rosella's butch, anyway. She'll stay."

But three weeks later, after my mother delivered the papers, my father broke into sobs at the McDonald's drive-thru. "I can't believe she's leaving me!" he wailed, pounding the steering wheel. I wrapped my arms around him. "That bitch!"

Before the first of endless psychological assessments, my mother, my father, and I went to Perkins. My father wore a skirt.

"What would you ladies like to eat today?" the waitress asked.

"Scrambled eggs." My mother shut her menu.

My father left a ten-dollar tip. I was never together with them again.

Logistics eroded all of my father's relationships. Because my mother wouldn't call him anything but Tom, their lawyers sent their kids to private schools. My father sobbed when I mentioned "my mom," or when his mother forgot he was now a woman. I started calling my mother "R" and he stopped seeing his mother.

Others tried to help work out the worms of the situation. Annalisa down the block gave me a VHS of a transsexual on *Oprah*. My cousin Jessica, who is 6-foot-5 and works for Planned Parenthood, brought my father garbage bags filled with her old clothes. "Have you ever watched *Oprah*?" she asked me. "They had a show on transsexuals. One of the kids said he calls his father 'Maddy.' It's a cross between 'Mommy' and 'Daddy.' Maybe you could call Theresa that." I started calling him "Mom." He just loved that.

In the middle of fifth grade, my father's girlfriend, Susan, moved in. I spent Wednesday nights and Sundays with my mom, digging through the Walgreens clearance and watching *Passport to Paris*, while my father and Susan cruised gay bars and bought cocaine. In the basement, while they shot methadone, I watched *But I'm a Cheerleader* and *My Summer of Love*. *Whoa, that could be me*, I thought, watching the young lesbians kiss. And then I went back to my scrambled-egg quesadilla.

I was everything my father wanted to be. At the Unitarian church's "women's night," complete with hotdish and drums, he whispered to me across the table, "When you menstruate, I'm going to throw a party and buy you a monkey." I didn't think it was *that* big of a deal.

As my parents' day in court approached, the promises grew. "If you come with me, I'll let you get a belly-button ring when you turn thirteen," he said. "We'll do it together. We're going to have a pool in Arizona." But when my mother won custody, we knew that an AMBER Alert would meet me at the state line.

So we hauled the mattress from the basement, unscrewed the bookshelves from the walls, tore down the kitchen table. My father smashed my piano with a Slugger. I carried the pieces out to the fire pit. He lit up a cigarette and then the edge of my mattress, whose flowers melted into its wire springs.

We watched from the patio, drinking white wine and vodka in Squirt, as the flames climbed, catching on the lowest leaves of our oak tree. I packed up the leftovers of my room into a garbage bag.

When the trees turned golden, my father and Susan picked me up from Marcy Open School in their red Ford F-150. With the sunroof open, my father raced me around the block at 80,

85, 90, seeing how fast we could go. We ate falafel on the tail-gate. We hugged good-bye. "I love you, Mom," I said.

There were no drums for my first blood, no dances, just a trip to Rainbow Foods for pads. The June air distilled into beads on my skin. I stuck my feet out the window. It was Father's Day.

– *Margaret Nietfeld*

Sequi

My brother: used to late
       nights, unknown
under a waxing moon, whose missing
quarter I felt I could see, if only
I squinted hard enough. I dream
       of those nights:
when I slept, blind, in a house,
in a bed, and he strode through
woods and over holes in golf greens.
       The scene is full,
the shadows mold his face, remove
his thick glasses: unbrother. Some nights,
I build his path with words, mortared
       in my mind;
others, I can use only
eyes, and the resulting wall stands
more steadfast than Hadrian's.
It is those nights that it's hardest
       to find him, to grasp
his vestiges in the fallen leaves. I can feel

him run, I try to follow at his side,
through paths and undergrowth,
car lots and Air Force bases, across
　　　the world
and back. But I cannot, I could not: my eyes
　　　were not open.

　　　　　　　　　　　　　　　　　　　– Shelby Switzer

Jedi Night

Your real name isn't Jedi. It's Geraldo "Jedda" Muñez. Don't ever forget who you are.

Don't ever.

Jedi is the name I gave you when I was ten. This was around the time the new Star Wars trilogy, the prequels where George Lucas shit his brains out, played in theaters. For a kid like me it never mattered. It was Star Wars, for God's sake.

But this story isn't about Luke Skywalker and Darth Vader or Chewbacca or even Yoda. This is about Order 66. Betrayal.

This story is about you, my favorite cousin in the whole wide world. Mi primo favorito.

You grew up in Washington Heights, the way so many Dominicanos do, and made your way through high school. You did okay and got into college in upstate New York. It's the path of many Dominicans — the path sociologists tell us we follow by nature and the path the media expects us to follow and the path the patriotic citizens of America want us to follow. It is our path. Yours, mine, the path of los Dominicanos. Whether you chose to follow it, to give in, is your own choice.

Not.

Hell no, it's not.

It's the choice of all those other people — the academics and media. It's the decision made by "intellectuals" and "journalists" and "true American citizens." Free will is a joke out of hell. Whoever thinks otherwise es un tonto.

The only way I ever got out was by playing the apple: colored on the outside, white on the inside. When you think like what you're not, you cheat the system. And yourself, I later realized. I always wondered why, when Luke Skywalker had his hand cut off and Darth Vader asked his son to join him, Luke didn't say "Sure, Dad, no sweat!" and then destroy the Empire from the inside. The thing is this: If you follow the set path, whether it's working through the inner ranks or on the cusp of "established" society, you lose your identity anyway. Being a subjugated people means you always lose.

That's what happened to you. By staying true to your path, you didn't stay true to yourself.

I was visiting your campus when the recruiter made his rounds.

"Serve your country."

He was tall and muscular but not domineering. He didn't cast a shadow or look down at you. He looked you eye to eye. Hombre to hombre. Like the guy you'd want to hang out with at the local bar. Like George W. Bush. You know.

You looked at him and nodded absently. He slipped a brochure into your hand. In wide, formal type, type that screamed it knew what it was doing and assured you it understood what was best for you, it read this: HOMELAND SECURITY. You shrugged and slipped it into your pocket, but letters kept coming and more recruiters and more e-mails. What else could you do in life? Paint houses? Mow lawns? Fix toilets? Run a decrepit auto shop in Washington Heights?

Here the path split. You could go that way. You could also try your prospects at policing or a federal job that really meant something.

But either way you lose, hombre. Either way you're screwed.

You don't decide your future. They do.

When you signed up for the Homeland Security job, they gave you a big gun and a shiny holster and a whole new desk to yourself. Of course your work was mostly desk work, but that was how it went. They give you the weapon; you feel the power; you're one of them, end of story.

They had your office in upstate New York, far from family and Washington Heights and los Dominicanos. You left the desk once a month to visit detention centers and talk with illegals. Their holding cells, gray cribs of concrete, stunk of cold piss. You'd go there, cell by cell, and make your rounds. Order of business.

Cell one:

"Jorge Rodriguez . . ." You paused. "Dominican."

The man looked at you, jaw clenched. His muscles tensed beneath his orange clothes. For a moment he looked like an angry clown.

"Sí," he said.

The illegal looked again at you with his whirling, brown eyes and reached for your clipboard and pen.

"Sign here." You pointed. "You are under federal law to speak the truth and nothing but the truth."

The illegal began to sign. The pen ripped the paper — a gentle shriek of tearing filaments and scratching, like a cat clawing at a door. You made him sign again. He was wasting your goddamn time. You clicked the pen once, twice.

"When did you arrive in the United States?"

He breathed.

"Ochenta y seis."

His voice was like nata, the strong layer of hardened milk that settles over coffee. You know that beneath the nata is flowing milk, boiling liquid that can spill or evaporate or swirl or tremble. Beneath is the chaos of hot fluid. You know the truth about this from all the times Abuelita served us café con leche when we visited her apartment. You know Dominicanos love their coffee so hot it scalds their tongues. It keeps us alive.

"English, Mr. Rodriguez. English."

For the third time, his fiery, dark eyes met yours.

"Why did you come here?"

His eyes swiveled toward the window, where light tumbled through the viscous magma of air saturating the holding cell. This light was a constant light, the light of day, and it did not flicker. This was the lightning without the thunder, the storm without the storm.

"Dinero," the illegal said, then corrected himself. "Money. Oppor-tu-ni-ty. Mi familia." He struggled with the English, but it was more than that.

"And?"

His eyes settled on the window. He didn't want to look at you any longer.

"El Jefe," he whispered, and you heard him curse under his breath. He crossed his shaking index fingers. "The Dictator. Trujillo," he murmured to himself. "Veinte años y el espíritu del Diablo nunca se murió."

"English, Mr. Rodriguez. English."

Your friends at work said Arizona was hell. Not that they'd ever been there.

"Goddamn Mexicans are everywhere," one of them told you. "The sons of bitches."

The other guy nodded.

"Yeah. It's like *Invasion of the Body Snatchers* or some shit like that. You can't get away from them. Scares the crap out of you."

Veinte años y el espíritu del Diablo nunca se murió.

Twenty years and the spirit of the Devil never dies.

Once I was at your place and we were in your room with a few other cousins and your buddies. You and the older boys were playing Resident Evil.

"Hermano," your brother Pedro said. "Cool it."

"You're on fire."

"No shit, Sherlock."

On screen your character was slaying zombies like mad. One hand wielded a mighty blue sword that decapitated beasts by the dozens. The other brandished some sort of giant machine gun that fired ten rounds a second; each bullet passed through the chests of two zombies in a row, at least, usually it was three.

You finally sliced the last zombie in half, holstered your gun, and thrust your sword into its sheath. Now it got interesting. You jogged to the side of the field of dead undead and retrieved a blue, pocket-sized machine from your belt. You pressed a button and tossed the device into the center of the vanquished zombies. It hit the ground, igniting into a frosty,

40

yellow mist. Minutes passed. The zombie bodies began to shift. Arms pulled heads to severed necks at the speed water would turn to ice if you pissed into the freezing air of that snow planet, Hoth, in *Star Wars Episode V: The Empire Strikes Back.*

"Shit no," a friend of yours whined. "No fair." His screen had been the first to fill with dripping red.

"Asshole." Pedro punched you in the shoulder.

You grinned.

Now the zombies stood before you, an unending field of conquered peoples: ZOMBIES UNDER YOUR COMMAND.

At this point my mother popped in to see what all the cussing and yelling was about, and when she saw me doing the dog-gape like the rest, she said to you, "Geraldo Muñez, you get here ahora. What the hell is this?" She reached over, got you in a death grip, and flung you out of the room. She pried me from the spot where I'd glued myself to the bed and held me like a mother grizzly bear protects her young.

"Geraldo, you playing these violent games with a ten-year-old around?" she demanded of you. She shook her head and began to mutter to herself. "Coño, niño. Hijo de gran puta!"

I tagged along, unsure of what was wrong.

"Tía . . ." You made your eyes big. "I didn't see him."

"You saw him. You did! Don't lie to me."

"But —" You sighed. "It's just a game. It's not real."

My mother pinched you in the arm. You flinched.

"Who are you to say what's real and what's not? Eh?"

You stood there holding your arm like un tonto as my mother walked toward her bag.

My mother pulled two lightsabers from her bag, put the first in your hand, and wrapped your stiff fingers around its warm

41

hilt. She handed the second to me. My face lit, and I squeezed the lightsaber. She didn't have to force me to hold this, oh no she didn't. I moved into position, beckoning with my free hand.

"Let's fight!"

You shook your head.

"Oh, hell no, Tía. Hell no. I ain't gonna do some kiddie crap —"

My mother gave you the look. The one every mother's got, the one that burns through your soul and squeezes jugo de naranja from your brains. The one you know you don't want to shit around with.

I turned from her to you to her to you.

"Let's fight!" I exclaimed, not knowing what to do. "Duel!" I extended my plastic lightsaber. It was the green one. My favorite. You made your eyes bigger and faced my mother, but she wouldn't give.

"You play with your cousin like you ought to, Geraldo. You hear me?"

You shrunk and entered Spanish mode.

"Sí, Tía. Lo que tú quieres, Tía. Entiendo, Tía."

"The hell you do," my mother shot back. She stalked out.

Behind you I could see Pedro and the other boys peeking through your bedroom door, which you'd left ajar.

"Playtime, Jedda?"

You turned once — this would be the only time you would face them again that day — and yelled, "Shut the f—— up." You faced me. "Alright. So how does this work?"

You fumbled your plastic blade out. It was purple, like Mace Windu's. I always thought Mace Windu was hip since he was the only black Jedi, one step from Latino. He was also the first important good guy Darth Vader helped kill, but that's a matter you've got to take up with George Lucas, and George Lucas has got the whole Clone army, remember? You don't mess with him.

I waved my lightsaber about and you followed. Once I saw your eyes spin a little too far to the side, I swung my weapon into your crotch and giggled.

"Jeez, Miguel." You put a hand between your legs. "Don't play rough."

I jabbed my lightsaber at your bedroom door.

"You did." I smiled. Innocent, honest.

You rolled your eyes, dark suns arching over pale skies. Nevertheless, they were soon glowing moons that reflected the brilliant, white light around them. In the space of an instant you'd changed, forgotten your brother Pedro and the rest.

"Shut your mouth," you said, grinning. "You hit me in the nuts one more time, I'm telling Tía."

I flung the tip of my lightsaber toward yours.

"She won't believe you," I teased.

You shrugged it off, and we sparred.

"You're good," I concluded. "You're like a —" I paused, realizing the sheer gravity of what I was about to say. "You're like a Jedi."

It was Fourth of July weekend and the whole family was over for a barbecue at Coney Island. A good bunch of us hung around a rough wood table sitting in the hot, white sand, just out of the shade of the boardwalk. I was maybe fifteen. You were in your twenties, still working for Homeland Security. I don't think half of us ever thought much about it.

At this point I'd stuffed myself with enough junk food. I walked off to play with one of our younger cousins, kicking a soccer ball back and forth. The hot sun beat on us like hell from above, and the sand beat on our bare feet like hell from . . . from hell. It was Tatooine, home of Luke Skywalker, that searing desert planet George Lucas stole from Frank Herbert's *Dune*. The ocean attacked the shoreline in violent, green-brown cascades of foaming liquid and drifting seaweed.

As I plunged a foot into the freezing ocean, I suddenly heard Uncle Enrique's voice, screaming like the crashing waves, and on occasion Tío Héctor's quiet, accented English. The words themselves were impossible to make out at this distance; the air was thick and unforgiving to the hot turbulence of sound.

"Your f——ing culture!" Uncle Enrique was yelling. He sounded drunk. "Your goddamn f——ing culture and your goddamn f——ing language! You come here and think you can f—— this country to hell."

I stopped and looked. Uncle Enrique was looming over Tío Héctor, engaged in some sort of argument. More of a brawl than an argument, really. I'd never seen Uncle Enrique like this. He was a quarter Cuban, a quarter English, another quarter white American. Related by marriage. Maybe he hadn't always seemed, you know, Latino, but he was my uncle always and you love your people like they're your people because, well, because they're your people. I guess they'd been talking politics and shit, and Uncle Enrique had probably drunk a little too much beer.

44

Tío Héctor, on the other hand, usually didn't say much at all. Today, though, he had to say something back. He had to, short as it was. Even that turned into a bad idea.

"Enrique, you're ignorant." Tío Héctor kept it strong on the top, hot and boiling beneath.

"No!" Uncle Enrique's mouth was wide as a dog's, breathing alcohol and hate and fear. "No no no no no. You're the f——ing ignorant one, you bastard. You think you belong here. You don't. You belong in the Dominican f——ing Republic. You're infesting this country."

Tío Héctor's eyes weren't narrow or big — they were simply focused, hot, on his furious brother-in-law's face. He didn't say a word. He knew words would do no good. There's always a point in your life when your words don't do shit for you, and you got to act. Silence, that's action. Sometimes that's the best action there is, hombre.

Uncle Enrique stomped off drunkenly, dragging his wife with him. He did his best to make noise in the sand. However, sand isn't the kind of thing that booms; it ain't drums and sticks and goddamn percussion. Sand whispers, sand molds, sand burns, but sand does not ever harden.

As family gathered around Tío Héctor, Uncle Enrique reached his car and sped out. The black pavement shrieked at us. My mouth gaped like a dog's. So did yours.

You sat to the side, at that same spot on the rough wood table, no longer sipping your Coke. You'd run out. You had your badge on the table, and your eyes set on the warm grains of sand churning in the wind, which had gone hot as soon as the family clustered around Tío Héctor to offer him comfort.

The entire scene rotated about an indeterminate axis, as if we sat in a boiling cup of café con leche and someone had stuck in a sugar spoon and spun it around un poquito. There was the family moving hurriedly about, the incoherent banshee wail of Uncle Enrique's car, his cracked Budweiser spinning slowly but surely along the pavement. Even you, who sat so still, seemed to catapult through time. I could see your eyes unmoving one moment and flickering the next.

"Miguel, let's play," our little cousin was saying. He had the soccer ball in his hands.

I breathed for a minute and eventually nodded. He tossed the ball. We kicked to each other along a short distance, as if afraid we'd lose one another across the depth of space. Somehow he understood that something was wrong. Like the Force, a powerful interconnection between all things living and dead, burning and freezing.

The party broke off soon enough, and as I walked to my parents' car I saw your badge there on the table, melting in the silence and in the flaming sun. Screwed or not, you'd decided you could serve your country better by serving your people. Good choice, hombre.

I realized then that I was wrong about a lot of things. In a sense this story was more about me than you. I lived life devoid of any Dominicanos but you guys. I thought I was a hard-knocks intellectual, like so many Latinos and so many whites do when they tough it through the heart of a privileged suburban life in America. Meanwhile, you lived scavenging off the Latinos your friends rounded up like cattle.

In both cases, we got soul-f——ed.

So maybe this is about the two of us, and the paths we can

take. And about choices. Us Latinos, we're strong, hombre. We're boiling, we're hot. We burn your tongue and scorch the roof off your mouth. And we don't ever give up. No, hombre, we don't ever. The truth is Latinos always got their Obi-Wan Kenobis and Han Solos. The truth is you can decide your future. It's just freaking hard.

– Haris Durrani

Thread

Something about the way she cries into the phone reminds me of the time I tried to merge our skins together by pressing my hands into the soft of her cheeks. She had opened her eyes then, swept my baby fingers away like dust from freshly washed dishes. I forgave her, thought maybe it was an accidental reflex, uncontrollable. I pushed closer to her again — my eye to her nose — her ear to my mouth, but then she stood up. Sighing, she pulled on a sweater. She had just needed a few minutes to escape reality, to slip into peace and dreams, but it didn't seem like I could let her have even that much. I was her anchor, she told me from the way she picked me up. An anchor that held her down as she sank.

"How can you forget all those years . . ." she tells me now, her voice higher than usual, painful and fragile to perceive like cracked porcelain. I clutch the receiver. Finally, a thread that cuts deeply enough to hold us together. My hand shakes. I catch a tear on the tip of my tongue and wonder if hers is as salty as mine. Is it hereditary, the taste of sorrow?

We are silent for some time, and I hear her sobs recede. I recall a day on the beach when I ran after the ebbing tide, too slow to keep up with it, until it disappeared into the next wave. I had let it escape, lost it, powerless.

"Are you still there?" I whisper.

The flood is over, and now she won't talk anymore. I am not sure who cut the thread this time.

In the empty echoes of a wordless phone conversation, I want to, need to, hang up before she does. Yet in her reticence, I find a motivation that keeps me waiting, hoping, for just one more word.

Isolation, perhaps, so that I know we are together in being alone. So that I can be sure that sometimes, in the darkness that settles before sleep, she hears the voices of all those other children who used to surround me while I watched her retreating back, wondering when I would be old enough to go with her. The years ripened, the children grew up. Yet I still fell short, still stood rooted as she walked away, still lacked whatever it was that would allow me to leave with her.

Maybe *betrayal*, so that she could tell me she feels the way I did when she forgot about me on the curb for five hours. Sitting on the sidewalk, I told myself she had asked the drizzle to watch over me, to act as a shield, as a guardian, should anything bad happen to cross my way. Eventually, the sun emerged from behind the clouds, and I wondered if the rain had to babysit someone else.

Or just *sorry*, because she might be too proud to say it, but I will come running back to her if she tells me she wants me. If she whispers how she misses me, I will tell her I miss her too. If she asks me if I am happy by cutting her out of my life, I will say "no." I know, though, that should I say it all first, she will tell me she needs to hang up now, she needs to go, because something else is waiting to be done. And I will be left with the tone, the monotone, of being alone again.

So instead I say nothing and wait. I wonder if, like I am doing, she is sitting with the receiver pressed to her ear, scouting for the slightest noise — a shaky exhalation, the brush of hair against the mouthpiece, fingertips touching the phone and almost my face. I wonder if she has left the phone on the table to take a pot off the stove before the food burns, to take the washing out of the dryer before the wrinkles dry, or to close the windows before the moths creep in as the sun sets.

I wonder if she thinks I will still be there when she comes back. I press the red button, my lower lip quivering, and tear the thread to shreds. I might be younger than she is. I might be more unwanted than she is. I might be weaker, frailer, and more desperate than she is. But I am learning to let go. I am learning to turn away and leave, and I know — I think — I hope — I am doing it the right way.

I stand up and set the receiver back in its base. It glistens in the light, wet. I slide my wrist across my cheeks and glance at the clock. This conversation was several seconds shorter than the last. I slam the door shut on my way to the bathroom, so that if the phone rings while I am in the shower, I won't hear it.

Because I learned from the best.

— Ayesha Sengupta

An Open Letter to the Suicidal

Dear Person,

I don't know you, but you are the subject of most of my fears, strange as it seems.

I fear for those around you, for those who pass you by every day, taking note of your bright smile without realizing your dark secrets, and yes, I realize that that's cliché, but the point is they don't get it. See, people are supposed to be happy, no matter what, and they hate it when things don't go according to plan, so when they see you hurting, they just ignore it. Because that's not the way it's supposed to go. But I still fear for them, because I dread the day that will come when you're gone and in place of what they thought was a hopeful young person, they find a vast hole, a chasm of memories that they wish they could unremember, sounds they wish they could unhear, moments they wish they could unlive. But they can't, and they never will. And I fear for them, because for the rest of their lives, all they'll remember of you is what they wished they had done, even though they never could have seen it coming.

(I say this because I knew a girl who killed herself, knew in the sense that I spoke to her once freshman year at the squash

51

courts. She was short, with black hair and a mind that filled pages with the products of an angsty teenage life. I could have gone to the Columbia University writing program last summer, which she attended, but I didn't. Maybe if I had, I wouldn't have felt so weird about crying the night after she died. Her poetry was so succinct, so beautiful, the literary embodiment of her life. Sometimes when I close my eyes, I feel her tears.)

I fear for your best friend, the person who knows your thoughts better than most people know your words. Surely they will have some idea, some vague notion that you're pondering the worst, surely they must know, but they'll never say anything. Nobody wants to take that trip, nobody wants to verbalize that thought, because they're afraid of the answer, choosing to deny the painful truth rather than admit your agony to themselves. They would rather turn their backs on your torture than risk even imagining you gone. But surely they knew. And surely the moment they find out, they'll be inundated with shame, plagued by questions of whom to blame, which will, inevitably, be themselves. They'll beg, crying out to whatever god they believe in to please help, please bring you back, please wake them from this dream. But it won't be a dream. I fear that they'll be crushed by guilt, guilt that nobody should incur. They'll hear your voice in every song, see your face in every picture, feel your warm embrace whenever they shiver. Alone, cold, bombarded by the winds of life, they'll call out your name and wish, just wish, that you were there. But all that wishing will amount to nothing.

(I had a friend who almost killed herself. She was naive and beautiful, conditioned to laugh like every other freshman did. She was secretly dark and broken, tortured by monsters that she didn't deserve, the products of a splintered family and a taxing schedule. She couldn't take the criticism at home or the lack of understanding at school, so she cut herself until the blood running down her arms assuaged her deepest demons. One night she called me to say good-bye, and the next day she wasn't in school. Nor was she the next. She was OK that time, but I always wondered. Always worried that the next day she'd be gone, and there'd be nobody to blame but me. I used to lie in bed, unable to sleep in case she would call. See, I thought that if I answered the phone, I could save her life, bring her back from the edge of the cliff. Sometimes, lying there in the dark, I would reach up and try to hug her soul.)

I fear for the world that you will leave, for the people who will cry at your funeral, the ground that will be dug up to allow for your misery, the classes at school that will be tragically left with one more empty chair. I fear for the swings that will remember your juvenile laughter, hearing the joy you harbored in the years before life became a burden. I fear for the music you'll never listen to (at midnight, when the utter silence of your house starts to become overwhelming), and more importantly, the songs you'll never sing, the repressed notes that will never come out of your mouth as vocal representations of the self you never showed. I fear for the poems you'll never write, the verses that won't flow like blood through the veins of your pen onto the tear-stained page. I fear that the only short story you'll ever write will be the note you leave behind before it's all over.

(I believe in the power of music to save lives. It's a cliché, but I remember long nights talking to my girlfriend, YouTube-ing songs because that's how I could save her life. Some of them we listened to for hours on end, just hitting replay and being infused time and again with hope that the struggle wasn't in vain. Maybe it sounds silly but it really felt like every word was life or death, the latter approaching with each passing second and the former only possible through placing our trust in the power of song. I used to send her MP3s when she wanted to cut herself, like the lyrics were little pairs of lips that could kiss her scars and set her at peace, spurning misery with love and healing her wounds. I think sometimes they were.)

This will sound selfish, but I'm also afraid for myself. For the last four years, there's always been one point or another where someone was dangling off the edge, tempting fate in threatening to let go. Suicide has been a presence in my life, like the awkward friend who follows you around and whom you just don't have the heart to tell to go away, or like the teacher who constantly berates you on the idiosyncrasies of your work, keeping you up at night with worry. Suicide was my Minotaur; I often felt like Theseus, roaming a cryptic labyrinth in order to fight a terrible monster. Theseus knew that the Minotaur was stronger than him, and that given a fair fight, the Minotaur would win. He knew that he may never find the Minotaur, and wander forever in the labyrinth like a 1960s Beat poet on a bad trip. But he knew he had to at least try, because the only thing worse than getting killed by the Minotaur would be not fighting the Minotaur at all, and leaving Athens subject to the cruel caprice of its fearsome evil. As pompous as it is to compare myself to a Greek hero, that's what I often felt like. I felt as though I was locked in a battle, David versus Goliath, for the sanity and safety of my friends (and also myself), one that I could not afford to lose. Every day I hugged them, striking a blow, but every night the phone calls piled up and I was inundated with the guilt and shame of failure. I think that's why it hurt so much when the girl I didn't know killed herself. Because up until that point, I was winning, subjugating suicide with the meager weapons I have (words, love, music). But suicide got me back, and that hurt. So I hope you won't be insulted that I'm afraid for myself. Perhaps you think it's silly or even disrespectful that I, one who doesn't know you (maybe), would claim to have such a personal stake in your struggle. It's just that I'm not sure I can look at myself in the mirror and claim victory over suicide. And victory over suicide has been all I've really wanted for the last four years. So please forgive me, but I fear for myself as well.

My fears aside, I have some questions. I hope you won't find it disparaging to be questioned on such an intensely personal matter by a high school writer whom you've never met (probably), but I've had four years to think about suicide, and the questions in my mind regarding it are numerous. Questions like, What will happen when you die? Not in the sense of the afterlife (or lack thereof), but in the sense of what will actually happen. What will it feel like? Will it be like a Band-Aid, ripped off quickly without full awareness of what's happening? Like falling asleep, your mind slowly taken away into the realm of nothingness to which we all return someday? Or will it be like a dentist's appointment, the feeling of dread setting in as the dentist rakes your teeth with instruments that vibrate in a torturous rhythm, the intrusive discomfort that invades your entire being just before the tools are removed and a cool calm washes over you, a smile returning to your face. Is that facetious of me, to compare suicide to a dentist's appointment? Perhaps, but the question remains: Does death come quickly, before you even realize what's happened, or does it come only after the enormity of the decisions you've made has occurred to you?

The question that always occurs to me is, Who do you think will find you? My biggest fear in eighth grade, bigger than the fear that my friends would stay home and never come back, was that I would find one of them, sprawled out in some room in the basement, eyes closed in peace, feigning sleep. I wouldn't have been able to handle that, because what could I do then? Look on in disbelief, as if standing very still would change the scene in front of me? Cry? Tears for me always tasted like salty defeat, their presence streaming down my face like the most fragile effusions of my soul flowing out and enveloping me in weakness. The sight of a friend in front of me, killed by their own hand, would have driven me to insanity.

(It almost happened once. That girl, the pretty one I mentioned before, she handed me a note, crumpled and folded like the cruel partition of her life. It was about 7:45 in the morning, and she walked out of the room just after giving me the note, like she was going to class. I unfolded the note, and read what seemed to be an irrevocable ultimatum: "I'm sorry. Bye." I ran, carried by legs of desperation to the room in the basement where I knew she'd be. I knocked once. Silence. Twice. Silence. A third time. The door slowly swung open, the motion dripping with reluctance. There she stood, eyes flooded with tears and a knife in her right hand. Pushed to the brink, but alive. For the first time in what seemed like hours or years, I exhaled.)

But the biggest questions in my mind are the ones that I can never answer. Questions like, What led you to this? Every high school life is tenuous, like a bird holding on to an electric wire during a storm, but what led you to let go and allow the storm to take you under? It might seem strange that I ask that question, but it's a wonder to me, how quickly stress turns to coping turns to depression turns to thoughts of suicide. Perhaps it's the psychologist in me, or perhaps it's just some twisted side of my conscience that longs to understand what drives us to the edge, but that question, the question of why, is omnipresent in my thoughts.

Maybe it's because I want you to understand. Let's face it, even if I understand why you want to kill yourself (sounds scary when you put it that way, right?), there's not much I can do. Ultimately, the decision is yours. So maybe I'm just hoping that you're questioning whether this is really what you want, whether the accumulation of miseries that you've encountered sums up to this. Does it scare you to think about it? My friends always told me it did, that the notion crept into their thoughts like a silent bandit, tortured them with demeaning slurs, and absconded with their peace of mind, leaving them more scared and alone than before. It's a scary word: suicide. It reeks with the putrid prospect of impending catastrophe, singing eerie tunes into the ears of those who hear it. Just that thought, "I want to kill myself," is not one to be thought lightly. In some ways I feel for you, you being those who have had that thought before, had it recurring like the jingle of a bad commercial in your head. I feel for you because I cannot possibly imagine how terrifying it must be to have that thought on a daily basis.

I think that happens to the rest of us, too; we all realize when somebody is struggling, but nobody wants to take that step, nobody wants to say the S-word, because that makes it real. That makes it possible, and nobody wants to think that suicide is possible. Realizing that someone wants to kill themselves is the worst feeling in the world. All the questions I've asked here pop into their heads like flashbulbs, stalking them with the unremitting fervor of a virus. Stress is inherent in the high school experience, so it's easy to brush off someone who's been crying. It's easy to pretend like suicide is only for the crazies, not us (because we're all perfectly normal, right?). Even like it's something to be invoked in jest (how many times have you heard somebody say "I have so much work tonight, I'm gonna kill myself"?). I think in the back of our heads, we all realize that it's possible, that it's really just an additional symptom of the stress syndrome we've all inherited by becoming a part of the "higher-education system." It's easy to see high school as a four-year battle with tests and papers, fought in order to win the privilege of fighting a harder battle with harder tests and harder papers, and in that context, it's difficult to see the end. I think we all realize that some people would choose to forfeit the battle, and in doing so reinforce the magnitude of it. But nobody wants to acknowledge it. Nobody wants to make it real, even when we all know that we have to. Sometimes, given the choice between saving a person's life and upsetting the delicate equilibrium of our own, we choose ourselves, simply out of a desire to remain ignorant of the harsh realities that the battle entails. When the girl killed herself earlier this year, I think everyone at my school took a step back, and realized what was actually at stake. We all wished that we had stepped off the battlefield for a second in order to help one of our own. We all regretted our incessant obsessions with our own lives. We all took a second to reflect on the fragility of the balance upon which we walk. But mostly, we all took a second to wish things were different.

At this point, you're probably wondering why I'm writing this. Sure, I've told you a lot about my past and my general musings on suicide, but I wouldn't be writing this if that were all I wanted to do, right? There must be a point. And really the point is that I want you to understand a few things.

First, you're not alone. I know, it's cliché, but often our most trying endeavors can feel in vain, simply because it seems like nobody understands. Everyone feels that way sometimes, no matter how they choose to cope. The world moves at light-speed, and sometimes we all feel left in the dark. And when things get to the point where we decide to opt out, it can feel even lonelier. But hopefully you've seen in this that you're not alone; I am constantly thinking about you, praying for you, worrying for you. It may seem to be all in vain. Perhaps. But I don't believe so, because I believe truly that love will save the world. You feel the way you do because of a deficiency of love, whether that's from your parents, from your peers, or from yourself (most likely the latter). But if someone can be there to embrace you with all your flaws, scars, and fears, it is love that will save your life.

Second, killing yourself is not the answer. Cliché again, but it's true (funny how often clichés are true, and how often they are so false). Killing yourself doesn't solve any problems; it simply transfers the onus from you to those who survive you. As I said before, losing you will affect many more people than you would expect. They'll miss you, long for you, cry for you, but most of all they'll regret. Regret is a demon that allows no respite, no repose from its malicious claws. They'll fall into the hole that you've dug for yourself, assuming your burdens and wondering what they could have done. It's ironic. You'll be the one causing all of this, but they'll be the ones who would never forgive themselves.

The last thing that I hope you take from this is that this is just one moment in your life. And sure, it's dark, but the beautiful thing about war is that those who survive one day fight the next stronger than they've ever been in their entire lives. And it's the same in this case. I know you're struggling, everybody knows it. But push through this, and you'll soon be Theseus after he slayed the Minotaur: conqueror of the most tenacious demon, fearlessly sailing into the future. In short, keep fighting, know that you are loved, and stay strong.

Sincerely, with love,
EBG

– Evan Goldstein

Cara-Soma

The first time we kissed was innocent.

As we walked along the sidewalk toward her elementary school, the old streetlights dimly showing us our path, she slid her hand into my own, which she often did. It was a cool, windy summer night and she was sleeping over. Her parents were out that night; it was before they divorced. They were out dancing, I think, or drinking. I don't remember which.

We weren't supposed to be out of the house, of course. We were only eleven and ten respectively — her birthday was before mine — and my parents were understandably quite paranoid.

"The moon is pretty," she said to me as she stared out the window, her hands tapping lightly on the pane.

"Yeah." It was Link's third time defeating the giant spider on the first level of The Ocarina of Time and I was well on my way to the second level when she came over and stood in front of the television screen.

"You're not even looking at it."

"Looking at what?"

"The moon!"

"Oh." I rolled my eyes and paused my game, setting the Nintendo 64's controller down on the macaroni-spotted carpet. I dusted off my ripped jeans and shoved my hands into my pockets as I casually strode to the window. I stood before it and poked my head forward, looking up at the round white moon that adorned the sky.

"Isn't it pretty?"

"Yeah," I replied, this time sincerely.

"I bet the moon kingdom is having a party right now, huh?" she asked as she leaned against me. I remember taking a sharp breath then and not knowing why I did it, but recognizing that I did not want her to move away.

"The moon kingdom doesn't exist."

"Yes, it does."

"No, it doesn't, silly."

"Don't call me silly," she whined, rubbing her nose against my shoulder.

"Then don't say silly stuff." My heart was beating faster.

"You're the one who watches Sailor Moon!"

"I do not!"

"Do too!" She moved away from me and I immediately felt colder, calmer. I turned around to see what she was up to and watched in horror as she rummaged through my video games and movies, taking out one by one my Sailor Moon VHS tapes.

"Put those back!" I exclaimed, rushing over and grabbing the tapes from her warm, pale hands. I shoved them into the back of my collection. She stood up and walked huffily back to the window. I stayed beside the TV. We were silent.

"I'm sorry," I said after a moment, standing up and putting

my head onto her shoulder, leaning down a bit to match her height.

"Don't call me silly." I could hear the pout in her voice.

"Okay. I'm sorry."

She continued to stare at the moon and I continued to lean against her shoulder.

"I want a better view."

"Okay."

I lifted up the window and pushed out the screen, the way I often had when my mom had forgotten something at our house and needed me to sneak into my room, so that we wouldn't wake up the drunken giant, my stepdad.

I was the first to step out of the one-story house and then helped her out of it.

Though the elementary school was only a ten-minute walk from my house, our short legs felt as though we had been walking for half an hour. We both jumped the gate and headed toward the playground.

We sat beneath the hood, right at the top of the slide, the way we had many nights before without our parents knowing. The moon was always pretty at the top of the slide.

"It's prettier when you're outside," she said as always.

"Yeah." I still wasn't looking at the moon.

"Sorry you had to stop playing your game."

"It's okay. I beat it already."

"I know. But don't you think it's pretty?"

"Yeah."

"Do you think the moon is having a party?"

"Yeah."

"Do you think it's pretty?"

"The moon?"

"No, the kingdom. Do you think the kingdom and princes and princesses are pretty?"

I laughed. "Princes can't be pretty!"

"A prince and princess are probably getting married, right now. Like Serena and Darien, huh?"

"Yeah, like Serena and Darien. They're probably kissing right now!"

"Ewww!" She made a face of disgust and giggled quietly. "You know, my mom says that my name means 'Dear Moon' or 'Beloved Moon.' Cara-Soma. Maybe that means I'm a moon princess too!"

"You'd make a pretty princess," I replied, and blushed a bright red, noticeable even despite my dark skin.

"I think you'd make a pretty princess too," she said shyly. "I wonder if two princesses can get married?"

"No," I said. "Only a prince and a princess can get married."

"Why?"

"Because only a prince and a princess can kiss. That's what my mom says."

She was silent for a moment and looked back at the moon. She was scratching her left arm, like she often did when she was in thought.

"I think you'd make a pretty prince." Her voice had gotten quieter. I said nothing.

Then —

"Well, so . . . kissing is gross."

"Yeah."

"We should go back."

She nodded and walked around me, to leave the playground.

"Hey, Evey?" she said, before her departure.

"Yeah?" I did not expect my voice to be as hoarse as it was, nor did I expect the chaste kiss she planted on my lips before slipping down the giant yellow slide, giggling the whole way down.

I had a giant smile on my face as I followed her.

You would think that, after something like that, some things would have been realized. For Cara, things had been. Her second kiss was in the sixth grade with a geeky brunette named Sarah Foster, who Cara had befriended after being partnered with her for a school project. She had her first girlfriend in the eighth grade. Her name was Jeanette Mitchell, a tomboyish blonde who had a thing for matches, Edgar Allan Poe, and The Cure.

All the while, we stayed friends and nothing more, growing closer as the years passed with Cara teasing me about our childhood kiss and how I had yet to add on to my experiences with any "lucky" boys . . . or girls, she would add coyly.

She came out to her parents right after she broke up with her second girlfriend, Winter Brigs, and pursued a more serious relationship with a girl who was two years older than her — a senior in high school. My mom and stepdad had divorced when I was twelve and by this time, both of her parents had divorced and were seeing other people.

Thus, she sat down all four of her parental figures on the long couch in the living room, with me on the loveseat, ready to defend her at any time.

65

"Are you sure you want to do this?" I had asked as she prepared in her room several minutes before. "They don't have to know yet, you know. You could wait until college or something. When they can't kick you out." I knew Cara's parents were fairly laid-back, much more so after their divorce. Happier, I guess. They were "non-practicing" Irish Catholics, unlike my deeply Evangelical mother who loved me but would surely cast me on the street if I ever pulled a stunt like this.

"They won't kick me out," Cara coddled as she patted down her clothes and checked herself in the mirror. Then she turned to me, flashing a brilliant but nervous smile, and kissed me on the cheek. "Wish me luck!"

I remember wondering, with an acute sense of anger and overprotection, why Lindsey, the new girlfriend, hadn't been there to give support. But I didn't voice my thoughts.

When Cara announced, with little preamble, that she was gay, "a God-fearing, woman-loving, girl-kissing, college-bound straight-A lesbian," the room was silent for about a split second before her father's girlfriend, Rebecca, shrugged and asked anyone if they were hungry.

Her mom smiled encouragingly and said, "Oh, that's nice, dear. But it was rather obvious with that other girl . . . that friend who used to sleep over all the time and suddenly disappeared . . ."

"Winter," her dad offered.

"Yes, her. See, sweetheart? We're not as blind as you think we are. Now then, since you gathered us all here, let's not waste a nice Saturday afternoon. Is everyone okay with sandwiches? Rebecca, come help me in the kitchen, will you?"

And the adults dispersed, leaving me wide-eyed and open-mouthed as Cara stood front and center in her living room, staring at the empty couch that her parents had just occupied.

Then she broke into a laugh. "That was awesome!"

It was, indeed, awesome for her. She continued to have a myriad of other relationships soon after Lindsey, with whom she parted ways after the older girl went off to college. She even brought a few girls home to meet her family. And me, of course.

As for my personal life, I continued to live vicariously through Cara, having little interest in the boys around me and never daring to look at another girl, though I found it increasingly harder to do after each volleyball game as we showered and changed in the locker room. Instead of dating, I found solace in studying and working hard, making Varsity Captain in my senior year and becoming copy editor for the school yearbook. I didn't make straight As like Cara — God knows how she did it, what with her being too busy getting caught with her girlfriends in the bathroom all the time. But she was a hard worker too, and a charmer to boot. There was never evidence on her record of any sexual misconduct.

My grades and activities helped land me a spot in the freshman class of San Francisco State University; of course, Cara got into UC Berkeley. We never did like being too far from each other.

In the summer before we would be leaving our homes and going off into the world of college undergraduates, I began dating a boy named Luke Skylar. I'll admit that I was more attracted to his name than his looks, but he was a handsome boy. Tall, with curly brown hair and light blue eyes, and pants that fit a bit too snugly. He was going to attend the California College of the Arts and loved to make plans, especially ones that concerned us. Cara didn't like him and he wasn't too fond of her either.

After our third date, our relationship was consummated with our first kiss. When I told Cara that I finally had my second kiss, she wasn't as pleased as I thought she'd be.

"Oh," she had said as she thumbed through the latest issue of *Entertainment* magazine. I expected her to jump up excitedly and tackle me to the ground, demanding details. How was it? Did you like it? Was there tongue? How'd it happen? Tell me, tell me, *tell me*!

But there was none of that. Just a simple "oh" as she lay on her bed, her long white-blonde tendrils framing her face.

"Yeah . . ." I said, unsure of how I might continue and decided to keep talking, to fill the awkward silence that had ensued. "We uh . . . he walked me to the door and just sort of leaned in and that's it. It felt weird . . . like, I felt awkward because I was a little shy, you know? I had never kissed anyone before . . . I mean, never *really* kissed anyone. You don't count." I tried to laugh at this and expected her to do the same, to begin teasing me as she had done so many times in the past.

Still, she remained silent, her lips in a thin line as her eyes stared hard at some article the magazine was opened to.

"Uhm. So yeah," I continue, "there was tongue, but that got a little awkward too. It felt good, though . . . the kiss, I mean, overall. I mean, it didn't feel bad. Not really what I expected a kiss to feel like . . . with like fireworks and that whole 'butterflies in your stomach' feeling but it was . . . you know . . ." I started getting nervous again. I didn't know what to do with the reaction, or lack thereof, that she had provided me with.

68

Then suddenly she closed the magazine and stood up, stretching a little as she did so. "Well, I'm happy for you. It took you long enough!" She gave me a weak smile. "But I'm tired now, so I think I'm going to bed. Do you want to stay over the night?"

"No . . ." I said, somewhat confused. "Ah, no, I'll just . . . I'll go home. You rest. I have to start packing anyway." We hugged and I departed.

We didn't see each other for three weeks after that, which was the longest time interval our friendship had ever experienced, not including when she left for cheer camp the whole summer of eighth grade and I cried for two days straight. I tried getting in contact with her, but she always had an excuse or was doing something else, too busy for me.

During that time, Luke and I got closer and kissed more frequently, making me feel much more like a pro each time. Still, that butterfly feeling had yet to overtake me. It was merely an action of affection to me, like holding hands.

When we finally did see each other, Luke and I were on a date to the movies. Cara was in the concession line with a girl I didn't recognize. Our eyes met and then she saw Luke. The girl tugged on her hand and she turned away, toward the cashier, without another instance of acknowledgment.

We didn't speak for another month and this time, I didn't bother trying to call her. When my parents asked about her, I would merely shrug and say we got into a fight. It was true, sort of. I mean, we hadn't really fought but something was clearly wrong and I wasn't sure what I had done to cause the rift. Confident that I had done nothing, I wasn't willing to subject myself to punishment for it and instead focused on my relationship with Luke.

Then came the weekend before I would depart for college. Cara and I had made plans months in advance to take a road trip to San Francisco together, something we had always wanted to do since we were younger but our parents hadn't trusted us enough. However, since we had barely spoken in two months, I didn't have any expectations for such a journey with her.

My mom's boyfriend, Jesse, and I were loading up my car and my mom was crying behind me, asking him if he remembered little things from my childhood, like when I first learned to walk or when I used to fall asleep in the backyard. I suppose she forgot that she and Jesse only started dating when I was thirteen, but he didn't seem to mind. They both had been more than hesitant about letting me drive to Palo Alto on my own, but I convinced them that I was a big girl and that this was their first step of letting me be an adult. I'm sure they weren't convinced, but somehow they agreed to let me go anyway.

"My little girl is leaving me!" my mom wailed as she flung herself into Jesse's arms. He gave me a wink as he tried to comfort her and led her inside the house, probably so that she wouldn't chase after the car as I left.

"You be good," he warned in his warm fatherly tone before embracing me in a giant bear hug. "Luke is meeting you in Bakersfield, right?"

"Yeah, his parents are going to drop him off and we'll drive together from there."

"And remind me again why this boy isn't meeting you here and driving with you the whole way through?"

"Because, *Dad*, his family wants to see him off so I don't know when he's leaving but it'll be later on today and I will be okay because I can defend myself. You taught me well."

70

"It's not about defense! It's just you, at least with Luke or Cara —"

"Yeah yeah yeah, strength in numbers, I know." I kissed him on the cheek. "I gotta go if you want me in Bakersfield before nighttime."

"Okay, okay. Be safe. I love you!" He headed inside as I got into my car, revved up the engine, and left my home of fifteen years.

I didn't get very far down the street, however, before a car started honking at me from behind. At first, I thought it was my mom, wanting to ask if I needed a pack of pads or something, but then I recognized the car to be Rachel's, a friend of mine and Cara's from school. And in the passenger seat was Cara.

I slowed and parked at the curb with Rachel doing the same. She didn't leave the car, but Cara popped out and jogged over to my window, which I rolled down for her.

"Hey."

"Hi?"

"What're you up to?"

"Just . . . going to college . . ."

"Awesome. Can I come with?"

I stared at her for a second and realized that despite the amused smile playing on her lips, she was dead serious.

"Are you serious?" I had to make sure.

She just laughed and instructed me to pop the trunk before jogging back to the car and lugging out two huge suitcases and shouting at Rachel to "get off her lazy ass" and grab the other two.

"Do you mind helping, babe?" she called from behind as she stood beside the trunk of my car. I nodded numbly, unbuckling

71

my seat belt as I got out and helped her and Rachel rearrange my things to accommodate her bags.

I took a second to admire the flexibility of my small car's space composition and then took another minute to pray to God that the car itself had the same level of endurance.

Cara thanked Rachel and took up residence in my passenger seat. I stood beside the rear of my car and looked at Rachel, who was heading back to hers.

I was giving her a "what the hell" look, but she only responded with a shrug and a smile before driving away. I walked slowly back to the driver's seat and started the engine. I looked at Cara, but she offered me no explanation and turned on the radio, which was blasting Mika. Too shocked and confused to be remotely upset, I put my car into "drive" mode and headed off toward Bakersfield.

I had miscalculated the amount of time it would take me to get to the city, what with a few unexpected twists in my plans. We ended up stopping to eat at Denny's after I found out that Cara hadn't eaten, and that took up about an hour and a half. Still numb, I didn't bother questioning her then and neither of us spoke much to each other for the duration of the car ride. It had now been four hours since I pulled out of the driveway of my house and the sun was beginning to set. I knew I should've called Luke to let him know what the delay was — it only takes about two hours to get to Bakersfield from Glendale. I was sure he had called too. But he was really the least of my concerns at the moment. About twenty minutes away from the city, I finally cracked under the pressure of my own thoughts and pulled over into the driveway of a Wendy's.

"Okay, Cara, what the hell?"

"What?"

"Why are you here?"

"In the car?"

"Yes. No. I mean, what are you doing in the car? With your luggage as if everything is totally peachy keen with us?"

"What are you talking about? We've been planning this for years."

"We haven't spoken in months."

"Only two."

"Oh my God." I shoved open my door and slammed it shut before stalking over to the railing in front of the restaurant.

For a moment Cara stayed in the car, and I leaned against the railing before I heard the soft click of the passenger side door. I didn't acknowledge her when she placed a hand on my shoulder.

"Evey."

I continued glaring at the street.

"Evelyn."

My eyes bored holes into the cement.

Finally, she put her arms around my waist from behind and laid her head on my shoulder. "The moon is pretty tonight."

"You can barely see it," I muttered, spotting the faded moon that was overshadowed by colors of dusk.

"It's still there. I can tell it's going to be pretty."

"Cara," I groaned, looking away from the sky, "will you please tell me what the hell is going on? Why did you ignore me for the whole summer and then randomly appear out of nowhere on the day I'm leaving?"

"I was mad at you. But I wanted to see you."

"For what? What the hell did I do?"

"Nothing." It was her turn to lean against the railing, her back facing the street.

"You threw away our friendship for an entire summer — the summer before college, the last summer we have to really spend together with just us — for nothing?"

"It wouldn't have been just us."

"So you threw away our friendship because you have something against Luke."

"Yeah. After you two started dating I didn't want our friendship anymore." She was looking at an older couple through the restaurant window.

"Why? What do you have against him?"

She shrugged. "Nothing. I just didn't want him to be your boyfriend."

"Why?"

"Because . . . because you're a dumbass."

I blinked in surprise. "I'm sorry?"

"I didn't want our friendship anymore because I didn't want Skywalker to be your boyfriend because I wanted to be your girlfriend. Seriously, Evey. It's not that hard to figure out."

I stared at her. And continued to stare. I didn't know what to say. "I . . . I'm not gay, Cara."

"Right, because you read *Playboy* for the articles."

"I do! I mean, I don't. I don't read *Playboy*."

"I guess you forget that I've known you for fifteen years, and your collection of random crap. Sailor Moon stuff behind your PlayStation 3 games and both *Playboy* and *Maxim* magazines in your underwear drawer — bottom one on the left."

"They're . . . not mine. They're . . . uh . . . a friend's and she . . . if her parents found them . . ."

74

"Which friend?"

". . . Rachel?"

"Okay, fine." She pushed herself off the railing . . . only to push me against it. She placed a hand on my cheek and pressed her lips to mine. Immediately, my stomach was attacked by butterflies of every species. I gasped and she took the opportunity to taste my tongue. I didn't know what to do, but I knew I didn't want her to stop. Instinctively, I placed my hands on her hips and brought her closer to me. When she tried to pull away, I groaned in protest and deepened the kiss. So caught up were we that we didn't notice the couple inside cheering us on with waved arms.

We pulled away from each other to catch our breaths and I leaned my forehead against hers.

"So. Not gay, huh?" she whispered, her hands tracing up and down my sides.

"Fine. Okay . . . so I . . . like girls a little. It's not that serious."

"I don't know about you, but I think that kiss was pretty serious, and I was sensing some serious repressed desire just now. From both of us."

I moved and buried my head into her shoulder, and she responded by wrapping her arms around me and caressing my hair. "It doesn't matter. We can't do this."

"Why not?"

"My parents . . ."

"No. No, no, no, no, no. We aren't doing this right now. We aren't talking about them right now. I don't care about your parents, or Skywalker, or the strange old couple giving us the thumbs-up sign behind you. I care about you. And me. Do you like me?"

"Yeah," I laughed, "yeah, something like that."

"More than Luke?"

"I thought we weren't talking about Luke?"

"Just answer the question."

"Way more than Luke."

"Cool, okay. Then. That's settled."

"What's settled?"

"I'm your girlfriend."

"Wait, what the hell?" I pulled away just enough to look into her eyes.

"What? You rather obviously like me and you like me more than whatshisface."

"Yeah, but we can't just —"

"Yes, we can. It's our lives, we can do whatever the hell we want." She looked at me pointedly and I just started laughing. After a while she did too, and we stood there, holding each other and laughing.

Several minutes passed, after the laughter subsided, and I held her against my chest, lost in thought. In less than an hour we would be reaching Bakersfield and Luke would be waiting for me. When we and Cara made it to San Francisco, I would be breaking his heart and officially embarking on a journey I never thought possible with the person I had been pretty close to being in love with for nearly fifteen years. And after that, we would have to deal with the knowing smiles that would likely come from her family and the wrathful consequences that would come from mine.

Cara always knew how to get us in trouble.

But she was right. For now, just right now, she was the only person that mattered to me and I was the only person that mattered to her. For right now, we would do whatever the hell we wanted. So, instead of thinking of consequences and talking about what may be, we said nothing and only enjoyed each other's presence as the sky grew ever darker and the moon took over her reign as queen of the night.

"See? I told you the moon would be beautiful tonight," she whispered to me.

"Yeah, you were right." I wasn't looking at the moon.

"You know what else I was right about, Evey?"

"Hmm?"

"You make a very pretty prince."

I laughed softly. "And you make a gorgeous princess, Cara-Soma. But I rather think I'd make a better princess."

"I thought you said two princesses can't kiss?"

I pulled her closer to me once more and placed a feathery kiss on each side of her mouth. "I was wrong," I whispered, and kissed her gently on the lips.

– Erika Turner

77

I Wanna Hear a Poem

I wanna hear a poem
I wanna hear a sex poem
A weed poem
An "I make my wrists bleed" poem
Not no cheesy poem
But a sleazy poem
A poem that'll make your lips curl like an Elvis CD
I wanna hear a cold poem
A hard poem
A "Here, take my card" poem
A poem that'll make me go to the edge of my seat
Because it's so damn good
You don't care who or what is reciting it
I want Scooby-Doo to come by and whisk me away with his
    un-understandable speak about how sad he is 'cause he ain't
    got his Scooby snacks
I wanna hear Rihanna talk about how unfaithful she is
Or Eminem's shovel digging his mother's grave

I wanna feel the hot lava of the words gushing through the
   margin of the paper because the poem is too strong for it to
   obtain it
I wanna hear the poem of a bored watch cop
Or a mad detective
The dreams of a troubled kid
Or a lunatic mother
I wanna hear a crazy lifeguard's poem
Or a simple rock star's poem
I wanna hear a poem about a great adventure
An adventure to the outskirts of a war site
I wanna hear a soldier's poem
About his best buddy's violent death
Or that terrorist's poem whose head got cut off
I wanna hear such an extreme poem that'll make me wanna
Jump on a ski boat in six degree weather
A poem so wrong and twisted
It'll make me have nightmares
I wanna hear an unusual poem
A poem that'll make me go "hmm"
To top it all off,
I wanna hear a love poem
From a cow to a moose
A silly poem
I don't care just don't make it a déjà vu poem
Or a cliché
Show me a poem that'll make me think
Give me a poem so good, bad, disgusting
That'll make my poem seem like trash

Try, but I'll accept a friendly quit
Just give me a poem that'll take my time
Not waste it, just give me a poem
A poem, a poem, a poem I wanna hear

– *Yadiris Valdez*

Louis Congo to a Man on the Wheel

I rule this ridge
where gators rest and bow
their heads, where cicadas
sing for my ears only —

in the distance, a drum beats
Congo Congo Congo
each time my knuckles crack
your hips — my skin and yours

tear, but I will deliver you
away from this strange land,
away from my strange hands
that beat beat beat

and never cease these days
when sunlight drifting
through the mosses appears
as in an unending dream.

So when I finally steal your breath
that tries to bend the tall grass
brushing against my shins,
I will gaze into the bayou,

scrub the blood from my thin fingers
until, stiff and raw, they strike away
my image from the water that carries it
off in ripples, that brings it back

and when I'm swallowed in sleep,
my heart's pulse will murmur
Louis Louis Louis,
knowing before I wake

my hands will grope for your limbs
and piece them back together again.

Louis Congo in Love

I.
For you, ma fleur, I toil
on the route of these slaves' escape:
15 pounds a head, planted on pikes
along the levee's edge. I wish the slaves
had chosen another route to follow,
one through the swampland,
one you'd never find;
I hope you don't bring home,
limp in your arms, the lengths of rope
I tied them to the table with
and used to wipe the blood
from the blade after it sliced
through each neck.

II.
Through the window, I watch
you sidestep the rotting magnolias
that mark the path to our home.
I remember then how once you turned

my hands over and over
as though you'd lost something there.
But you never mentioned
the red crust I couldn't clean
from beneath my nails some nights.
You'd just turn my hands over again
and watch them drop to my sides.

Louis Congo's Bride

This is our season underground:
you press six seeds between my lips,
watch them slide down like rubies.
You slip your body over mine.
We sweat through our Novembers.
And when your fingers scratch my skin
like little treasure hunters,
rubies rise across my limbs
encased in feverish welts.

Louis Congo's Wife

Waist deep now, I tread
unsettled waters,
my skirts floating up
like swamp gas. I drag
your limbs behind me,
mon cher, a yard of twine
tethered to your ankles.
My feet sink
into curdling mud.
My breasts, dark-studded
with droplets that catch
the sunlight, heave
up above the water.

Chest deep now, I climb
onto your body, a raft
barely held together
under my knees,
floating just below
the bayou's surface.

The stitches that hold
thigh to hips have loosened,
and I tighten the threads,
pulling the free ends
taut and knotting them.

As the sky begins to darken,
I float past narrow banks
of muddied land
I'll never return to,
where a pair of torches
flashed like kaiman eyes
through warped glass
and eight blistered hands
dragged you from our bed
by the ankles, the way Set
captured Osiris.

I've picked up every piece of you →
toes, knuckles, lips scattered
across the swampland — every chunk,
swollen and gnawed upon,
pushed up by the bottom feeders.
And still, still! you drift
away from me, demanding
blackberries and tafia,
libation for the dead.
Tugging the threads that keep
you together, I watch them
slice through muscle and skin.

Your fingers, ribs, balls,
and calves pull away like crabmeat
pecked from the shell
and I sink through.

– *M'Bilia Meekers*

All or Nothing

After nearly putting my eye out, Rachel Weiss quit the marching band. Rachel hadn't wanted to join in the first place, as she
pointed out every time we had afternoon practice. She was first
chair oboe in the concert band — another fact she often pointed
out — and all concert band members were required to march at
football games. The other oboists played percussion for marching band, because oboes have a tendency to explode when
exposed to excessive heat and football season began during the
hottest part of the year. But Rachel insisted on playing the oboe,
and she insisted on playing her oboe, an ornate wooded one her
parents bought for her when she made All-State orchestra. Mr.
Harding, our director, caved into her demands, which really
irritated the rest of the band, especially the other oboists who
were playing triangle and xylophone at every football game. No
one in band liked Rachel anyway. Mr. Harding didn't even like
her, but she was the best musician we had so she always got what
she wanted.

For some reason Rachel seemed to like me, or at least made
frequent efforts to start up a conversation. Will Buchanan said
it was because I was the only one in the band who was too polite

to tell her to shut up. Will played the saxophone and had a tendency to make thoughtless comments, though his observations were almost always accurate.

"You just don't know how to stand up for yourself. You always want to make everyone happy," Will told me as I assembled my clarinet on the sidelines before halftime at one of the football games.

I shrugged. "What's wrong with that?" I tugged at the high collar of my jacket, pulling it away from my sweaty neck. Mr. Harding insisted we wear full uniform every time we marched, although the bands from the other local high schools got to wear T-shirts and jeans during August.

"It makes people like Rachel Weiss talk to you," Will said. He didn't even check to see if Rachel was nearby, but I was relieved to see she wasn't. Mr. Harding motioned for us to stand and prepare to march. I stood in front of Will, and Rachel took her place in front of me, holding her prized oboe. I couldn't see a drop of sweat on her face or neck. Apparently Will had also noticed Rachel's immunity to heat, because he leaned forward and whispered, "It's a lot hotter in hell where she comes from."

The buzzer rang for halftime and I followed Rachel onto the field as we started to play. We were almost done when something hit me in the eye. I couldn't tell what it was, but I kept marching. Mr. Harding would never forgive me for messing up the routine. We were forming a lance because a knight had proven too difficult. Mr. Harding thought there was no way we could mess up a straight line, and I wasn't going to be the one to prove him wrong. It wasn't until we got back to the bench and people started gathering around me that I found out what had happened. Apparently Rachel's oboe had exploded and one of the wood shards had flown back and hit me.

"Are you okay, Sarah?" Will asked, pushing me down on a bench. I nodded. "Let me see," he said. I lowered the hand covering my left eye.

"I think it's just irritated," Will said.

"Oh good. Now that I have your expert medical opinion I won't have to worry anymore. Isn't there a nurse or doctor somewhere around here?" I asked, twisting around on the bench. Rachel and Mr. Harding were standing nearby and seemed to be having an argument.

"Do you have any idea how much this cost?" Rachel said. Her cheeks were flushed and she clutched a pile of wooden shards, which must have been the remains of her oboe.

"That is beside the point, Miss Weiss. You may have caused Miss Pierce serious injury. You will play a different instrument when marching or you will be removed from the band." Mr. Harding always referred to his students by their last names.

"You can't remove me. I quit," Rachel said, turning and stomping off. Mr. Harding sighed and rubbed his forehead, then came over to me.

"Are you all right, Miss Pierce?" he asked.

"Yeah, I'm fine," I said. Mr. Harding nodded and walked away.

"I always thought the whole exploding oboe thing was just an urban myth," Will said.

By Monday my eye was completely fine, but Rachel still hadn't apologized to Mr. Harding. When she walked into the music room during concert band rehearsal everyone quit talking and stared at her. She ignored them and took her usual seat in the front row.

"All right, we're going to run through all the pieces for the fall concert in order," Mr. Harding said. He went to retrieve his conductor's baton and saw Rachel.

"Miss Weiss, I was under the impression you had quit," he said.

"I quit the marching band," Rachel said, looking up at Mr. Harding. "I did not quit the concert band."

"It's an all or nothing deal. You chose nothing." Mr. Harding gestured to the door with his baton. "Now please leave."

"You can't kick me out. I'm first chair. I have a solo."

"No," Mr. Harding said, "Miss Hayes is first chair, and Miss Hayes has a solo." Natalie Hayes turned bright red and sank down in her chair. Natalie was painfully shy and hated being the center of attention, but the only other oboist was actually a flutist who had switched at the beginning of the year, and sometimes she still held her oboe sideways when she wasn't thinking about it.

Rachel scooped up her sheet music and stalked toward the door. Looking over her shoulder, she said, "Natalie can't play my solo. It's too difficult for her." Then she left.

As hard as it was for all of us to admit it, Rachel was right about one thing. Natalie couldn't play her solo. Mr. Harding kept insisting she would get better with practice, but by the night of the performance she had not gotten any better.

"You just need to relax," I said. Our concert started in half an hour and Natalie was crying backstage. She hadn't even bothered to put together her oboe. I opened her case and started screwing the pieces together.

"Here," I said, giving it to her. "You need to get your reeds ready."

"I can't do this."

"Yes, you can. Go to the bathroom and wash your face, and then come fix your reeds," I said. Natalie nodded and went to the bathroom, and Will walked up beside me.

"This is going to be a disaster," he said.

"Sarah?" Someone called my name and I turned around. Rachel was standing behind me, wearing our black concert dress and holding what I assumed was her new oboe.

"We're saved," Will said, throwing his hands in the air. "I never thought I'd say this, but Rachel, I am so glad to see you."

"Is Mr. Harding letting you play tonight?" I asked.

Rachel shook her head. "That's why I need to talk to you. Can you talk to Mr. Harding for me? Tell him I'll play whatever instrument he wants when we march if he lets me join band again."

"What's with the sudden change of heart?" Will asked.

"I don't want to see you embarrass yourselves," Rachel said. Will rolled his eyes and started to walk away, and I followed him.

"Wait," Rachel said. "Please. I really want to play." She fiddled with her oboe. "I miss band. I don't even know what to do without it." She blinked and I could see her eyes were wet. "Please, Sarah," she said.

Will shot me a warning look, knowing I wouldn't be able to resist Rachel's pleading. "Those tears are probably fake," he whispered.

I ignored him. "I'll talk to Mr. Harding," I said.

Rachel smiled. "Thank you," she said. I went to look for the band director and Will followed.

"You need to learn to say no," he said.

"Shut up," I said. Will backed away when we reached Mr. Harding, who was directing the students setting up the chairs. He didn't hear me call his name over the clinking of the metal legs. I said his name again, louder, and he finally turned.

"Miss Pierce, can this wait? I'm rather preoccupied at the moment."

"Rachel's back," I said. "She wants to play tonight. She says she'll join the marching band."

"I'm sorry, but you can tell Miss Weiss it's too late for that. We are performing in thirty minutes and she has not been rehearsing with us." Mr. Harding turned back to the students setting up the chairs and yelled at one of the boys to adjust a chair in the second row.

"But Rachel knows all the parts already, and Natalie is in the bathroom having a nervous breakdown." I was surprised I was still arguing with him. Mr. Harding seemed surprised too.

"Why is it so important to you that Miss Weiss be allowed to play?" he asked, turning to face me again.

"Natalie doesn't want to play the solo. She's terrified. And it isn't fair to punish her for something Rachel did. Rachel knows the part, so let her do it." I had never heard myself sound so firm and assertive, especially not when speaking to a teacher. It was disconcerting. Mr. Harding must have thought so too, because he looked at me like he'd never seen me before.

"All right," he said finally, shaking his head as though to clear it, "tell Miss Weiss she will be playing the oboe solo tonight." I nodded and walked away. I knew I hadn't done much, but I couldn't help feeling proud. I had never spoken back to a teacher. It was kind of exhilarating.

"You know, when I told you to stand up for yourself, I meant for yourself, not for some pretentious oboe player who drives everyone crazy," Will said as he walked up beside me.

When I told Natalie and Rachel the news Rachel hugged me and Natalie started crying again, presumably out of relief. I barely managed to get Natalie's face dried off before we had to take our seats on stage. Rachel returned to her seat on the front row, all trace of pleading gone. She was in her element now. Smoothing down her perfectly styled hair, she crossed her feet at the ankles and held the oboe below her lips, a look of intense concentration on her face. Will rolled his eyes at me from across the stage. Mr. Harding raised his baton and I placed my clarinet to my lips.

The first two pieces went well, and I was feeling pretty good by the time we started the third piece, the one with the oboe solo. After the clarinets finished I lowered my instrument and joined the rest of the band in watching Rachel. Finally, the rest of the instruments faded out and Rachel took a deep breath and began her solo. She made it through almost the entire part without an error, and I breathed a sigh of relief as we neared the end. I should have known that Rachel wouldn't have a problem, but after listening to Natalie for the past few weeks I had almost forgotten what the oboe solo was supposed to sound like. Then Rachel missed the last note. It wasn't that obvious — I don't think anyone outside of the band even noticed — but Rachel looked horror-struck.

We finished the piece and the audience applauded, clapping even louder when Mr. Harding motioned to Rachel to stand as soloist. But Rachel just sat there, staring at the oboe in her lap as though accusing it of betraying her. The rest of the band got up and filed offstage but Rachel remained in her chair. She seemed to be in shock. I paused outside of the wings, and then walked back across the stage to her.

"Come on," I said. "Time to go home."

"I can't believe it," Rachel said.

"It was just one note. Forget about it. Let's go," I said.

Rachel shook her head. "You go ahead," she said. Will was waiting in the parking lot to give me a ride home, so I turned and left.

"See where being nice gets you?" Will said when I reached the car.

"It's not like she missed the note on purpose to spite me. Natalie would have been worse," I said, climbing into the passenger seat.

"So? The rest of the band's still going to be mad that you stuck up for the girl who messed up our concert," Will said, getting in beside me.

"Let them say what they want," I said.

Will raised his eyebrows. "Wow. What's gotten into you tonight?"

I shrugged. I couldn't explain why, but I was feeling almost giddy. "On the bright side, this might make Rachel a little more bearable," I said. Will shook his head and pulled out of the parking lot.

After the fall concert most of the other kids in band quit speaking to me. They actually weren't that angry about the messed-up solo, but they now thought I was friends with Rachel, which was enough to make me the band's resident leper. Will was the only one who was still talking to me, and we were standing together when Rachel came to my locker a few days later. "I want you to know," she said, in her most self-important tone, "that in spite of the fiasco you caused, I appreciate your effort to help me."

I managed to keep from laughing until Rachel had walked away. "The fiasco I caused?" I said.

"Hey, it's still the nicest thing Rachel has ever said to anyone," Will said.

There was a football game that night, and Rachel, as though determined to prove her worth to the rest of the band, volunteered to play the triangle. Even playing the triangle, Rachel had perfect form, hitting every repetitive dinging note perfectly, and smiling with each metallic chime.

– Taylor Davidson

The Dreambook for Inconsequential Lives

I. Unique Baby Names

You stand behind the cash register at Heavenly Hotdogs, thinking ludicrous thoughts. You smile because Kiley was forced to man the deep fryer today, which you hate for the bubbling burns it lashes at you, and because Kiley is a bitch anyway. She doesn't have a real excuse like you do to avoid the task. You knew how to make Henry the manager feel just a little bit uncomfortable in the way you whispered, morning sickness throw-up, yes that would be bad for business. You fiddle with the condiments on the gray-speckled counter, the salt shaker next to the pepper shaker. Remember how, back when your biggest worry was finishing all of the broccoli on your plate so you could have dessert, you would marry the salt and the pepper, sliding them across the table to a hummed wedding march. Ketchup officiated. The fries cried into their tissues in the pews, and the hamburger threw a party afterward where the pickles got drunk and the soda danced the electric slide. "Oh, hello. One foot-long, no sauerkraut, jumbo Diet Pepsi? $3.85." The register reveals its inner secrets with an explosive eagerness, almost like one of those pop-up books you still secretly love. You hand back the change in coins, sliding them across the counter with the tips of your fingers, making sure to drag the pennies and nickels through half-congealed puddles of grease or sugar along the way. "Keep the change? You sure?" You count the number of babies that pass by the restaurant's glass façade. They are suddenly everywhere. You think, my baby will be something special. Mustard. Straw. Napkin. You are less picky and more confused, really, as you store these words away, each a potential baby name.

II. Shopping Lists
Tampons.
Bread.
Underwear.

Watermelon.
No money. Shit.
Saltines.
A new man.

III. Drugs I Have Known
Who's to say I am a good girl, but I have never touched a drug. Not even Advil for headaches. Not pot or cocaine or heroin, and I am scared of needles, which means I don't have any tattoos either. I am clean. Except if I did get a tattoo, which I have not and would not, I would get one on my inner wrist. It would spell *Believe*.

IV. Prayers
Dear God, If you — I mean, You — know everything and all that, why do I have to take time and sit down and close my eyes

("Breathing deeply helps," Mr. Priest told me) and tell you all over again? Isn't that just wasting our time? But if I'm going to do this, I want to do it right. You know this. I want — the opposite of fear. I don't know what it's called. I just want to do what's right. I want to go to bed with dry eyes and a full stomach and a warm happiness all around. I want everyone to have these things. Even Kiley the fast-food bitch, because I guess she's not a bitch to you — You — anyway. I want these fry burns to go away from my arms. I guess I want money, too. So my kid will never have these kinds of questions.

V. Mondays

Her water broke while she was on the bus, headed toward Heavenly Hotdogs. People were packed in tight on the downtown-bound 2A. The bus rocked and sped, ignorant, and soon people started surrendering to the slick floor. A chorus of disgruntled voices obscured what was important, the cries of a girl who is contracting into womanhood. She never made it to the hospital. Were it not for an ex-cabbie who had experience in this sort of impromptu birthing, along with the help of several men and women who were parents and therefore understood the miracle of the impending event, the world might not have known a Papercup/Onionring/Milkshake Jones.

True story. But the child was named Junior.

– *Alice Rhee*

Hands

Once, when summer was already
beginning to forget itself,
my mother broke the neck
of a snake with only
the upwards flick of her
thumb.

I nearly didn't believe it.
Elsewhere in my memory
she is forever painting
baby swans. She contemplates
each grey feather that she
applies to the canvas.

I often wonder if she knows
of the grace she possesses
folding clean towels
and blankets, leaving
the sheets for my sister
to gather.

– Katelyn Long

What I Never Told My Father

I know a man loves me
when he makes sure I'm protected
in small ways: this boy holds
me steady on the school bus
as we cross the bumpy roads,
has the soft hands of a teen
and the hard jaw of a man.
Curled into a ball with my head
in his lap, my neck curves
awkwardly and my vertebrae
pull apart, gently,
as he anchors me
against the jostling.

It reminds me of the way my dad
would cover my ears at the first signs
of adult language. Not for little ears,
he would say. If only he really
knew me now. If he knew
I spoke like an adult, lived those nights

on the sand that stretched into
the morning, felt for this boy who
knows the scoop and sway
of my body, he wouldn't
understand.

He wouldn't be able to compare me
to the child he remembers
digging moats in the sand, cupping
June beetles in her palm. If I told him
about it all: the smoke that burned my lungs
under that canopy of birches, the times
I held my cousin's hair back
above the toilet, I'm sure his jaw
would tighten and his calloused
palms turn up to the sky.

In this moment, as I nestle my face
into this boy's lap, I'm sure my father's bedroom
is lit through the swell of curtains and he
is resting there. The *New Yorker*
sprawled across his chest lifts
up and down with his breath, holds there
like the last secret in the world
holds in the air before falling swiftly
to cover us all like a cold sheet of rain.

– *Emily Pittinos*

A Slice of Arizona Hell

From here the moon looks like something my five-year-old brother could sketch. I wouldn't even hang the thing on my fridge, but here it is orange and icy in the Arizona night. Everything around me is flushed a sickly orange. Orange runs down the Jeep like an egg yolk and soaks into the gravel parking lot. Outside, the shopping carts rattle like they are haunted by orange ghosts. A solitary orange Twinkie wrapper floats by, untouched. This is the tumbleweed of our modern age.

Above my head, closer than the moon and far more useful, sits a blinking sign. *Open*, it says in stalled whimpers. My brothers move like dusty snakes toward the grocery store. Their faces aren't clear to me in the darkness, so I have to make up their expressions. Mackie is unbendingly serious. Darryl smiles thinly. I hear a short, drunken laugh, and then all is silenced. In the window a cashier with large, frizzy hair counts orange money.

If Ethan were here he'd re-create the scene in colored pencil: the sign, the cashier, the insincere moon. He'd color everything dark purple, even my face. Right now, he colors everything a defiant purple. I don't think he'd repent tonight, even though I exhale orange ink and orange restlessness. For this reason (and others) he's not old enough for the grocery store. I asked the girl next door to watch him, and she agreed eventually. I thought she didn't understand at first, but I was wrong. According to Dylan, her eyes always look like lumps of dull, incomprehensive coal.

When the coldness bites, I hold my hands up to the shuddering car heater. Arizona always grows this cold at night. In land so flat, coldness must take a shape, or else be forgotten. Tonight it escapes my mouth and curls into thin, vigilant snakes. I am alone in the car with only smoky reptiles for company. The car stinks like sewers and roadkill. I don't like being alone on empty Arizona nights. I would sit with anybody, even Ethan. I'd talk about girls and shit and he'd draw picture after purple picture of my skeletal face. The pictures would be ugly as hell, but I'd tell him they were beautiful.

Through orange-tinted light, a beautiful scene starts to unfold before me. The calm of night has set into the grocery store. A lone cashier gives tired sighs as she counts loose change. She does not expect any more customers, and her eyes have shut down for the night. Fluorescent lights illuminate empty aisles and make the cold bite even more. I have never seen the nativity reenacted, but I can imagine what it feels like to watch. It's what I feel now: breathless wonder and inexplicable gratitude. I am so small and insignificant compared to the peaceful bounty before me. This scene should be captured in stained glass.

The grocery doors glide open, and my brothers enter in regal ski masks. They could be the Magi who followed some orange star to this godforsaken place. One of them sticks his gun to the cashier's back with such grace, such humility. I think it is Mackie, but I can't see through the mask. One of my brothers hands the girl a sack to stuff full of money. They wait so patiently. The cashier starts to cry perfect oval tears that make her face glisten. She looks out to the sky, unspoken prayers on her lips and haunted terror in her eyes. Her eyes look like she is carrying the child of God.

The woman speaks to my brothers. I cannot hear the things she says, but I know they are wonderful, godly words. She hands them the bag and still she talks on. Her mouth, made big by red lipstick, forms honest words. One brother holds the gun steady. The other looks for expensive liquor. They both listen with disbelieving mouths to this frizzy-haired woman. She is no older than nineteen, I'd guess. Her hands shake. Her lilac eyes look out into the orange night, searching for some kind of miracle. In all her anxiety she cannot see that this scene is a miracle.

I do not know what happens next. I blink for an instant and suddenly the world makes no sense. Blood trickles onto the conveyer belt and the rack of plastic bags. The frizzy-haired girl has a hole in her back, then two. Her holes grow as my brother pulls the trigger again and again. The glass is so thick I hear nothing. Soundlessly, the girl crumples to a heap on the floor. Her hair alone makes her different from the tiles surrounding her. I watch her limp body as my brothers flee the store. I watch the breath leave her body. Still the blood flows, thicker than before. I cannot see her eyes. I want to see her eyes one last time.

My brothers reach the car and beat on the windows until I unlock it. They throw the overflowing bag of money into the backseat and yell at me to speed away. They still haven't taken off their masks, and for a moment I think they are strangers. I look back at the cashier, but I cannot find her amid all the dusty tiles.

"What did she say?" I ask quietly.

"Just drive!" my brothers scream, and I do. "Anywhere!" they cry, "just get away from this place." I shift into drive and follow their vague instructions. The night is a gaping hole, waiting for us to fill it. Why didn't I see that before?

I don't glance back as we drive away. The scene is too beautiful to spoil with reality. I can't shake the cashier's face from my thoughts. Her eyes were fields of sprawling lilac, turned orange by the unrelenting moon. I want a picture of that face to hang on my refrigerator. I never want to forget a moment so pure and perfect in the grand scheme of the universe. Nothing has ever been so beautiful and nothing ever will be again. I tell myself this, and my breathing slows back to normal. I drive until the moon gasps, then flickers out. The orange glow melts away and the freezing Arizona highway turns a deep, pulsing violet like every other night. With a laugh, I think that Ethan has finally taken his favorite crayon and scribbled out all reality.

– *Peter Gray*

Wal-Mart Is Ghetto

Halls full of seventh graders talk and high-five
In their cashmere jackets and A&F polos
$170 jeans with the new flip-flops
Squeaks come from the new basketball sneaks
The fur cloth rubs from their North Faces
I'm different though
I wear the old, the thrift, and the unwanted
I take the $10 sneakers with thanks
And I sew the holes up on the cloth with ease,
Promising myself that one day
It would all be better.

The popular walk daintily
As I fight to keep my sneaker soles on
There is no one else like me
No one from the Ridgeville apartments
No one born on a couch
No one living in a leaking-roof condo
No one like me
Jenna What's-her-face walks by me

"Wal-Mart is sooo ghetto," she says
I want to hit her
She doesn't know
She really doesn't know.

– *Will Dodge*

Swamp

She always liked to mention it when we were together in a group or when we met someone new. She said it loudly, in a matter-of-fact way, and then she would press her body against mine, push my head sideways with a passionate force, and twist her lips with a squealing sound that made my head buzz.

It made her extremely proud that we had known each other since forever and our mothers' swollen bellies had bumped together seventeen years ago. With my cold hands in her warm chubby fingers, she named me without my consent her confidant, her pet, her sister, her best friend, stroking my curls that used to fall down to my waist and making me swear that nothing would ever change.

And it didn't for a while.

Hot summer afternoons were spent in her unkempt backyard. We would dive into her cold pool that really was more of a swamp, with its green mossy edges and floating bugs, and make ourselves mermaids. She made us search for a treasure at the bottom of the world that, once discovered, would eliminate the deep sea of evils.

But we never found the treasure.

Whenever I came out of the water, my ears aching from the lack of air and from struggling to press my body against the bottom of the pool, to exclaim breathlessly that I had found a wooden treasure trunk, she would disappoint me. "The treasure is not in a wooden trunk, sister mermaid. The evil octopus has disguised it again. Keep looking." Then her short stubby legs, tired from spinning in bicycle circles, would come to a halt and she'd let herself sink.

Tedious hours spent in a useless search exhausted me but eventually the rain ended the sessions. As warm drops fell, we got out of the pool, our blue scales fading to reveal the light hairs on our girl legs.

María. La Virgen María. La pura, la inocente.

Her parents named her proudly, like any good Mexican Catholic. They hoped that their youngest daughter would resemble a woman they placed in their living room with flashing Christmas lights hovering above her holy head.

María wears the name with indifference. "Why are there so many Marías?" she complained when put in a classroom with two girls who shared her name.

María wishes she were named Roxanne. Not a name that makes her another brown girl in a crowd.

But María is not just another girl in a crowd. She has a gift or a burden like her Holy Mother. She has more love in her than I have ever seen in anyone else. She expresses it preposterously, giving it out in overwhelming amounts, never measuring, and it's always too late when she realizes she has given more than anyone could ever give back.

I still do not know where this hollow pool of blind love she

111

let spill on so many came from. As much as she seems like someone who says everything that comes to her mind and yells it out inappropriately across hallways and in restaurants, María keeps her secrets, she has her sadness. On gray days they bind her to warm sheets. It's only after several hours that she learns to pull herself back together, shake it off, and wake up. When she untangles herself from a sea of blankets, she lights up a cheap cigarette and pours herself a glass of her mother's wine and sits on a balcony that looks out over her swamp pool.

Heavy eyelashes and red lipstick disguise her pain well. When she finishes covering up swollen eyes, she goes out with one of her many friends. María laughs herself to sleep. She wakes up again in admirable resilience, ready to love the world once more. She skims past imperfections, viewing them as personality quirks and amusing contraptions of human existence, not something she ever has to protect herself from.

And this I envy.

Dios te salve, María.
Llena eres de gracia:
El Señor es contigo.
Bendita tú eres entre todas las mujeres.

She lost her virginity young. At thirteen, I did not really understand why she felt proud of herself. I hadn't even kissed a boy. Holding hands with someone was a distant wish that made me nervous, that made my palms moist. María had just gotten out of her Pokémon phase and I had just begun keeping a journal. We were young.

María persisted in telling me more than I wanted to know, with her sly red grin. The way she described the whole ordeal made me nauseous. I disliked the thought of a young man I had never seen in my life breathing heavily upon her, caressing the slight curves of her bursting breasts, threading sweet webs inside her mouth with his tongue, while dragging his heavy hands across her. She said he had made her feel important.

María adored him.

Daniel, a tall, strong eighteen-year-old with dark eyes and a mustache, marked the beginning of our separation. He became the first in a long list of men and boys who tore her away from me. María would invite me to tag along with Daniel and his friends. "Daniel has a car," María would squeal through the phone. "We can come and get you." But I made up excuses. Hundreds of them. I felt like a girl, my breasts had just begun to ache, and I hated it when María would grab my hand and make me touch hers, soft and round. Like a woman's, she said.

Our daily telephone conversations died when María got kicked out of school. She had always hated doing homework and then she started to fall asleep in half the classes, bored out of her mind with equations and stories about people who lived long ago. She looked beautiful when sleeping. Her red lips looked fuller and her eyelashes longer. It was a shame to wake her up but I did anyway, getting out of my seat and pretending to blow my nose while giving her hair a tug. She always woke giggling.

Guiltily, I came to the conclusion that my efforts in creating our bond had been minimal. After she got kicked out of school, I only saw her on weekends. Each time, she looked older and there was something new to her: a pink streak in her hair, a hole in her ear. But then our outings diminished to scarce crowded nights where she would place her chubby, soft hand in mine to resuscitate our past. And then, in a whisper, she asked a question we both knew how I should answer. "How long have we been best friends?"

"*Desde siempre.*"

Daniel days did not last for long. They slowly morphed into days of names I would hear María mention only once, lovers saved for the darkness.

At fifteen, María's short body, overwhelmed with curves, shaped her into a girl who seemed mature and womanly. She carried herself well, thick black waves of hair against round breasts, her cat eyes honey yellow, and her bronze skin glimmering. María kept only her long hair and silver tongue-piercing throughout the years, giving her an ethereal gypsy look. Everything else about her matched whomever she shared a bed with.

By then I looked different. I stopped being scared of my body, and I let go of being a girl. María smiled every time she saw me and, like a proud Mexican mother, she praised my hips, my discrete curves, my long hair.

I do not think María really fell in love for a long time. She loved everyone, flirting with every gender, any age. She tried to be liked by all. With her intense nature she drove several away. But that didn't bother María because, even though not for long, people enjoyed her everywhere.

⁎   ⁎   ⁎

I knew Andres from school. He got good grades and liked to read, even though he pretended he didn't. He never brushed his hair but he always kept his sneakers clean. María had become his friend the year she got kicked out. He was not her type.

"Andres? Really?"

"You know I have always had a thing for him."

"No, I thought you were friends, not . . . I don't know, something else."

"When are you going to realize you only get one best friend, and for me that's always been you?"

María did not fall in love until she was sixteen. Andres was different. She did not cheat on him and he did not cheat on her. He wasn't like the others, who were always much older, much larger, holding María in their thick hands as she pressed herself against chest hair. Andres was still a boy, skinny, naive, but not innocent. He had had his share of girls, of one-night stands, of *putas*, but he never took advantage of María. They were equals.

They fell in love quickly, spoke to each other all the time. When María took a bath, she would put him on speakerphone and tell him how her razor was rising up her thighs and how soap had gotten into her eyes. Romance. Andres listened to all of it, maybe not to what she said but definitely to her voice.

Chiquita hermosa: No sabes cuanto te adoro y te amo. Gracias por ser mi mujer algo que para mí siempre serás. Quiero que sepas que haría cualquier cosa por ti porque eres la niña por la que siempre he soñado. Eres perfecta aunque tu lo niegues. Me haces la persona más feliz del mundo.

María shoved his love letter into my hand on one of those crowded nights. "Isn't it really corny?" she said, giggling in amusement. "He's like that. He likes to whisper things in my ear, when we are . . ."

I smiled, shaking my head while pressing my finger to her red lips. María put her mouth against my ear, indifferent to my expression of discomfort. I gently pushed her little body away from mine but then pulled her back in a hug. "Just remember to be careful."

María responded in a sudden storm of laughter, "You know I'm not, but don't you worry about me." She paused and looked at me in her usual flirtatious manner. "Plus, you'll rescue me if anything happens."

I let go of her and tried to give a serious look, as I had many times before. "María, I mean it." But she had already turned away, putting her hands into one of her friend's long blond ponytails, twisting the strands around her finger.

The summer it started to go wrong with Andres, the calls began again. I couldn't help but wonder why it was me and not one of her other friends, the ones like her, those wild night girls. We hadn't spoken for more than a couple of minutes on the phone for years, because really we had nothing to talk about. Nothing that tied our worlds together. We just called about the important news, the new boyfriends, my dead cat, her parents' divorce, stuff you might tell a relative out of obligation, out of politeness. But Andres was breaking her heart, and she was too proud to admit it to anyone in her world.

María clung to his presence. She had sacrificed other relationships to dedicate herself solely to him.

116

In her presence, Andres looked exhausted. María clutched his bony hand in hers, making his fingers numb and purple from holding on too tight. She manipulated his blood circulation, his breath, his time.

María foreshadowed their end with vague comments. He would get tired of her mood swings and uncontrollable anger. She realized she frightened him with some fits where she allowed herself to throw furniture and scream in excruciating sobs.

I didn't know what to say, so I told her that everything was going to be fine and that things happened for a reason. But I didn't understand the reasons. I didn't know about her anger, her sobs, where they came from, why they emerged. She had named me her best friend with pride and I didn't know her at all. I saw what I wanted to: the superficial, shimmering blue surface, not mucky green corners and the dirty square tile at the bottom.

It was the only time I have witnessed her tears. The catharsis lasted a few minutes. Her tears, short and quick, never trickled down her small face because she brought her chubby child fingers up to her eyes every time a teardrop emerged to fall.

I hugged her in a corner. She disliked the idea of anyone watching her weak.

María confessed to me in whispers that she had never felt so alone. She longed for simplicity, childhood, for the days I couldn't find that stupid treasure because there just wasn't one. She told me there was no one else anymore, I was what she had. Everything else seemed fleeting and fake.

She wrapped her brown arms around me, holding on as if I

117

would float away if she changed position. "Invite me to sleep over. I don't want to sleep in an empty bed tonight."

I look at my room to realize she has invaded it. María functions like a heavy storm coming every once in a while in a sudden swirl, moving conventional objects out of their place. No invitation, no warning, just thick wind shaking glass windows, making them tremble with riotous laughter.

Her clean blue sneakers lay uninhabited among my pile of dirty shoes. Her plugged-in curling iron heats up against my plastic beads, her crumpled T-shirt is on my carpet, and her drippy fuchsia nail polish lies on my desk. She will soon complain in forgetfulness that she has lost these things.

My toothbrush stained with red lipstick serves as a sign of our sisterhood, your saliva is my saliva, "who gives a shit?"

You are back, María, probably for sheer convenience and for a limited amount of time, but I don't care because I need you too.

I need you to love me the way that only you do. Ignorant of imperfections and ready to forgive. The way that I love you. We are willfully ignorant.

– *Loretta López*

Untitled

I.
My father is a fraud.
He is afraid of losing his identity
and love.
So he stays up late,
watching televised stories
about the similarities between lovers and lies
as he fingers his collar
with the button on the middle of his throat
that my mother sewed in steady place
so she wouldn't be tempted to slit it.

He doesn't know about that, though.
He only knows his childhood
and how truthful he was.

Sometimes he wishes
when we're all asleep.

II.
My mother is a dreamer.
She stands on the windowsill
and cleans between the panes,
praying to the God
to distract her eyes
from the pale way her daughter's face shivers
in scared contortions late at night.

III.
My brother is a hero.
He keeps two guns in a cardboard box under his clothing
next to the books he will never have the time to read.
The day he got his uniform,
he was nowhere to be found.
And now he sits cross-legged staring wide-eyed
in front of all the doors I close and lock.
Because what he doesn't know
will almost certainly hurt him.

He doesn't know me.

IV.
My sister is confused.
She likes to put on little plays
she doesn't know are true stories
to make me laugh about my mistakes
until she holds me by the waist
and makes my hands shake from crying.

She will never see.

V.
My friend is depressed.
She calls me in the darkest of nights
to whisper on the phone and then grow silent
because there isn't much we can do.
Little Benjamin draws her presents
of newborn frogs smiling
and suns with crudely painted rays
that reach out to all four corners
to make her stay in her too large bed at night.

She doesn't stay.

VI.
My love is alone.
He had another
until his car veered off
into the dying branches
and her breath
smelt of permanently crushed glass.
Now I beg him to keep holding my hand
whenever we go down long staircases
because they spiral down in unnatural patterns
and I'm scared his legs from the accident
would kill him on the way down
and his hot breath would smell of the cold concrete
beneath.

VII.
I am a liar.
So I write until my fingers
smell like the tired hum
of the computer.
The letters fade off the keyboard and disappear
because all my pencils are broken
Just like everything else I own.

I am alive.
As I sing along to the voices
that always knew more than me
and try to look up meanings
because I don't understand
and never will
but they all try to make me
keep going to feel the sad fate of my poetry
and read things
that would make them love
their own decrepit lives.

I am hope.
Between 12:35 and 3 A.M.,
wondering if I can be as productive as my hands
that caress the drunk words my love slurs
between gasps of vomit
and uncomfortable sleep.
As I continue singing the meaning
of every song in my head to him
until it hurts enough to sleep

and dream of silent colors that don't have the courage to ever
    exist
and things so impossible to say
to the lies living with me.

– Nadra Mabrouk

Glow

There's a little string of lamps, bobbing up-down in the dark, tiny yellow suns swinging back and forth on the coal miners' shoulders. They trudge home under the cover of night, replacing the brilliant light of the sun with small lightglasses, wan light shoving the hands of dark out of their eyes. They cling to the bulbs with their sore and swollen hands, black dust carved into the lines of their knuckles. Coal soaks into their hair, dyes threadbare trousers and boots and mittens, smears across their faces. The seamstresses leave in gaggles, the white of their sweat-stained shirts stamped brazenly upon the night, trekking across muddy streets to melt into their homes, eyes strained, backs hunched and aching, fingertips sliced red from loose string.

We can see them go, wending their way home, desperate for their families — see it all from the windows, glassless blocks of nothing, letting in gusts of dry, warm air and thick, heavy dark. We work by the light of the furnaces, burning brightly orange behind bars of black, and look wistfully over our shoulders at the homes.

"Almost there." Ada's got the mold cradled in her hands,

inch-thick protective gloves making her fingers look weirdly large. The heat swells, pulses up into her face. She says, "One more."

My lips purse tight over the opening in the pipe; cheeks blowing out, they inflate ruddy-pink as my breath runs down, the orange in the mold cresting up.

"It's full. Pull it out."

The blowpipe eases out, twisting free of the glass like glue, giving a little pop when it shrugs loose. Ada is quick to stab in the funnel, before the hole closes, and the glass sighs, enveloping the wood into the folds of its flesh. The Glow shivers into the funnel and down, breathes life into the glass. Together, they whisper sweetly, pulse once, again, again, a newborn heart beating swift and sure.

She hurries to the lehr, and as the first lightglass rolls out soft and gentle onto the cooling racks, I bury my pole deep in the womb of the furnace, and the heat scorches my mouth dry as bone. When I come away, there's a fat glob of molten glass on the end, angry red, and Ada's waiting with the cast, watching me step up onto the bench.

Down the line, girls like us — the gaffers — scuttle back and forth, from the furnaces to the lehrs and back to the benches. Blowers stand up tall on chairs, pipe pinched between chapped lips; holders squatting low, the heat from the mold and the glass bleeding through thick gloves to their callused hands. The younger girls, one or two or three years spent here, sink their arms deep into the Glow, stirring the batch with heavy wood paddles, loading it again-again-again into the blistering heat of the furnaces. We all do our jobs fervently, as steady and intense as the pulsing, never-ending fires.

"Ready?" I ask.

Ada snaps the mold closed over the blowpipe, swallowing the little blight of orange whole, and wipes a layer of sweat away with her sleeve. She nods, once, wearily. "Okay," she says. "Blow."

The younger girls clamor around the window, shutters flung wide, their downy hair illuminated gentle white from beams of moonglow. They're whispering, or attempting to — harsh and brassy crow-sounds grate in our ears, excited murmurs, ten-fifteen-twenty girls all huddling close.

"Can you see anything?"

"No. If they would move their fat heads, maybe —"

"Oy," Mattie hisses, her stare sharp, teeth bared like flint. "Shut up. The furnace-men are downstairs. If they hear you all tramping about like cows, we're dead."

Some of the girls shuffle their feet, toes muttering darkly on the floorboards. Mattie glares. "Clear off. To your beds."

They all listen. She has that power, Mattie. Always has. Once they drop grudgingly onto their ticks, golden straw jutting mussed and sleepy out from the sheets, Matt takes my arm, tows me to the window. Ada and Charlotte shadow us, their hair peeling up from the backs of their necks in the breeze. One of the younger girls grumbles, complaining, and Mattie shushes her.

Charlotte breathes, "Someone's down there."

We can hear them downstairs, beneath the guttural chugging of the furnaces gnawing sleepily at the coal, fires banked. They're talking, muttering words we cannot hear, meaningless sounds clawing up in between the boards of the loft, spreading across the ground like blood. Mattie and I press our ears flush against the floor, straining to listen. Nothing.

126

The voices draw nearer, and we're able to make out snatches of conversation. "This . . . where you'll sleep . . . the lehrs . . . furnaces never go . . ."

Mattie's head snaps up, her eyes clouding smoky gray. "New girl."

"Damn it, girls, *look* at that mess."

The seer's face is angry purple, spitting venom at Fern, the new holder. She sets her jaw and stoops to help one of the younger girls up, both of them brushing batch from their skirts. Sand spreads thin fingers across the floor, spilt from the pourer's heavy pan. "Don't help her, you lazy cow, just keep working!"

Like she can't hear, the new girl scoops up the spilled batch with cupped hands, sand leaking from her closed fingers in gauzy threads. "Blanche," I hear Mattie call to me, the only factory girl not gluing her eyes to her work, pretending not to hear the seer's shouts. Her gaze burns hotly on my face. I don't know how I'm supposed to help, but I abandon my bench anyway, take Fern's arm in my fingers and pinch hard, steering her away.

Fern glares at me. "I'm trying to help," she says. The seer looks about ready to throttle her.

"Forget it. Come on."

Fern Scott is my partner now. Usually, the new girls work three or four years in the Glow, building their skins thick and leathery so when they get up to the blowing and the holding they don't burn alive, char to ash. But Mattie's partner got sick and had to leave, and we needed a new holder.

She looks silly in her long sleeves, thick gloves stretching up to her elbows. Sweat gleams on her like a second skin. I cart her back to our bench, tell her to kneel and keep her head down and

127

set up the mold. She does, but I see her hands shake and her cheeks turn the color of the kilns. She snaps the mold open so hard the hinges shriek.

The others pretend not to notice. All but Mattie, who watches us sharply.

"Stop that," I say, hissing as I jab the glowing end of my tube into the cast. "Do you want him to hit you?"

Her voice is heated. "That girl fell because I tripped. I'm supposed to leave her there and look the other way?"

"Yes." I pause between breaths, my cheeks puffing out. "You are."

She lifts her gaze up, away from the fluttering heart in the mold. "*Why?*"

I sigh. Fern can be very trying company, sometimes. "Because. You don't work, lightglasses don't get made. The city isn't lit. You don't make money. Your family doesn't eat. Got it?"

She blinks, her eyes honey brown, warm and glossy in the fiery light. She isn't paying attention to the mold. I can see the red of the heart pulsing, angry, swelling up.

It spills over the lip of the cast. "Hey, watch it. *Fern*, the *glass!*"

"Just hold still, will you?" Mattie cups Fern's face in two hands, tenderly, squinting into the black-blue pulp that is Fern now. "Give me the thread, Blanche."

I hand it to her, coarse yarn threaded through a needle's eye. "Here," she says, "hold Ada's hand. This will hurt."

"Not that hard, Fern!" Ada yowls, prying her fingers from the vicelike grip. Fern shudders as the needle enters her skin, weaving in and out to sew a cut over her eye. I press damp clothes to her lip, smeared with shining blood.

Today Fern spilled a bowl of Glow, knocked it over while she was reaching for the funnel. The seer took her outside and beat her till she was huddled on the ground and left her there. We found her an hour later.

"He shouldn't have done that to you," Mattie says fiercely, strength in her words like the heavy wall of heat from the kilns. "Someday, I'd like to beat *him* bloody for a change." Everyone laughs but me. I know she isn't jesting.

"Mattie," I warn, but she barrels on.

"I mean it." She looks wounded at me, turns her gaze slow onto the others. "Did you know once, when I was little, the seer knocked over a pan of Glow and beat me for it so the manager wouldn't know he'd done it? It's disgusting, how they treat us." Around us, thirty pairs of eyes, all the girls, watch us from their ticks, blinking wearily up at us. Some of them just look exhausted, irritated with our chatter. But others — others, they've caught her fire. I can see the anger burning in all their eyes.

The girls' loft isn't lit by lightglasses. We have a wide-mouthed copper bowl set in the center of the floor, stumpy tallow candles blighting its insides like a cluster of mushrooms, dozens of little flickering flames belching orange light, sputtering and gasping with each gust of breeze punched in from the windows. I wonder then, what would happen if the bowl were tipped on its side — would the fires catch, dance across the floorboards, and devour the straw of our beds? Would its columns of smoke fan out and choke us all?

"It's time for bed, I think," I say, and many of the girls yawn and sigh, sinking into their beds slow and dreamlike.

Mattie blinks. "Yes," she says. "I suppose it is."

We all curl on our sides, the heat from below us swallowed up by the floorboards, easing into us, flooding our skin. I can see, through a haze of lashes collecting firelight like dew that Mattie and Fern still sit up. Mattie touches her hair. "If he ever lifts a hand against us again . . ." The furnaces groan happily, pulverizing coal in their jaws, and I hear nothing else.

Fern has been here three weeks, and the seer's only beat her once. She and Mattie have been practicing sometimes at night, adding an extra two or three or four hours onto their twelve-hour workday. The younger girls join them, too, saying they want to learn. Fern doesn't spill the Glow anymore, and she only occasionally forgets to tell me when the mold is filled.

Mattie and Fern are inseparable. Their friendship has become exclusive, and Charlotte and Ada and I are often left out. They don't seem to mind. I pretend not to.

But sometimes, when they're all down by the kilns at night, the girls' voices are louder than the furnaces'.

"Come on, Blanche," Fern singsongs, "pick up the pace."

I tell her to hush, partially because I am annoyed, mostly because she's the one slowing us down. Our kiln is only filled partway, lightglasses dark on the shelves.

She laughs brightly and twirls on the lehr, drops one of the globes down indelicately. I wince. "Oh, Blanchie," she's singing loudly now, "Blanchie, Blanchie, I'd like to hit her with a branchie."

"Will you shut up?" I hiss. "The seer is going to —"

"What's going on over there?"

The seer makes his way over to us, squinting meanly down at Fern first and then at me. I keep my face to the furnace, dig the pole sharply into the liquid glass pooled there. Fern stares back at him, her teeth glinting sharp in the light. "Get to work," he says tiredly, and I think Fern has had a stroke of luck. Then she opens her mouth.

"I *am* working. A little song can't hurt anyone, can it? It does make things more cheerful around here."

His eyes glitter, jet-black. "Just be quiet and do your work."

"Aw," Fern pouts, her lip flushing bright pink, a little dimple from weeks before where she'd bitten through it. "Was your mam always too drunk to sing to you? Is that why you don't like it?"

"*Fern!*"

She was so close. He's tired, weary from tramping around all day. She would have been fine. His mouth splits into an ugly line and he glowers down at her; she looks small and fragile, kneeling beside the mold. There's a bat on his belt, a slender reed of a stick, swelling to a fat, heavy end. "I guess a little song can hurt somebody. I'll close your mouth for you, seeing as you can't do it on your own."

When he hits her, we're all watching. Every girl has stopped what she's doing to stare, the furnace light turning their looks of sympathy to mean, small little stones. Mattie's standing up on her bench, her eyes blazing. Fern yelps, the bat cracking hard against bone. He hits her once. Twice. Five times.

"Blanche!" Mattie screams, and my gaze flicks up. She's holding a lightglass in her hand, clutching it so tightly I fear it'll break. From the heat of her skin it flares to brilliant life, the

131

Glow searing white beneath the brittle casing of glass. She swings her arm back to hurl it.

I don't know why I do it, but my hands find the seer's back. I shove him, hard, away from Mattie's lightglass. The globe shatters against the door of the lehr, Glow flooding out white, blanketing flecks of Fern's blood like spilled cream. The seer bellows, groans. "Oh, God." I say, "Oh, oh, God."

When I pushed him, I knocked him flat into the furnace's side. His face is a furious blister, skin melted like candle wax. The stench of charred flesh pervades the warehouse. Fern cups a hand to her eye, blood trickling through the gaps in her fingers, and beams at me. "Thanks, Blanchie."

I drop my blowpipe to the ground, shudder, and vomit on the bench.

The managers are strangely quiet about what happened. None of us have been fed in three days, and the new seer beats us just for talking. Fern needed more stitches.

We don't know what happened to the seer. He was taken to the medic's on a gurney while Ada and Charlotte and the younger girls cleaned up the broken glass and spilled Glow, and I threw up again.

Our skin is smattered blue, puckered like rotting fruit. The seer hits us for moving too slowly, for talking, for standing too long at the furnace or the lehr. Mattie has been beaten the most. She is one livid bruise.

The sky has darkened, shrouded smoky black, and we are all stooped over our benches, our hands and our backs aching from the work, hunger a throbbing distraction.

"Hello, girls." The manager steps into the kiln room, eyeing the stacked crates of lightglasses with approval. "I hate to see you all worked so hard. But poor behavior must not be ignored."

He looks all around the room, his gaze prodding fresh wounds. "It would seem we have a bit of a rebellion on our hands. This will stop. Today. I —" His eyes slow on Mattie, stooped oddly over her bench, peering down into the mold. "Miss, is there a problem?"

Mattie's hands scrabble madly for the cast, fumbling to open it. Unable to pry it open, she shoves it away from her, the wood wheezing on the concrete. The hearts of her eyes swing up, horrified, to the manager, watching her coolly. She breathes, "What did you do?"

And then the lightglass, fetal in its mold, cracks. We hear it. The pulsing heart shudders, constricts in on itself. And it explodes. Red, on the ground, on the kilns. Mattie drops, wordless, to the floor. Ada screams and keeps on screaming.

The manager lifts his chin, looks on as if nothing has happened, his gaze sweeping back and forth, touching on all of us, like shards of glass stabbed deep between our eyes.

"They did it to her."

"I know."

"Mattie would never let anything get into the glass. She's always so careful."

My eyes open.

All around the loft, the girls sleep, creamy faces smooth in their dreaming. The soft light of the candles rubs the skin of

133

their arms and shoulders and neck and back, make the bruises look like playful tricks of the light. Mattie's tick is empty, the curve of her spine permanently embedded in the straw.

Fern's, beside me, is also empty.

Far below, normalcy reigns. There's the furnaces, snarling in their beds, content with their night's meal. The light they give, warm and red, floods out and slinks up between the loft boards; the scratch of a dry breeze gushing through the windows, battling the tiny stars of fire in the bowl. And there is something else. Something sugary-sweet, tinkling glass-laughter. Glass breaking.

"Fern?"

She's standing in the storeroom, aglow from the thousands and thousands of lightglass. Not even the ink from outside can perturb the white-light; it's thick and syrupy, hard to breathe. At her feet, the dusky, smoky-gray of the concrete floor is awash with white. Her hands shimmer like pearls, slick, translucent white. It's splashed on her dress, in her hair and on her face.

"Fern, what are you . . . ?"

Several of the crates have been pried open. Two are empty. Reaching in, she clutches six or seven lightglasses in both hands, turns to me slowly. There are silvery tracks down her face, akin to the Glow but softer, sadder. She drops the glasses onto the ground, hard, and they shatter, one after another after another. Glass cuts her hands. Glow leaps onto my ankles, burns where the acid touches.

"It's better this way," she says, "I'd rather live in the dark."

– *Katie Knoll*

134

The Falconer's Daughter

She dreams of sleeping
In the arms of skybirds.
Each dawn she is drawn
Trancelike to her window;
They sail like arrows above her
Circling, circling, circling.
To her, the sun is a yellow eye —
Branches, gnarled talons —
Her home, a hollow nest.
If they really are omens,
Her heart should hold more
Than ceaseless days at the window.
Her life should be more
Than a frail house,
Circled by protectors.

– Lindsay Stern

V-Day

The sky is on fire. Beads of light flicker off towers of glass. Red, blue, and green streak across the sky in a dazzling waltz before disappearing into space. With each burst of orchestrated flame, great pillars of smoke and gray contrails are illuminated for an instant against the empty backdrop of the sky. Some things are too good to be true. Tonight defies that statement. Tonight the world is alive once more; everyone will sleep sure of what the next day brings. Yesterday was a day of war, tonight is a night of victory, and tomorrow is a day of peace. This is V-Day: the end and beginning of all things. The old world has been torn down and a new one has taken its place. And although the everyday struggles of life will be there tomorrow, all is right in the world for a few brief hours.

You live in an apartment on the thirty-first story of the Worchester building; it overlooks First Street and the park. At 10:32 P.M. you lean on the windowpane with your forehead, pressing against the thick glass. Below you are the main launchers, near the fringe of the park. They have been hurling rockets right past your window for two hours now. As each missile flies by, there is a sudden tense vibration, and a dull *thwump*. The next thing you hear is a cracking noise far above your head. You can also see that throngs of celebrators, partyers, and soldiers are still parading through the street, on foot or in "victory cars," which blare loud, rhythmic music and wave the many banners and streamers of the military branches. The city, so coarse and disjointed in nature, is celebrating in a strange harmony.

You, on the other hand, are not celebrating. You are not outside. You are inside because life has not stopped for you. Your mother is in the hospital. She has been diagnosed with some disease you can't pronounce that could compound the effects of the white flu. When you think about your mother or the flu that runs in both of your veins, you begin to sweat and fidget, so you try not to. Your sister, Natalia, is supposed to call you from the hospital in the town you grew up in. She was supposed to call at least thirty minutes ago. To take your mind off things, you decide to boil up some noodles. You always eat too much when you're nervous.

Setting your phone on the marble kitchen counter, you pull out a pot, fill it with water, and set it on the stove. The igniter fires several times before setting the gas stream aflame. About a minute passes before your phone rings. With a degree of panic you rush across the kitchen and bring the phone to your ear. Somehow you are already out of breath.

"Hello?"

"Garin? What's wrong?" It's a man's voice; you sigh in relief.

"Christ, you scared the hell out of me. I was just waiting for my sister to call me. My mom's in the hospital. They think it's the white flu but they don't know how serious it is yet."

"Did she forget to take her shots?"

"No, she wouldn't do that. Forget about it, man. What's up?"

"Are you at your apartment right now?"

"Yeah."

"Can you be at Pauli's in ten minutes?"

"Yeah? Wait, what is this about?"

"Something has come up that I really think you should know."

"What are you talking about? You sound like a crazy person. I can't leave. I need to talk with my sister. Just tell me now." Working for the government makes some people a little too serious about things.

"Garin, your entire family could be in danger." Your heart skips a beat.

"Wha-what?"

"You need to meet me at Pauli's. I'll tell you there."

"Wait, no, why can't you tell me —" He has already hung up. You put the phone down on the counter and stare at it for a few seconds. Either it could be elaborate bullshit he wants to play on you, or it could be something else. You don't really know which it is, but you have always been on the paranoid side, so at about the same time the water begins to boil, you put out the stove.

You drop your cell phone into your left pocket and pull on the navy jacket you bought a few weeks ago. The plastic mask you pull over your face stifles you at first, but with the flick of a switch, air begins to cycle through. Three clasps secure several elastic bands around the back of your head. You check your watch; it is 10:56.

At 10:59 you step through the revolving glass doors of the Worchester and into the cool night air. A blue headlight on the forehead of your mask automatically switches on. You walk

138

east down First Street. Pauli's is on Alahuac Avenue, about two blocks down and on the right. Tonight is a good night for a walk; being out on the street helps you clear your mind. Your thoughts drift to the towering skyscrapers and the crowds of people streaming in every direction; they all are smiling through their masks. They all are singing. V-Day, just the thought of it makes your skin crawl, in a good way, of course. It doesn't seem real, but you know it is. It's V-Day; the world is being given a second chance. You're smiling.

At the turnoff for Alahuac Avenue, there are two men leaning on a beat-up taxi. They are wearing black suits and solid masks with vertical LED strips. You try to ignore them, but as you pass you can feel their eyes tracking behind their blank facade. You know who they are. They are part of the liberation party — a bunch of crazies, in your opinion. They are racists and criminals whom nobody takes seriously; however, you know to keep your distance. They aren't exactly the people you would want to run into in a dark alleyway. Only twenty steps later you have forgotten about them and have resumed your daydreams. If it weren't for an especially loud victory car distracting you, then you would probably have missed Pauli's altogether. It is 11:05; you are five minutes late when you step through the front door. He is sitting in a booth to your far right, taking a sip of his coffee as he sees you. You walk over and sit across from him.

"Well, what's so important?" There is something wrong with his eyes; it bothers you, but you can't look away from him.

"In about one hour you're going to be put on the blacklist."

"I knew you would pull this stupid cop bullshit on me." You laugh, but his eyes are aflame.

"They believe — we believe you have been making calls into the occupation zone."

"This is ridiculous."

"Garin, what stupid shit are you up to?"

"Nothing. I don't even know anyone stationed in the occupation zone."

"They were civilian numbers."

"What? See, that's just — Christ, do you actually believe I did any of that?"

"You tell me."

You pause and lean in to whisper.

"I have made no calls to anyone in the occupation zone whatsoever. I don't know anyone stationed or living there. Now you tell me, am I going on the blacklist? Because you better be goddamn serious because this is not the time."

"Garin, you are going on the blacklist, no bullshit. However, I think I can help you out."

"As if things couldn't get worse. What's the plan?"

"You're going to get out of the city, while I try to sort things out. You'll probably need to stay hidden for a day or two."

"No phone calls?"

"From this point onward." You lean your head into your hands; they slip across the front of the mask. "No masks, either. They can track it."

"Well, I would much rather risk getting caught than dying from the white flu. In case you've forgotten, I have Type C."

"Don't worry. I've got you covered." He pulls out a packet and hands it to you; there are three green capsules inside. "These will do fine for a day."

"Are you sure these work? I thought . . ."

"You think, Garin, but I know. These will work fine for now. I'm already sticking my neck out too far for you, so I'd be a fool to give you the faulty medications."

"I guess you have all this figured out."

"Damn right I do. You need to take these now, but keep wearing your mask. Go to the metro station on Jordan Street." He slides a ticket across the table. "Put your mask on the southbound, and then go northbound until the stop at Fairbanks. Someone will meet you there; you can trust him. He'll take you somewhere safe until I get all of this wrapped up."

"I thought the metros were closed?"

"They just reopened. Have you had your shots today?"

"Yeah."

"Good. Take the pills and get out of here."

"OK." Lifting the mask off your mouth, you open the packet and pour the capsules into your mouth. He hands you a glass of water; you drink it, and the medicine washes down your throat. "I don't know what's going on, but I guess I don't really have a choice."

"It's a bad situation, Garin, but it'll be OK." You stand up and walk to the door. Out of the corner of your eye, you can see he's firing an inhibitor shot into his arm. As the cool night air surrounds you, you break into a fast walk, hiding in the shadows of a nearby alley. You fumble through your pockets, grab your phone, and then hurriedly you dial your sister.

"Pick up, Talia, pick up." The tone sounds several times. "Goddamn, pick up."

"Hello."

"Talia. This is Yuga." It's her answering machine. You swear under your breath and clench your teeth as it grinds on to the recording tone. "Talia, I know you can't talk right now, but you need to know something. I have to leave town. I — I — I don't know what's going on, but I have to leave for a couple of days and you won't be able to reach me. Please do not call me. Something bad could — I'll explain later. Tell my mom I love her, and, um, yeah. I'm so sorry, but I can't explain it all right now." Your gaze moves to the other end of the alley. Two men are standing side by side. Are they watching you? "I've got to go."

You slip the phone into your pocket and casually walk the other way. Your heartbeat speeds up. You exit the alley and walk thirty steps before looking behind you. The two men are now standing at the entrance to the alley, clearly facing you. They must be the two liberation guys trying to pull something. You face them. "Listen, guys, I've got no deal with the liberation party, OK? I don't mean any disrespect, but I just want some privacy." They don't move. "You're not with the . . ." You start backing away. "Christ, guys, I didn't do anything. This is a mistake. Go talk to —" You turn and begin to run. You can't hear if they're following you, but you don't care. Your body is burning up, your head is on fire, and your heart is pumping like mad. Paranoia takes over.

When you reach the metro station, you can barely breathe. Leaning over to catch your breath, you look down the street and see that the two men are gone. What were you thinking? You don't go on the blacklist for another hour. You pull yourself together and walk up the metro station steps. Few people notice that you're breathing heavily or that your eyes are wildly searching the crowd. It's V-Day. They have bigger things on their minds. You scan the ticket at the entrance and move onto the first platform. People are already filling up the southbound

142

train, and you can see through the doors of the metro that the northbound has just arrived on the platform beyond. You step through the metro doors, drop your mask, and calmly walk out.

"Hey, man, you dropped your —" The door shuts and you move onto the second train. You manage to navigate the crowds and sit in a booth at the back of the car. As you get yourself comfortable, you can feel the train begin to move. The train picks up speed and the platform rushes by. Just as the platform disappears, you see something that makes you jump. On the edge of the platform you could swear were two men in solid black masks. They must've followed you; they must be tracking you. You curl into your booth away from the window. The position you find is extremely comfortable. Shuffling to prop your feet up, you relax your neck muscles. You're falling asleep. Funny, you weren't even tired only moments before, but now you can barely keep your eyes open. As your eyes open and shut, you can see several men coughing across from you. You fall asleep.

You jump yourself awake. How long have you been asleep? You can see you're still on the train, but it is no longer moving, and now you are alone. A sudden wave of fear hits you: You slept in an open area without your mask on. You scramble to pull out your inhibitor case. You take off your jacket, and jam one of the needles into your shoulder. For a second it stings as the fluid rushes into your body. Discarding the needle and the jacket, you walk outside the metro car. You are in a suburban neighborhood, one that overlooks the city, and one that you have never seen before. It is dawn now, and the sun is piercing thick clouds with light, engulfing the whole city in shades of red. In the distance you hear a chorus of police sirens, but the place you find yourself standing in is totally silent.

Out of nowhere, a car pulls up beside you: a beat-up old taxi that you remember from a distant nightmare. The driver leans out from the driver's side window.

"Get in, Yugarin." You don't see any point in arguing with him. You are lost, and any hope of getting out of the city is pretty much gone by now. The second man opens up the door to the backseat, and you climb in. The car ride lasts about five minutes. The two men are silent; their black masks reflect your face like a mirror. Seemingly identical houses pass by your window, all cast in horrific red. You don't even think about talking. The car stops at a house that looks just like all the others. You get out and walk to the front door, the two men flanking up the sidewalk. The door is unlocked, and you open it, stepping into the foyer.

You see me standing before you. Of course you want to know who I am, as you have never seen me in your life. In these extraordinary circumstances, the answer to the question is very hard to explain and will lead you to ask another question.

Picture your life as a book, a novel if you will. It is a novel about a very unusual place that doesn't make all that much sense. Naturally you would be in disbelief of this world; you would believe the book to be a silly fantasy. However, as you begin to read it, you are mesmerized. This impossible landscape quickly sucks you in; you can see it, feel it, touch it. This once impossible story becomes reality to you. You believe in it, and cannot disbelieve it. What makes you attached to this world, this fanciful story? The writing, of course; it must be descriptive and convincing. Behind this orchestration of words lies the writer, the unseen narrator. In the simplest terms possible: I am the narrator of your life.

This is truly the simplest way to describe myself, but now you want to know what all I just said means, so I will elaborate.

You were born in the occupation zone. You volunteered to undergo an extensive psychotherapeutic program, which, through multiple waves of drugs and hypnotherapy, would make you believe you were someone else. I made you believe that your name is Yugarin, that you have a sister named Natalia, or that two other mysterious men are standing in this room. This is effectively a lie, but I make it true because I tell you that it is true. After being transplanted into this city, you became our insurance policy for the war that turned against us; you became an undetectable living weapon of mass destruction. Today, this war was lost, and you were turned into a biological factory of a white flu mutagen. This mutagen, spread by your train ride, turned the white flu from an immune deficiency into a killer. Ninety-five percent of this nation is infected with the white flu. Ninety-five percent will die. You are the hero of our people, the unknown warrior who succeeded where our armies failed. You are a wolf playing a sheep.

You think I'm crazy. You think I'm talking lunacy. Turn around. Those men who drove you here are not there anymore. You turn around and they have vanished into thin air. Your name is not Yugarin; it was, but it is no more, because I say it is. I am the narrator and you are the unknowing protagonist.

Now, due to chemicals introduced into your bloodstream several hours ago, you go into cardiac arrest. Your body begins to tremble; you can't feel your left arm. Your legs buckle, and

145

you pound your chest with your right hand, shaking erratically and gasping for air. You eventually collapse to the floor, your glazed eyes staring at the ceiling.

The last thing you see is me, standing over you. Did you really shake erratically? Or did I just tell you that? Did you even go into cardiac arrest? Or did I just make that up? This whole episode could have been the ravings of a madman, and you would never know it. You accept what's in front of your face no matter how unreal or insane it is. Such is the power of the story-teller. Today is V-Day, the end and the beginning. I am smiling.

– *Merrick Wilson*

boy

(for Jamaica Kincaid)

witness the three guys march right in and take what they
   want, hold
my aunt inside her bedroom and close the door. i want you

to muffle her screams, terrify her children, turn away from
   youth,
        survey and make final this lack of justice in discovering

hidden horror. someone please find the way i drive ambiguous.
        the world's fastest man can go and never stop just like a
        train,

so lay one sister tied up on a track and store the other with her
        so they may die together. i don't know why cousins kill
        cousins

in front of convenience stores, only that a violin allowing a
   bow to go

147

      against its strings seems to me as conventional as
      bulletproof glass

enclosing a movie theater, that when my cousin, age ten, takes
naked photographs with her cell phone posing like a girl

in a rap video, her deadbeat dad should come out of the
   woodwork
and call whatever mess he's made the twenty-first century.

– Da'Shawn Mosley

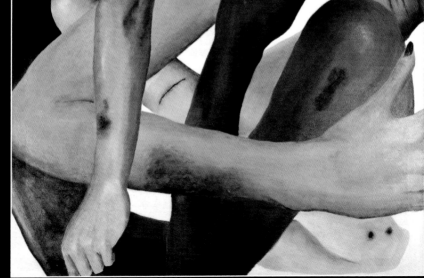

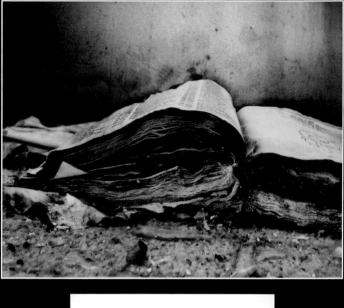

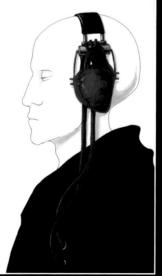

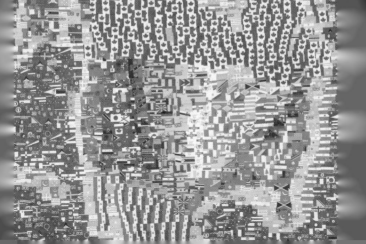

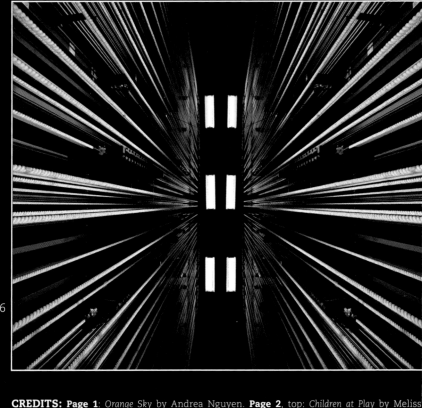

Maps

An aged atlas, skin-wrinkled pages
laced with boyish scrawls, childhood
sketched out in ink. I study the names of distant,
sand-covered cities: Tripoli and Pretoria.

The shores that a child aches for. Maybe
as the roundness of your cheeks melts away,
you forget there is life beyond your front door.
You forget how the rivers in India

look like the veins in a hand, how the men
and women on an island in the Pacific scar their backs
with seashell pieces to say *We are not children anymore.*

The tides of the Atlantic stop ebbing
at your brain, and the Andes peaks become
no more than a flowering of triangles on a map.

– Victoria Sharpe

Experiencing Adolescence as Tantalus

The House on Solitude

I remember moving to the house on Solitude. I carried a fish-bowl between my feet on the drive. Upstairs was so big and white and open and bright. It looked like Heaven, just lightness, with one big mattress in the middle. My room was pink. It made the carpet look pink too. It was the inside of an eraser. A Necco Wafer. I painted over it. Purple, like a bleached grape. Then green, like key limes and Granny Smiths. Even though it changed, it was never quite right. It was always infantile.

It has a minuscule window. I hated it. Going from the empyrean luminosity of the top floor to the Pepto-Bismol dungeon was like being condemned. Trudging down stairs covered in a carpet that does nothing to make the floor more comfortable was a jail sentence.

The yard is big, with two chicken coops and a gazebo that is covered in moss. I always wanted to live inside the gazebo, my own little house; an adult in a poofy dress, throwing tea parties. I wanted to run away from home once, so I decided to live in the chicken coop. I never did. It smells awful in there.

The best part is the raspberries. My mom looked at houses for three years. I never thought we would actually move. I stopped caring. Then we went to one. The realtor was late, so we just ate berries in the yard. I love raspberries. They are the best part. The house is a house. It has a roof. But I love the berries best. They felt like home even before we lived there.

My brother used to have a lizard. We fed it crickets. Some escaped, and then they lived under the furnace. I loved listening to them because when I did, I was in the tropics, slumbering in a hammock, surrounded by monkeys and jaguars and grand kapok trees. I always imagined that under the furnace they had a metropolis, with twinkling lights and trolleys. I miss that sound.

If You Die Before Your Dinner

Dessert before dinner. My aunt always orders key lime pie before dinner. If you die before your dinner comes, at least you'll have had dessert. I like that idea. It keeps you in the moment, optimistic. I don't understand the other things she does, though.

My aunt sniffs crayons. She has boxes and boxes: small, large, and jumbo. Thirty-two colors, sixty-four, one hundred and twenty-eight. Each one like a Technicolor mountain range. They hide in their boxes, little towers, temples of friendly pigment, ready to conquer the world. But she doesn't color, she just smells them. She prattles on about them, the waxiness, and the palpable odor of color. Waxiness like candles, candy corn, the smell of dental floss without the mint flavor.

She also sniffs artificial grapes. I visited her once and she took me to a hobby store and showed me a certain aisle. It was covered in plastic grapes, a vertical vineyard. They are maroon, like albino rat eyes; black, like licorice; and green — a pale, sickly green, like snot. They are shaped like boat buoys, and overly shiny. On the two-story-high wall, they are like polka dots on lush virescent fabric. They are a caricature of fruit, a travesty to the starving. They are made for kitchen tables and mantelpieces. Temptation without reward. She rubs them between her fingers, like they were long-lost jewels, found after years of searching, or bloody battles and conflicted succession. She floats her digits below her nose, like she is sniffing a fine vintage wine. She is a connoisseur of grapes and crayons. I don't know why she is so connected to her nose. Maybe smells are a constant for her, dependable. They are always the same. Maybe it's the only thing in her life that doesn't change.

My Name
I looked up my name once. It means "universal." Usual. Typical. Boring. Like paste, useful, but overly sticky and funny-smelling. Tacky — like a carnation. My name is an ugly red mug from an office Christmas party. Functional — like pea gravel. When I was little, I wanted to be named Eleanor. Like the first lady, something strong and elegant, like a tiara. Back then, I loved the color pink. Things change.

My mom told me I was going to be named Graham if I was a boy. Like the cracker. I like Graham better. She also told me she wanted me to be Grace or Iris. Yesterday I walked into a room without opening the door. Grace is not the name for me. Iris is wrong too. It is tall, slender, delicate, and purple. I am a traffic cone. I am not quiet, or dainty, or feminine. I do not own a dress.

152

My name did not set me up for success. I wasn't named after anyone. I saw in *Time* once that Emma was the most popular name in England. I was one of the many. Apparently Jane Austen's *Emma* was written so no one would like the protagonist. When I wasn't universally ordinary, I was unlikable. I'd never liked the name anyway.

Then I started German class. The teacher saw my name and was surprised. He said that I should have kept my name instead of choosing a German one for class. I didn't know Emma was German. I used to think of Germany: guttural language, lederhosen, and potatoes. But I love the language, and now I am special. Singular. Sensational. Now I accept my name. It is a mask of putty, hiding the color and intricacies below. Simple, but enigmatic.

Terrifying Brilliance

She is intimidating, especially to the unprepared. She talks much faster than I can take notes or even comprehend. Her mind travels from topic to topic like a Ping-Pong ball. She can explain anything and offer her opinion as well. She has an almost fictional strength of character. She knows who she is. She is a novel made of iron, carved with intricate designs, poetry, controversial ideas, and clarity. She is a desk lamp — when asked, she swivels over to shed light on that of which I am ignorant.

She is always on time, always energized, always wearing a vest. She always writes in cursive, and she always writes with a fountain pen. She says pens are like toothbrushes: You don't use anyone else's. She always drinks Earl Grey tea, and always recycles. She is always going, gleeful, glorious, sagacious. She talks

153

with her hands, like an interpretive dancer; literary analysis in 6/8 time.

She is Einstein, Herodotus, Ovid, and Chaucer. She would climb to the top of Mt. Everest and theorize about the ascension of a mountain being a Christ symbol. She taught me to never say "hopefully," or leap out of my seat chirping "boink!" in the middle of a novel. She introduced me to the archetype. She taught me the meaning of i.e. and e.g., and why the number thirty-three alludes to Jesus. She gave me Jane Austen, John Knowles, Eric Remarque, Harper Lee, S. E. Hinton, Joseph Conrad, Chinua Achebe, and — most of all — William Golding. She is the fountain of knowledge, spurting ideas and information whether it is wanted or not, like the fact that the Hanoverian royal who married into the British monarchy brought a fat mistress and a skinny mistress. She taught me that the oven is not related to the muffin.

She also introduced my class to God. She discovered we were raised as heathens. She says she grew up giving ten cents every week to save the pagans in Africa. Little did she know we were right here. She has educated us on Christian history, from the stories of David, Bathsheba, Lloyd Douglas's *The Robe*; from the Church of England and the Puritans to Martin Luther and his ninety-five theses. She has saved us from ignorance. She is a veritable force of nature, typhoon Susan. I want to be her.

She has taught me more than any teacher I have had. She still scares me a little, though.

Annotation

My teacher asked me where my notes were.

"On this piece of paper, right here."

"They're not in your book?"

I couldn't write in books. They were so perfect, so clean. Whiteness, punctuated by prose: so intelligent, so strong, so enviable. Who was I to mar that clear beauty? I could never match them, so wise and important as to be published. I dreamed of writing — wished and fantasized. Writers were clouds. Idyllic. Writers were statues, fixed in glory, messiahs over me, one so young and ignorant. I absorb, praying for osmosis. . . . I would not dare to mutilate that poetic paragon of prose. My wobbly words were half-baked cupcakes from a box in comparison to a writer's twelve-tier wedding cake replete with pearls and orchids.

How will you find a quote? How do you remember what you thought later? How will you know where to look? I could not answer. My thoughts felt stupid, childish, frivolous, undeserving of being immortalized. Minuscule. A pea next to the country of Bolivia.

But I was under orders, so I took a pen and attacked that pristine ivory. My pen was an assassin's dagger, the ink spreading like blood into the page. The page was ruined and it was conquered. Writers no longer sat on pedestals, their faces intent, philosophical and grayish. My thoughts were good enough. I had grown into someone large enough to stand next to an adult, and still keep my head above water. My word next to theirs was still a weak, pea-brained puppy next to Lassie, but it could stand on its own feet and bark loudly.

I have always wanted to find books with writing in them, to see what others thought, to marvel at their grand ideas. Perhaps someone will find, deep in a last-chance sale bin at a used bookstore, a book that I have annotated and they'll think I am clever.

Identical

"All right, Emma. Let's try 'Minuet Three' again."

I released a sigh that would have sent the Leaning Tower of Pisa tottering on its foundations.

I lift my flute up, the metal covered with sweat and saliva, like a disease. It is warm in my fingers, growing heavier with each repetition of this song. I begin to play. The notes are heresy to my ears.

"Again, again — one more time. Let's see if we can clear this part up, shall we?"

It rings in my ears, the eternal echo of my shortcomings. Her patience is both comforting and infuriating. As I continue to slide below musical perfection, I feel like I grow shorter. I am a squalling infant, incapable of what is proclaimed as simple.

And finally I reach it: tonal obedience. I have reached the standard. I sound like a recording. I have reached this perfection, but my thirst is not quenched. It is her perfection, not mine. She says in an infantilizing, falsely encouraging manner, "This is how it should sound." I must play it at the right moment. Just like everyone else. In a group, we must play at the same time. If we are perfect, it sounds like a single musician. Identical.

I stare at the flute. It mocks me from its case. It is nestled in black velvet, relaxed like an arrogant old man in swim trunks by the pool on his private island. If I raise it to my lips, I must do it correctly. It must be at the right angle. The sheet music lies there, the lines of the score as rigid as the expectations set by music teachers. The notes are flies, buzzing around my head as I try to focus.

"*Again*," they whisper. "Do it just so."

Then I tried acting. And I was a balloon released — a butterfly liberated from captivity to stretch its sticky wings and glide into the sun. With a play, I am given a word, and — sometimes — a general direction at which to aim it. With it, I can fly. I can holler it from rooftops. I can whisper it beneath a pillow. I can mumble it in front of the class. Every time I say it, the word is different, and it is perfect for something else, just maybe not this.

A note is concrete. It is right, or it is wrong. "Here is what you say, when you say it, how long it takes you, and even how you say it." *Dulce.* Sweetly. Obediently sweet. No love. No joy. No passion. No sweetness. Only discipline, a soldier marching in time.

Then I knew — I could never work in a cubicle. I cannot do something just like everyone else. I do not want to play it over and over, only trying to achieve someone else's idea of perfection. A note is always someone else's. It never belongs to me. I can make a word my own.

Fear of Failure

"We're at places," I murmur into my headset. "Okay, Lights 103.1, go."

For me, adolescence is running the projections for the play *The Laramie Project*. My leg bounces, the only moving part of my body, anticipating that first cue. As it arrives, I twitch with anxiety, fervently praying that the screen that will appear is

157

correct. I concentrate, for it is essential that I press it flawlessly, at the right moment. I wait in a minuscule corner, walled by hundreds of vertical ropes like vines, a pale fluorescence, twisting faces into gaunt ghosts. A hard, metal chair is curling my body into contortions. I am chained to the constant fear of having the wrong scene appear, constant dread that I can't do it right, that I will fail. That I am a failure. And then, like the inevitable sunrise, signaling another day, another show, another show to screw up, my cue comes. "Pro H, go." And I hit the button. The nine key. If it's right, I am on cloud nine. If not, there is no cloud and I fall down, down, down. I tap it, a tap that is simple, swift, subtle. The screen advances, fading steadily and . . . it is correct. A sigh rattles my stiff body. I have another chance.

Yet when I do make a mistake — my finger too chilly to execute an action, an order too early or inaudible — Armageddon begins. An opportunity for total success and perfection is stripped away, like peeling paint being obliterated by a power washer. Before, it was fixable, it was forgiven, it wouldn't decide my future. That one misstep, that gaffe can cause the entire show to plummet. I will go home, berating my sobbing self for not reaching a goal that seems so simple, for not achieving perfection when it is dangled beneath my nose, like a melon before the face of Tantalus.

I know I can do this. I want myself to succeed. I need to succeed. I am not in over my head, though I feel suspiciously wet and light-headed. I expect perfection in timing, but I cannot achieve it. It is a glistening, golden apple. The snake says I can reach it, and I am so hungry.

In the end, the projections are simply a complement to the actors, an afterthought. But they are all I have. Progressing from screen to screen will not decide my fate, but every time my finger twitches, every moment of guilt and self-flagellation, the ashamed profanity mumbled just offstage, pulls me further from the ideal I crave.

– Emma Funk

The Incorrupt Body (From Utopia)

For five days during the summer I was born, my father was the most famous man in America. Years later he would remark, "I went into the mine a poor son of a bitch and came up again a mill-ion-aire." He was proud that he had survived the mine collapse, proud that he had gotten to give an interview to CNN. People crowded around him as he emerged from the dark hole, struggling to touch him. Like Jesus. My mother sobbed and wiped her eyes with the sleeve of her dress before clinging to him, her clawlike fingernails scratching the thin fabric of his work shirt. The day after he came out of the mine, she went into labor with me, and was overwhelmed with flowers, some of which came from, she later found out, the president of the United States. My parents spoke fondly of those days, and after a while, the abject terror my father felt while he had been trapped in the mine was replaced by a faint sense of nostalgia. He reminisced about it, joked about it with his buddies. Very early on I was aware that I had arrived into the world at a miraculous time.

When I was ten, after the money from *The John De La Barre Story* had run out, Dad decided to run for mayor of our town, Utopia. West Virginia is a state where you get elected both for looking like John Kennedy and for being a good union man, and Dad had both those qualities. I went with him in my pink Sunday dress to the Nu-Way Bakery, to the First State Bank of Utopia, to the Carraway Theater, its bleached paint peeling. I held a sign with the UMWA logo and the phrase "De La Barre Raises the Bar." Dad was young and handsome and he waved a lot, brushing his hair back from his head. I fell in love with him as much as every other constituent did, breathless with the thought of some new blood in Utopia at last.

When CNN heard that John De La Barre, the mining miracle, was running for mayor, they sent someone down from the office in Charleston to interview him. It was an election year, and one of those election years where suddenly everything anyone says becomes a comment on their patriotism. I would like to think that my father knew this, that he said what he said because he wanted to be radical, just for once. Even at the age of ten, reading his quote over and over again in the newspaper, I didn't want my father to say what he said because he actually *believed* it, and still think he'd get elected. I didn't want for him to be that stupid.

What he said was, "Personally, I don't think the president could give two shits about the people of Utopia *or* the people of West Virginia."

The president was a Republican, so it was dangerous in itself, but I think it was the "shit" that really got to them. The man they had envisioned on his knees in the blinding dark, begging God to relieve him of his labors, had said "shit." About the *president*. When he lost, Dad merely shrugged his shoulders, said, "Well, I didn't want the goddamn responsibility anyway," and went back into the mine.

I thought about the quote years later, when my brother, Elijah, called me from Morgantown and said, "You've got to do something about Dad."

I was in Lexington, standing at my kitchen counter, watching coffee drip into the pot.

"He went to work today," he said.

"He goes to work every day."

"Yeah, well, that's the problem, Cara." I could almost see him rolling his eyes. "Just drive back to Utopia this weekend and tell him he's an old man and he can't work."

It went like this: Elijah had driven down one Friday afternoon and had witnessed my father pass out upon stepping out of his truck. The blackouts were, according to my mother, something fairly common in recent months and had something to do with the fact that my father refused to use his inhaler for his work-induced asthma.

Elijah said, "He's got to stop working. Let him live off the movie residuals and the mine pension. He's not dumb. He's doing this because he's a mean son of a bitch who's afraid to die."

I saw his point. But I didn't want to drive to Utopia. "You do it."

"Aw, Cara. He loves you. He doesn't love me."

This is Elijah's thing. He avoids any family responsibility by claiming that Mom and Dad have never shown affection toward him, and so he owes them nothing. I imagined him sitting in a half-drunk stupor up in Morgantown with his WVU buddies (all unemployed), whining at me to "do something about Dad."

"I mean it," he said. "There is absolutely no affection there."

"Elijah," I said, "are you drunk?"

162

"Yes, ma'am, I am," he said. "I surely am a little bit drunk."

"I'm hanging up now, Elijah."

As I put the phone back on its cradle, I looked at the Post-it note of my parents' phone number I kept on the wall. I hadn't called them in ages. I wondered, vaguely, whether my father still thought the president — any president — didn't give two shits about Utopia.

I called him.

Driving into Utopia feels like driving onto the surface of the moon. You turn off the interstate and go over an old industrial bridge bruised with soot, while under you the muddy Guyandotte trickles its way to the Ohio. The town itself juts up into the hills, and the roads sharpen into points and dangle over the dusty downtown streets, casting shadows over the Nazarene church and the Utopia Society for Crippled Children and Bob Barker's Income Tax Service and West Virginia Gift Shop. At two o'clock in the afternoon, downtown Utopia is silent, except for the occasional thundering *chucka-chucka-chucka* of the CSX coal train as it roars its way to Tennessee. Not long after my father came out of the mine a hero, Utopia began to go silent. I could actually hear it as I grew up, walking to the Kroger to get something for my mother. Quietly, the voices of my neighbors drifted away into the dark rooms of their houses, and emerged only on Sundays, when they would sit on their porches and glare at one another.

"A ghost town," I would sometimes say to my friends in Lexington. "I come from a ghost town."

My family lived on Miller Road, at the head of the Hatfield-McCoy Trail. Miller Road was a good street to live on, because it wasn't on a cliff and no one sold drugs on it and it wasn't a far walk to the Kroger. So we lived well enough, but we were still poor. Everyone in Utopia is poor. But growing up, I never thought of my family as such. We lived in a white clapboard house with a sunroom where Elijah and I would sleep in the summer, sharing knockoff Oreos from the Kroger and whispering late into the night. When I left West Virginia, I sometimes thought back on the house fondly, especially the little creek that ran at the bottom of the hill that crested off the back porch. The Old Regular Baptists would baptize their faithful there, and even though we were plain old Southern Baptists and therefore weren't supposed to associate with them, we would open the windows on Sunday afternoons, listening to their strange and beautiful singing piercing through the heavy air with their foreign melodies.

"Guide me, o thou great Je-ho-vy," Dad would sing, throwing his head back. *"Pil-grim in this barren la-a-a-nd."*

But I had heard the Old Regular Baptists had moved their operation down to the Guyandotte, and as I turned onto Miller Road it was silent, except for the occasional barking of a dog in someone's distant yard. I pulled into the makeshift driveway, the tires crunching on the gravel, and I saw that the white paint on the outside had begun to peel, that my mother's flowers were shriveled and dry. My feet were sweating in my boots, and, as I put my hand up against the side of the house and paint flaked into my hands, I felt a thick sense of shame.

I rang the bell hard, because I knew Mom wouldn't have her hearing aids in, then knocked twice for good measure. Someone was watching *The 700 Club* deep within the house.

She appeared at the screen door. Mom was a strikingly beautiful woman, Miss Utopia 1970, and she still had all of her hair and her teeth and her good figure. When I was very young, I thought she was Barbie. But now she looked hard and careworn, a Dorothea Lange photograph come to life.

"Hello, Mama," I said.

"Oh, Cara." Her embrace felt bony and forced. "Oh, Cara. You've got to do something about your father."

He was plopped in front of the old Naugahyde lounger in the living room, watching the TV. This was always my image of him from about the age of ten onward, after he lost the election. He would come home, and, without even showering, he would sit down in his lounger and flip on the news and call for Elijah or me to bring him a beer. Around 9:30 he would fall asleep, and the three of us would tiptoe around, trying not to disturb his sacred rest.

"Goddamn politicians wouldn't even bother coming to Utopia," he muttered as I put my bag down in the doorway. "I don't trust either of those slick-talking snake-oil salesmen as far as I can throw 'em."

"Don't listen to that *700 Club* Bible news, Daddy," I said.

He turned himself around in the lounger slowly, and broke into a fit of coughs before thumping his chest soundly.

"Sorry," he said. "Feelin' a little under the weather lately."

"Daddy," I said, "we need to talk."

"Did Elijah call you from Morgantown?" he asked.

I nodded.

"Aw, Jesus," he said.

"Daddy," I said, "how big is your mine pension now?"

165

"Hell, Carrie."

"I'm just saying, you could retire real nice. Maybe you could even move out of Utopia."

He reached for the remote and shut off the TV. Obama's picture died into black.

"Girl," he said, "I'd advise you to shut your mouth."

He took dinner in his room. Mama and I ate split pea soup standing over the sink, in silence. The soup looked and tasted like baby food. She told me that ever since the collapse, Daddy couldn't stand to eat much else. Then she yawned, said she was going to bed. I slept in my old room, my old posters peeling off the wall. The bed was too short for my legs, and my feet poked out of the blankets, icy-cold even in summer. My room was right next to my parents', and because I couldn't sleep I stayed up all night, staring at the ceiling at my glow-in-the-dark stars forming the constellation of Orion, listening to Dad cough and then sigh.

It was almost five in the morning when Dad poked his head into my room, fully dressed.

"Get up, Carrie," he said. "I wanna show you something you'll never see again in all the days of your life."

I made coffee on the stove — they didn't have a coffee-maker — and we drank it, black and bitter. Sometime in the night, my mother had gotten up from their bed and settled down on the couch. The blanket was drawn up around her, over her head. She looked like a corpse. I shuddered.

"Let's not dillydally any longer," Dad said, tossing the rest of his coffee in the sink. "Got a long drive to Aracoma."

The Aracoma mine was named for Princess Aracoma, the daughter of the Mingo chief whom the English first made contact with in these hills. Every summer, my family would make the pilgrimage to Logan to hear the story of her love for Boling Baker, the Englishman, and her subsequent death. It was amateur theater, but it always left me breathless and full of admiration of their love. When I got older, I found it amusing that they had given the Aracoma mine such a romantic name. It belched up black smoke and foul-smelling fire, and the people who staggered through it looked like ghosts caked in ash. After the collapse, the UMWA had managed to get it closed down, and a few years later it reopened, and it looked much better — at least on the outside. Mines bothered me. They possessed all kinds of spiritual questions about whether humans were meant to go so deep into the earth. If you dug far enough, would you eventually hit something?

It was 7:30 when we reached the mine. It was Saturday, but there seemed to be an unnaturally large amount of people around. Getting out of the car, I noticed Lyman McKenna right away. He was a friend of my father's, and used to come over to sit on our front porch, drink beer, and watch the WVU games with my father. I always had considered him a man who kind of surpassed joviality and was more boorish than anything, but today he seemed nervous, jumpy. Suddenly it was cold, and I vaguely wished that I'd remembered to bring a sweater.

"Johnny," he said. "Miss Cara. When'd you come in from Kentucky?"

"Yesterday afternoon," I said. "Been trying to convince this one here to give up this fire and brimstone."

I said it cheerfully, as if to be funny. Neither of them laughed.

McKenna invited us into the manager's office and poured us more cups of coffee. Then he and Dad retreated into the backroom and shut the door. I drank my coffee and flipped through the copy of *Newsweek* someone had left on the manager's desk. There were lots of articles about the election and how each candidate would do in each state, but they'd apparently forgotten West Virginia. It was so predictable I didn't even roll my eyes.

After a while, Dad and McKenna came back in, both rubbing at their temples as if they had terrible headaches.

"You own a handgun, Miss Cara?" McKenna asked.

Dad laughed and shook his head. "Naw," he said, "she ain't got no gun. She's one of those liberals who don't *believe* in guns."

McKenna pursed his lips in distaste and shrugged. "Well," he said, "she can do what she wants."

There were voices coming from outside the office, voices I couldn't easily identify. Dad went to the window.

"Lordy," he said. "Oh, Lordy, Lordy."

I got up to follow him, but McKenna put his hand on my arm.

"Now, Miss Cara," he said, "you don't want to see about that."

"What's going on?" I said. "Dad?"

Dad turned away from the window and stuck his hands in his pockets.

"Well," he said, "it seems a bunch of folks from up north got wind of the fact that this mine ain't exactly up to *snuff* when it comes to the standards of the Environmental Protection Agency up in Washington."

I looked at him blankly. "What are you talking about? They fixed it up a while ago. I thought it was fine."

Dad shook his head. "No, not that."

"Then what?"

McKenna wrung his hands together. "This ain't a standard mine anymore," he said. "This mine is a *strip* mine now."

Strip mining. Since I didn't live in mine country anymore, mining issues were very rarely on my mind, but I *did* know that in Utopia it was something of a black-and-white issue.

"People need to eat," McKenna said. "Strip mines feed 'em."

"Goddamn Yankees," Dad said. "What the hell they know about West Virginia?"

"They know it's beautiful," I said. "They don't want to lose the mountain."

Dad's eyes rolled so far up into his head I thought they might get stuck there.

"What the hell I care about the mountain? They could pave over the mountain tomorrow if it was gonna give my kids a better meal at night." McKenna's voice was sharp and angry. "The mountain is for people who can *afford* the mountain."

The door opened, and several more men came in, wearing UMWA jackets.

"Nina Floyd's out there," one of them said, "and she's half-naked in front of God and everyone."

"Nina Floyd?" I asked, perhaps a little too breathlessly. Nina Floyd had won an Oscar the year before for her role in a dark comedy that had been shot in Lexington. I'd served her coffee, and she'd tossed her long red hair over her shoulder and said "*Thank* you-u-u," in such a way that I had tried to emulate it for weeks after. All it had done was make my boyfriend ask me if I had a cold.

"Yeah," said Dad, with a little suspicion in his voice. "Nina Floyd. She's been poking around here for months." He shook his head.

One of the men who had come inside reached into his jacket and pulled out his handgun. Handguns were a fact of life in Utopia — you saw them everywhere — but still, the nonchalance with which he handled it unnerved me.

"Why do you boys have to have your guns out all the time?" I asked. "They're just protesting."

"We protect what's ours," said McKenna darkly.

After a while, it was decided that we would go out and face the protesters head-on, block the entrance so they couldn't get into the mine and engage in what McKenna called "their fool tricks." They opened the door and filed out, one by one. In the parking lot there were dozens of others — men, women, and children, most of whom I recognized. But I didn't want to talk to them, so I kept my head down and walked along silently, like a ghost.

The protesters had gathered outside the mine gates, now padlocked shut and guarded by the state police. They were all young and white and thin. Actually, they all looked a lot like Nina Floyd. And *clean*. The first thing that struck me was how clean they were. Living in Utopia gives you a kind of unwashable grit in your hair and nails, as much a part of you as your teeth and eyes. They were all chanting, wild, loud chants I couldn't pick out. And at the front was Nina Floyd, her shirt showing her midriff toned by the best hands in Los Angeles. And she ran her hands through her hair the same way she did in the coffee shop.

I pushed past Dad and McKenna, ignoring their cries of

protest until I was as close to the gate as I could possibly get. I wanted to see Nina Floyd again, in the flesh, her body incorrupt by ashes.

Someone behind me turned on their car radio.

> *You're so condescending,*
> *your gall is never-ending . . .*

Dad worked his way up to the front, beside me. He was panting now, gripping his chest in pain.

Nina saw him. She held up her hand.

"Mr. De La Barre," she said. Her voice drifted smooth and unctuous through the gate. "I wonder if you'd like to come outside and address the crowd. About the dangers of mining."

"To *hell* with you!" he shouted, and the crowd outside erupted in boos as the crowd behind us erupted in cheers and hollering.

She smiled, the kind of smile my mother used to give me. "But," she said, "it was mines like these that almost killed you."

"Only thing that killed me was you goddamn hippies chaining yourselves to the equipment for the last twenty years," he spat.

"Fuck the mine!" someone behind Nina shouted, and they cheered again.

Dad stuck his finger through the iron bars of the gate.

"I would just like to know," he shouted hoarsely, "just how many of you folks are from the mountains?"

"You don't have to be from the mountains," Nina said, "to care about them."

"Sure," said Dad, shrugging, "but you don't know nothin' about what it means to *live* here."

171

Nina reached into the loose canvas bag hanging at her side. "Let me give you the card of the Southern Appalachia Conservancy Group . . ."

"Where's that group headed up, Miss Floyd?"

Nina tossed her hair again. "Charlotte, North Carolina."

"Wouldn't hardly call that *rural*, would you?"

She ignored him. "Mountaintop removal is hazardous to the environment. Mountaintop removal is when —"

"I know what it is, Miss Floyd. I do it every day."

He said this with an air of exasperation. You get used to it after a while, especially when you're from where we are from. People assume you live and die by the mine, that you're either illiterate or just unwilling to read the literature the environmental groups from the North send down.

"And you're destroying the Earth!" a boy in a stocking cap next to Nina shouted.

Dad held up his hand. "Folks, I don't pretend like I don't know what strip mining does to the mountain in the *geographical* sense. But the fact is, people gotta eat. And if strip mining's gonna save our economy, then I think the good people of Utopia and of Appalachia are gonna be doing it for a long goddamn time."

Nina turned her nose up in the air. "We don't want you making money," she said, "at the expense of *our* future."

A surge of white-hot rage shot through me. It was her voice, her perfect unaccented *voice*, with the hint of self-absorption a person of her caliber earns. Us and them, us and them. What did she know about us?

In the days and weeks that followed, I thought long and hard about what happened next. About how I might have taken

172

her slender, pale, clean neck between my two fists and shook, hard, until Dad and McKenna dragged me off of her, how she fell to the ground clutching at her breastbone, coughing. About how Dad coughed harder on the drive back from the police station. About how Nina Floyd had her article in *People* about her savage attack by West Virginia miners, too dumb to know what was best for them, showing off the purple bruises around her neck.

"Some girl did it to me," she said. "Some girl who just didn't know any better."

And, most of all, I remember how much my father looked like John Kennedy in the coffin, the cheap powder scaling his cheeks and nose, and, when they opened him up, they found everything in perfect order except his lungs, which were black as night. From the mine or from the cigarettes? We would never know.

Dad *did* live and die by the mine, in a way. His was the Utopia success story — a man can get rich through faith in God and hard work. His American dream. It might have killed him. But hell, it kept me fed and sent me to college and made him proud. We have so little in our lives, don't we? And maybe it made me mad that Nina Floyd, with her muchness, with her money and her talent and her car, would try to take that away.

We protect what's ours. We live and die by it.

– *Rachel Rothenberg*

With You I Climb Mountains

With you I climb mountains. We begin in the morning, when the air is cool and thin, and the cicadas have only begun to stir in the candy-like glow of the rising sun. At one in the morning, just hours ago, you planned this; at seventeen I'm fiercely nocturnal and responded to your sleepy voice with fervent noises of agreement, fueled by gasps of caffeine and displaced, late-night laughter. When asked later by my mother where I am going, I tell her, *nowhere, I just need to get out of here*, and she lets me go, mumbling adolescence adolescence oh those adolescents under her bacterial breath.

In the morning, the real morning, I take a taxi to your high-up home with the stairs carved out from the side of the *yama*, the mountain. You meet me at the door and you say, still kind of asleep, "Walk with me."

There are gallons of energy drinks stored away in my veins and I don't know what to say. Surely even if I said anything it would ruin this quite perfect moment, all dawn and eager eyes, so I nod, I nod twice, and you take off down the green stairs. I can do nothing but follow. The moss here is slippery, like my heartbeats when I'm with you, and by the bottom of one sloping road there is a runoff of what I think is algae, pools of liquid ecosystems throbbing between your exposed toes. My irises move to follow the outline of your hand, moving backward instinctively to push gravity in my favor, and eventually your fingers fumble, in their amateur, boyish way, for my own cold hand.

This is how they did it in the movies: the girl says, my hand is cold. And the boy smiles a smile that he has practiced since conception, so it is fine-tuned and regularly polished with pheromones and pearl-paste. He says, don't worry, I can fix that. He takes her hand in his and squeezes it, not too hard but not limply, either, and everyone in the audience sighs (the women audibly, the men, not so much). They go home wishing for romance. Those who already have it wish their partner knew how to do that, and that night they spend the bedroom hours talking about how I wish you were better to me — but I am, I am, dear, can't you see? I warm your hands whenever you want me to. You just don't notice until someone points it out, you ignorant woman.

"I like your hand," I say, testing out the theory. "It's warm."

You don't answer. Maybe I have failed at this, and the movies are just meant to stay on their silver screens, but later on when you lean me up against the telephone pole as the little crosswalk man is stalled at red you say, "I like you."

And then, in a whisper: "Still cold?"

My footsteps are like frogs. I feel clumsy trailing after you; I've never been on your mountain and I don't know a thing about where I should step or how I should go about the downward roll we're currently traipsing on. I feel like my feet are twitching, their mouths opening wide, skin pulled taut, waiting to leap to the next point in our tiny journey.

We amble through tunnels lined with slick leaves and puddles of standing water. Here, the road goes down, down, down. You're walking like the steepness is already worked into your legs, and I don't doubt that it actually is, but my bones only know one level of elevation and I am getting tired already, at eight in the morning. You're looking forward, mumbling about which way we should go, and I can see the sweat standing out at the nape of your neck and I want to touch you but we're on an adventure. We're *trekking*. Those kinds of things come in the aftermath, when the hero has his arms around the ex–damsel in distress and the orchestra plays.

An old lady, an *obaa-san*, passes us, walking slowly with occasional dips and pauses along the way, and she nods — the casual bow — in our general direction. But she's smiling, and you know her by the way you bow shyly back, shoulders sloping and head dropping forward. Then she takes a look at me, at the color of my hair, and the mood of her smile shifts from daily-hello-boy to oh-my-foreigner. I can't help it: I blush, feverishly red, not the cute pink that the Japanese schoolgirls on my street emit when they giggle in hush-hush tones on the sidewalk, pleats sagging to their natural length.

I'm momentarily embarrassed, and look straight down at my shuffling frog-feet, willing the rampant dinosaurs in my stomach to just evaporate back into my bloodstream already. It's just like my mother said — everyone knows, honey, that you are not from around here. And that should be obvious, with my flaxseed hair and my freckled skin. I'm not Asian even though the shape of my eyes suggests otherwise. Sometimes I keep my head up and my hair back just so I can attempt to look like an Eastern beauty, and during these times you kiss my eyelids and tell me, "But you are just what I want."

Your grip on my hand tightens, fingers pressing firmly into my knuckles, or perhaps I'm just imagining it. I make to move forward, to continue on our journey and forget about this minor relapse, but you keep me back. We wait as the *obaa-san* ambles slowly past us, taking care to stare pleasantly at the gravel below her feet, her one set of eyes held carefully away from where we stand. But the other is on us, staring like it's never seen anything better, like we are some detached fragment of modernism — so disgraceful, yet at the same time so beautiful.

Japanese folklore tells me not to fall in love with mountain men. Women wail of disasters that befall mountain-made marriages — "He's never home, and my lonely days live on forever." In my head I imagine these men as backpackers, with hairy beards and beady eyes barely poking above a thick scarf, their whiskers gloriously iced. They huddle in the nooks and crannies of the mountains for months, and then they come home for a day to sing these songs with the gentle *shamisen* instrument in the background plucking away notes like the tears on these old women's papery cheeks. I came upon such lyrics accidentally in a museum and could feel your breath down my neck. You didn't say a thing, but I knew you were telling me: *I'm a mountain man. I am a mountain man. Fear me.*

I told you that I wouldn't, but I may have been lying. Directly beside your mountain lies the ocean, and that is where I am from. It takes years, eons, for water to erode rock, but we of the water are patient and strong. In our case, however, it may just turn out to be the other way around.

I am thankful that you are patient with the ups and downs of my ballooning heart and looming figure; that you are not opposed to the way I fawn over you in my blonde head, because I'm not so sure you're used to me yet. It's like when we first met and you asked me in broken English where I was from, and I told you the East Coast.

"The East — ?" you repeated, mouth swallowing the foreign word, though you knew it was familiar in some other way. "*East?*"

I learned later that your teachers taught you that the country of Japan was in the East. What they didn't tell you is that there is a part of America that is also in the East, that is also a long line of coast. Did they tell you about the oceans? I asked you then, during our first awkward moment, when you looked at me like I was spouting geographical lies. Did they tell you about the Pacific, the Atlantic?

"Of *course*," you said, grinning slowly. "But why would we need to know about that?"

I laughed, you laughed, and we went to the punch bowl together in search of more conversation topics and a dull ice pick to break through our language barrier. Later, I will want to tell you that you needed to know about the East Coast because someday you may travel there, someday you may travel there in search of golden fruit, of unreachable bounties and uncountable riches. And, maybe, me.

*   *   *

We trot down nature-made staircases and I almost fall three times. I want to see packs of stray cats, I want to stop at a convenience store, I want to make my way down back to Earth with you by my side — I want all this and so much more right now. What I do not want, however, is to have more elderly people stop and stare at our bizarre show of unspoken romance.

I think about it, though, and I know: even the cats stare when we walk together. Truly we're not that special, this happens often — I can show anyone the babies to prove it. We are simply overstepping time and writing new history textbooks with our tongues and young fingertips and strong, angular memories. But when your eyes meet mine, and my hands hover over yours, and our heartbeats start to dictate the silence, I can hear above all else the trees around us whisper.

This is why I stop on the stairs.

The question mark hanging over your head reaches your lips and I barely hear you ask me why I've stopped. But what can I tell you? That I'm too insecure to be with you? That I'm far too in love with you, but also too conscious of what the trees think of us?

"I'd like to stay here for a long time," is what I say instead. "A long, long time."

"I know," you tell me.

"But I don't want people to stare," I whisper.

"Well," you say. "*Well.*"

You take my hand and we start to walk again. After a few minutes you start to sing; anything you know, from haiku set to spontaneous tunes to things you have learned over time. One of them is the mountain man song, and I unexpectedly find myself humming along.

My sister tells me that I dream in the night. I don't remember any of them, but I know for some reason that they are for you. From this I can safely say that I yearn for you even in my dreams — the safest place in the universe, where I am a version of myself stripped of everything I think I should be.

But neither of us lives in that perfect place. Instead, I am forced to convene with you in reality: where I go to one school, behind military-issued fence, and you go to another, in the heart of the city. We speak two different languages in a country that you were born in but that, at first glance, culture shocked me into a near paraplegic state. Your family takes their shoes off at the door and mine treks dirt through the house, even onto the bathroom tiles. The only thing that we have in common is our connection to the East, but even there our shared trait is not really all that shared.

Still, I love you. Somehow (because who can really explain the complicated process of tripping into love?), I saw your heart in my dreams and followed it all the way to the peak of a mountain. I like your hands and I like your warmth and I like the way you want me even if we are so separate from each other, in height and culture.

In Japan the mountains grow like children in the country, and the children on these mountains run through their lives like rivers running from the winter freeze. The mountains watch these children embark on summer vacations, to the convenience store to buy rice balls, to endless years of secondary schooling.

Your mountain, I tell you as we round more corners and nearly fall down gravelly slopes, probably watched you take your first steps as you followed your mother's beckoning hands all the way around the house. Your mountain observed through the clouds as you battled several typhoons just to buy ice cream at the store, and then two years later it saw you cry furiously when your dad called to say your little sister (not brother) had just been born.

"But I love my little sister," you say at our sixth crosswalk, obviously crushed at my accusation that you once refused to accept the existence of the now two-year-old Yumi.

"Yeah, but at the moment, you didn't," I say, smiling widely.

We are comfortable here. *I* am comfortable here, with my hand in yours, where I can see the city looking back at me from the tops of the staircases. I wonder aloud if you feel the same way.

"Comfortable?" you say, and I can see that you're racking your brain for the Japanese equivalent of the word. Unfortunately, I don't know it either, and since we're not in school I do not have easy access to a Japanese-English dictionary. I just hope that you'll remember.

And you do. "Oh!" you say, and grin. "Yes — that. Of course I am," you tell me, swinging our arms between us. "I like this very much."

A pause, then two pauses. I can count the number of moments that pass by the wind that seeps lazily through our entwined fingers, and I can't take this anymore. I turn to you and I blurt out, "But would you be more comfortable if I were somebody else?"

More pauses come our way. Clearly, we are not the most rushed people in the world.

"Honestly," you answer much too slowly — too slowly, and I start to lose my breath — "maybe I would."

I try to stop walking; I try to keep my heart from throwing itself into my stomach. But you squeeze my hand tightly, reassuringly, and keep walking.

"But I don't want you to be somebody else," you continue, looking back at me. The sun hides half of your face and I can only catch some of your smile, but I can see it in my mind and I know how much it says, *you are such a nonbeliever.*

"Silly you," you whisper to my hand, and each of my fingers tingle when your lips touch them. "Silly, silly you."

We reach the bottom of Mt. Hikari in record time: two hours and twenty-three minutes. You tell me that it normally takes you just twenty minutes, but I choose to ignore that comment and focus on returning back to the real world instead. Stepping off that last stair feels like I'm jumping, headfirst, into a completely new world. In less than three hours we have somehow come from a land full of curves and greenery to a flat expanse of tall buildings and clumps of cigarette butts.

In those few hours I have counted three *obaa-sans* staring at us, two packs of elementary school children pointing and squealing from their vantage point by my knees, and three middle school girls giggling quietly in their pleats. Every time, I wished to be someone else, someone more soft-spoken and shorter and sweeter. I wished to be from the East, and not just the East Coast.

But even in my thoughts I can hear you laughing, I can feel

182

your hands on my face and your thumbs on the corners of my eyes, then your lips brushing over where your thumbs were. *Silly, silly you,* my dream-you says, skipping through my distorted thoughts, grinning through even the ugliest of my notions. *How many times must I tell you that you are exactly what I want?*

One for every stare, I say to you in my head. One for every time someone thinks we are odd. And only one more for each and every time I forget that if you don't care about the stares, I shouldn't, either, because we two together is all that matters.

Our schools met for a cultural exchange once, a one-day extravaganza hosted by our respective Interact Clubs. Mine told all of us to speak in whatever Japanese we knew, and yours instructed your class to use English no matter what. It was probably because of these demands that most of our classes stayed homogenous huddles near the finger foods, determined not to make a fool of themselves for the sake of a high school reputation.

But we were the brave ones, or perhaps just so deprived of each other for a very long week that staying away seemed absurd. I crossed the room to offer you a pig in a blanket ("I don't have any room in my house for a pig . . . in . . . a blanket"), we talked.

And did I care then? Did it matter to me who saw the way I touched your elbow or the way you put your hand on my shoulder to show me something? Surprisingly, it didn't, and the only thing I knew in that room as our two vividly separate classes attempted to mingle was that we were together. We had breached some kind of wall, and only managed to do so because I wanted to — because I wanted you. I wanted to take you home and show you to my parents, even though I knew it would take five minutes for them to get over how very not American you were. I wanted to meet Yumi and pinch her cheeks and help her climb the monkey bars. And I wanted us to walk together on your mountain, fingers laced, eyes turned toward the journey ahead.

So here I am, now. Here is my hand in yours. Here are my amphibian footsteps trudging through day-old dirt and fallen leaves. Here is my heart, dancing furiously in your fist. Here we are — two pieces of the jigsaw puzzle, where I am the funny-shaped one and you are the inlet where I belong. I truly have no room to complain.

– *Melissa Tolentino*

Nine Things She Thought About
Before She Jumped

1.

She thought about the hammock,
The one she had heard her ninth grade teacher talk about in
That heart-spun tale of practice makes perfect.
How the flea-infested man from India had spent his final
     months
In his hut weaving the hammock,
Taking twine and faded clothing and the fabric from the sofa
     cushion he had found at the side of the road,
Weaving a row each day.
She thought of the day he finished the hammock, when all the
     town came to revel at his ingenuity,
How he slung his masterpiece between two trees by the last
     green patch of grass he could find
For the untouchable children to play on.
And how that night he curled up in the newspaper-covered
     corner of his hut where no memories flapped moth wings
And died.

She thought about how the story didn't make sense to her at
the time,
Like a fickle flirtation that reality used to charm the hope in
her schoolgirl soul.
She still didn't understand, even after her body grew to inhabit
working clothes and her eyes began to fade.
When the man had reached the end, the perfection, he
decided to die.
Why?

2.

She thought about the vibrator she had uncovered, age
nine, while looking for cough drops in her sister's dresser
drawer (she always hid them with the underwear).
How she had held it in awe, a pink plastic pickle,
Never knowing the criminality of such a thing until her sister
came in and saw her
And her eyes grew an inch and she started to cry, took it
from her, and buried it under the blanket so it might
repossess its secrecy, begging her all the while,
Please-don't-tell-mom-she'll-kill-me.

She had looked away, embarrassed, at seeing her sister's
panic.
How does a buzzing piece of plastic teach you to live
ashamed?

3.

She thought about the secret door (now that was a story) she
    had found playing
Flashlight hide-and-seek tag at her friends' house.
And how she had stumbled upon the rotating wall in that
    stone-and-moth basement,
Into the room with the old paintings propped against brick
    walls
And polaroids on the shelves from the times when Russians
    walked in Afghanistan.
And she had left the door open so that her friend (Lissa or
    Sally or Meggie or Jean) found her, an equal look of triumph
    and wonder at the discovery of the new hiding place.
They looked at the faded photographs together.
Her friend pointed to the boy in every picture, not long out of
    high school,
That's-my-dad, she'd said.
But the pretty girl he had his arm around,
That's-not-my-mom.
And they marveled at the brave idea that love was not like
    lightning.
It could strike the same place twice.

4.

She thought about the game of Clue with all the pieces
    missing,
No pipes or pistols or Miss-Scarlet-in-the-ballroom-with-a-
    candlestick.

But her family made their own characters, her mother and
    father and sister and her,
Sitting at the table on flickering-candle nights.
At age eleven she learned all the ways you could kill someone.

5.

She thought about the bricklayer who had held her six-year-old
    self,
A stranger, but not the kind in the good-touch-bad-touch
    handbooks of her youth.
The kind that held you up the two feet you needed to spread
    the mortar icing onto the sweat-and-brick cake of the
    skeleton house.
Her mother had smiled and taken out her pride-and-joy camera
    to capture her daughter, busy at her honest work, her height
    a gift of the gentle stranger.
She learned that kindness was not as rare as a kindergarten
    safety class made it out to be.

6.

She thought about the light in the back of her third grade
    science classroom,
Flicker flicker flickering the last hour of the day as her class
    played with their plastic microscopes,
Laughing at the cellular hierarchy of their fingernails.
There was a new girl who came on a Thursday and sat next to
    her in the last row

Under that flicker flicker, as if it was counting with them to
the end of the day.
And once, between learning Celsius and Fahrenheit, the new
girl stopped taking notes,

Shoved her notebook off the desk, began to raise her hands in
all directions,
Her eyes retreating to the back of her head.
And how the teacher screamed and dropped the thermometer
and ran,
Don't-put-your-hands-near-her-mouth! as if they would do such
a stupid thing.
She was shooed away from the manic case, so she walked over
to the ground and began to play with the little marbles of
mercury instead,
rolling playfully on the floor, completely calm in the face of
panic.
If she looked close enough, she saw her fickle reflection, the
baby fat still there.

7.

She thought about the rope that had failed her twice,
Like the dress-up necklaces of her childhood, always breaking
when the pull got too hard.
She had tried other ways, but couldn't swallow pills, even with
water
She didn't want to be creative about it,
Didn't want to be remembered solely for how she died,

And all the Sylvia Plath crap.
She didn't want to remain a brackish-water memory to the
world, just a name on a gravestone.

8.

She thought about the yardstick her father had held walking
into the Barnes & Noble,
The weird glance the shelf-stackers gave him as the two of them
walked to the poetry section, the intent solid in her father's
head, liquid in hers.
She put her index finger down where the first yard stopped so
he could lay the next one.
One and a half yards! he had cried. One and a half yards for
two thousand years of extrapolated thought!
And then he would laugh at the waning lyricisms of the world,
and she would laugh with him, not knowing that he wasn't
laughing because it was funny.
And then they would go to the Starbucks and she got hot
chocolate with an extra swirl of crème and he got coffee
black as the night, sipping with a distant look in his eyes,
Thinking that all of society could be measured in yardsticks.

9.

She thought about the first raindrop that had gone skiing
down her nose
On the day the weatherman had said
The-drought-is-expected-to-go-on-for-another-month.

She thought of the glitter-smiled children who ran through
 Swiss cheese screen doors and
Threw their hands up to greet the sky's lifeblood
As the fantastic stars shed wholesome tears, pouring,
And the quicksilver puddles made way for flower-patterned
 boots.
She was there too, witnessing the new joys, slack-jawed at the
 marvel.
Everywhere she looked, life began again.
She jumped in those puddles as well.
She would have sworn she'd seen a pigment in that water,
The moment before she landed, shattering its crystalline
 likeness,
The color of a fleeting thought.
She jumped in those puddles.
She jumped.
Like a diver,
Into the water,
down
        down
                down to the end of the page.

– *Luisa Banchoff*

The Song of an Unopened Bloom

Rodney was known for playing his banjo. He'd sit on the front steps and pick nonstop, and you'd see he was just like the instrument: one peg shorter than the rest and couldn't keep his strings tuned. You could watch him all evening and forget he was even playing — fingers wild and eyes steady. Daddy was born and raised on bluegrass, and even he was proud of Rodney. He'd say to the neighbors, "The boy ain't good at much, but he can play the banjo, that's for sure."

No one liked to think Rodney was a problem kid or anything, he was just always alone. I never spent time with him, seeing how I was four years older and always had a boyfriend around, but I could still see what was going on. You couldn't ignore someone with eyes like his, wide and open but not really looking. He didn't have friends, didn't have grades. Some days he came home with his shirt ripped or a black eye. The bigger guys at school would tease him for sitting alone on the bus, or never going to football games. I never took to him well, mostly because I hated that he never did anything with himself. He wanted to disappear as much as he could with each day he wasted. The only time Daddy would ever talk about it was when he looked out the kitchen window at Rodney sitting in a rocker while he picked on the banjo.

"If he don't do anything else in his life, at least he played music."

No one in Waynesville had a whole lot then, just acres for farming. Seasons changed with the harvest. Wintertime was brought in by Christmas trees, spring had strawberries (they were always my favorite). Tomatoes gave us summer, and fall, pumpkins. Years were marked by how good the crop was — Uncle Dean got married the year the Tentons sold the most Fraser firs, my best friend Kate moved to Boone when Dad wouldn't let us carve jack-o'-lanterns 'cause he had only enough to sell.

Pastor Dave was one of the three pastors in town. He built his own church that sat a mile or so behind seventy acres of Christmas trees. Farmers showed up to church if they could afford to, both time and land being sacrificed. On Sundays, when the plate came 'round for offering, some people would throw in a few dollars, maybe a check — never much. But at the end of each season, if a farmer had had a good crop, you'd see him scribbling on the back of an envelope, "3 acres, 1036 Cherryhope Road, Wes Burgess." They'd only offer their land if they had just finished a selling harvest. They wouldn't even think of giving the pastor dead soil. You'd see that on the General Store's sale bulletin board the next day for a large sum of money. I asked Daddy one time why he never gave Pastor any land. He said, "We ain't had a season worth giving to the Lord yet."

There was a competition in the town to find the first pumpkin of the fall season. It wasn't official or anything, just a game that started at the Farmer's Market one September. Our dads would bet — put money, land, even hunting dogs on it. It was our job as sons and daughters to actually find the pumpkin. You'd drive by farms and see small heads weaving in and out of vines, looking for the tiny thing. When we were younger, me and Rodney always thought it'd be full-size the first day we found it, like we'd wake up and see it round and orange when we looked down the hill. The first and only time I found the pumpkin, it was dark green and no bigger than both of my fists put together. Daddy would never bet any money. He just patted me on the head and mentioned it in passing to Mister Anderson at the deli, who had lost five German shorthair puppies the year before.

He loved it when we searched for them, seeing his kids and income come together, everything he lived for growing before his eyes. He told us to count all the pumpkin flowers we could find, saying a good farmer always knew how many blooms there were; it was most important to him. Of course it wasn't — how something begins to bloom can never tell how it will finish growing. But we believed him just the same and would count yellow petals on our fingers, tallying every ten in the dirt.

This was before anyone noticed something wasn't normal about Rodney. It was the fall we counted more than 200 blooms, line after line drawn on the ground beneath our feet. Rodney was six, and I was ten. The sun had almost set behind our house on top of the hill, the eyelid that slowly closed over daylight earlier every day. Momma had called twice for us to come in, but I was still crouched in the vines counting flowers.

Rodney had gone and sat on the porch steps. He just sat there staring at his leg in front of him. It was mid-October, the time when ticks leave their homes in the woods and skin to hide in dirt 'til spring. When I came to Rodney, he was watching one burrow into his calf muscle, growing bigger from his blood. I moved to get matches from Daddy's toolbox to burn it out, yelling that Momma would whip him for sure if she knew he hadn't picked it off the minute he saw it. I started to light a match when Rodney told me to stop, saying it needed to eat, it had a long winter ahead of it.

"It ain't a grizzly bear," I told him, pushing his arms away to get to the vermin. He yelled at me to stop, and sat as calm as could be, watching it wiggle its body into him. I told him I wouldn't be sorry when he got a wooden leg after his real one got cut off, then I went inside. I didn't tell anyone.

He told Daddy the chain-link had cut him when a scar started to shine where the tick had been. Daddy searched the front fence looking for a wire end to fix. I didn't have the heart to tell him he wouldn't find anything. I don't think he could have stood the idea of anything hurting his son that he couldn't see, even more that Rodney could have stopped it. Something so easy to pluck away, but he let it eat at him, slowly making him disappear.

Daddy had always been a farmer. It's all he grew up knowing, so it's all he grew up to be. It wasn't a bad thing, but it's hard to base life off of something you don't know how to predict. He believed the usual farmer's myths: a bad season of strawberries means a good one for pumpkins, rain the day before you sow means thicker Fraser trunks, and other sayings that had no real reason attached to them. But I think they were more like prayers, a way to convince yourself that everything will turn out better than you think. Farmer gossip was the most heartbreaking

195

thing sometimes. They were always so hopeful. They'd grab at any kind of straw when their income came from the sun and rain. My friend Mac Thomas's daddy would water his strawberries with moonshine on Easter Sunday. He said it added to the color and flavor. I think he was just a drunk.

But every time I overheard a story about a new way to grow pumpkins or trees, I thought of Rodney, and how we always wanted to believe that he would be okay. But no farmer's false hope at the beginning of a season could match what we had for Rodney.

The hardest thing was seeing Daddy's face that October. He held up a long vine with holes big enough in the leaves to see his disappointed face on the other side. "Some kinda bug," was all he said, kicking off his boots at the back door. He didn't eat dinner that night, so me and Rodney ate in silence with Momma, except for the occasional question about school she had for him. Momma was never a talker. A lot of me thought she didn't really want to be living with us.

I had a story set up in my mind that I expected to happen: We'd wake up to a note on the kitchen table where she always sat for meals, written the morning after Rodney graduated from high school, and that would be all we had left of her. I knew why she was still there, though. Rodney was holding her back. I could tell she favored him over me, for sure. She just wanted to see a diploma and know he would get on okay without her. Rodney had just started high school, and I was working at the General Store selling makeup. I wanted to tell her about the lipstick sales that day, the new shade of powder we had gotten in last week, anything that would relate us in the world of womanhood, but she continued with questions for Rodney. It was useless, really, with answers all generally the same. "I don't pay attention to girls much, Ma," "I don't listen too much in class, either." She'd look down at her sweet potato with the same disappointment Daddy had in the pumpkin leaves, with even less to hide behind. Momma had plans for Rodney the way I did for her, 'cept hers had an ending with a good future and pretty wife for Rodney. At least my prediction was somewhat realistic.

Eventually Momma got up to fix Daddy a plate, humming an old bluegrass tune. She had a way of doing that — putting herself in the background like a low-volume radio that became unnoticed static. Rodney got up to play his banjo outside, and soon enough, the song that Momma had been humming floated through the screened door, mirrored perfectly and crying.

The next day, he woke up early, just like he did every day. There wasn't ever a real reason for him to wake up before the cock crowed, but he did just the same. He had a purpose that morning, though. He was out in the fields, even before Daddy. He was crouched over, hands disappearing into vines and leaves every few steps. He finally came in for water, and Daddy asked him what in God's name he thought he was doing. I knew he had started looking for the first pumpkin, something I thought we'd outgrown after elementary school. In high school, boys placed bets the way their dads did, growing up before their bodies had time to catch up. Rodney must have put money on it; he was always one to stash allowance. He went back outside without a word, Daddy not far behind him with the tractor keys. He had planned to till everything up and start a late crop in place of the failing one. "They'll be ready to pick just before

Thanksgiving," he said. "The other ones just bloomed too soon. The soil wasn't expecting 'em yet." Daddy said he'd wait 'til tomorrow to finish with the tractor, just to make Rodney happy.

That night, I heard footsteps come across my room. They were slow and heavy, waking me as soon as they were beside my bed. He smelled like fermenting fruit. "I found it," Rodney said, leaning down by my pillow. I told him to go to bed, that it was just a damn pumpkin. "I got it, though. I found it." He kept saying that, and wouldn't leave 'til I got up and led him out of the room. "Just wait 'til I go to school tomorrow," he said before I closed the door.

The next day, Rodney came home while I was getting ready for a date. A guy that worked in the hardware department at the General Store was taking me out, and he was gonna be there any second. Rodney walked into the kitchen. I hadn't even heard the screened door when he came in. His clothes had orange clumps sticking to them and tiny pieces of white. He smelled twice as bad as he had the night before. He got closer to me, and as he turned to go upstairs I realized it was the inside of a pumpkin. I almost started giggling. I had no idea how he could have gotten the guts of a pumpkin all over himself. I opened my mouth to say something rude most likely, but instead told him that I was leaving as I heard a horn outside. I remembered later why he had come into my room last night. My date asked me what was wrong, said my face turned blank when I realized that the first pumpkin in Waynesville had been covering my brother.

*　　*　　*

The next day at the makeup counter, a few high school girls with too much eyeliner and blush leaned against the glass cases. I overheard their conversation.

"Could you believe it? The retard at school found the pumpkin, and he actually thought they'd give him the money!"

"Yeah, Tanner and Miller said they smashed it and really let him have it. They said it was rotten. Must have come from a dump of a farm."

"I heard he bet his life that he'd find it."

They thought that was funny.

Momma found Rodney in the toolshed. "Only one bullet went through him," the police said, "nothing else to call that but suicide."

Daddy threw the handgun Rodney'd used into our lake out back, metal sinking into mud. Me and Momma cried, but for different reasons — there's different tears for a son and for a brother. She left two weeks later, and I could almost feel my heart sinking the way the gun did through pond scum — slow without knowing any other fate. I couldn't tell you if Daddy took her leaving well — the only feeling he ever wore on his sleeve was pride. Everything else was buried below the dirt he lived off of, the same way as his son.

"Only fifteen years old?" the sheriff asked as he got into his car. He really said it to me like he couldn't believe it. "Didn't even get through the first year of high school."

I told Daddy about the boys at school, the story I had heard at work that day. I almost saw him flinch at the thought. I tried to picture what was going through his head — two things that seemed to be growing fine on the outside but were dying on the inside; the two things he wanted to love, his harvest and his son. In the end, they came together, head on, and revealed what had been rotting inside of the other. At dinner I'd mention something about him, say I missed the banjo music from the front porch. Daddy'd grunt in a way that meant "I know," and that he was thinking of his childhood, "the real bluegrass days" he called it — the time that he looked back on and the time Rodney blew away. He kept farming and didn't bother to clean the blood off of his wrenches and screwdrivers.

I went out later one evening to wash them, finding the silver beneath his blood. I cursed his ghost in that toolshed, saying, "I hope you're happy with this bet you lost to yourself."

At the end of December, I found myself looking over Daddy's shoulder at church one day as he scrawled his offering of all but one acre we owned on the back of a grocery receipt. He had told me the night before that he used to have dreams at night about farming. He had seen himself riding a tractor, hearing it pop from just being oiled, the green tips of leaves poking through the soil, the big orange harvest we sold on the roadside, and his two towheaded children parting vines to find tiny yellow flowers for him. He said that none of those pictures came to him anymore. He said, "The day it don't come to me in my sleep is the day it ain't a part of me."

But I knew what I was watching as he placed the crumpled paper in the plate that was being passed from pew to pew. Daddy was letting go of all he had wanted since he bought our farm twenty years ago: a wife who kept her vows, a son who would take up the farm after him, fields of pumpkins that would only spread with time. Nothing came at night anymore. There wasn't

200

Momma to slide under their sheets after dinner, wasn't Rodney to come in my room with good news like the night he'd found the pumpkin. He was leaving his ex-wife, dead son, and ruined soil at the Lord's house — a place he wouldn't return to for the rest of his life. I never asked him if our land was good enough to give to God, because I knew it was. His son was good enough, and the land where he lay was too.

– Aubrey Isaacson

Date of Release

It's when the first rays of strange eastern light hit a distant sky-scraper that I know this place is no longer mine. I don't recognize its thousand twisting streets that all sound the same, all mono-syllabic, all empty. I flinch at this foreign new sun stamped upon jagged steel horizons, this newly acquired dirt beneath my fingernails, at the screeching quality of these sidewalks. My mother told me it would be easy to remember, that it would be like riding a bike after ten years of letting it rust in the garage, but she was wrong. Nothing quite belongs.

I've read up on hutongs for Trivia Bowl. I know that they are relics from the Qing and Ming dynasties, ancient alleyways that sprawl across the city, traversing main streets and shopping malls to intersect at the red-walled, forbidden nucleus. But it is a different thing to see them wake up. When faint red light descends upon pocked walks and broken shingles, the streets stretch their cobblestone spinal cords and mewl softly, a thou-sand battered, smoke-gray cats. The old women emerge with their chamber pots and shuffle to the public restrooms emanat-ing the unmistakable stench of urine. The merchant rides through the hutong on his bicycle, his deep, braying yells of steamed buns and corn drowning out the creak of the bicycle wheels.

Jet lag has kept me up and I'm sitting on the bamboo slats in my underwear, trying to ignore the persistent calls of steamed buns and finish *Wuthering Heights* for Trivia Bowl's literature section. It's hot already and this strange blood sun is in my eyes. Soon it will hemorrhage, the harsh scarlet paling to a brittle gray, barely distinguishable from the sky upon which it's superimposed. Soon my grandfather will get up. His hands, bony and graceless, so like my own, will grasp at a bed corner and his spine will unfurl in the already-humid air. He will haltingly make his way to the kitchen to boil a pot of water to make the tasteless porridge that always leaves me hungry, no matter how many bowls I eat. And then my grandmother will awaken to take her place on the black leather sofa. The moment she sees me she will ask me if I want new clothes. She's asked the same question for a week already, even though I've given the same answer each time. I'll finish brushing my teeth with green-tea toothpaste in the cramped little bathroom and as soon as I stick my head out she'll accost me from her perch on the black leather sofa with suggestions of skirts and blouses and pants.

I'll always say no. I never mean for her to get that look on her face; I just don't want her money wasted on my awkward breasts and gawky shoulders. I try to say it without a hint of condescension, with no downward tilt to the corners of my lips, but the Mandarin comes out wrong; my voice is exactly the sort that you'd expect from a person who is trying to convince someone that they are not growing old.

This answer will always anger my grandmother. She'll tell me with shaking hands that she would buy me beautiful clothes, not the American crap that I wear. Here, women are fashion-able. Don't I trust her? Do I think she is useless?

Today I'm tired and I agree to a pair of shoes. After all, on some days I like my feet; a boy once told me I had cute toes. "What color?" she asks, the turbulence of her features soften-ing. I let her pick.

I don't know what kind of birds they are. Trivia Bowl doesn't have a section on zoology so I never bothered studying birds. They're small and jewel-bright, fluttering, useless. Like the hundred shining baubles my mother and I hung with gritted teeth in an attempt to resemble the kind of families we saw on television, these birds are ornamentation, the sort that are always in cages. There are two of them. They have pert black masks and small beady eyes ringed in blue. They sit in a small, round, wooden cage in the corner of the living room. The fan is pur-posely pointed away from them, my grandfather explains, because they're from the tropics and can't stand too much cold. As I twitch a finger through the cage bars they scatter in a pan-icked gold and green blur of wings, hopping to the higher bars.

My grandfather comes in with the birdseed, sprinkling the granules of millet and rice into a minuscule tray. They peck eagerly and mindlessly, twin daubs of rainbow gluttony. The tendons in my grandfather's neck lose their tension and stop their minute vibrations, like the slackened strings of a violin. It is then that he turns to me and tells me to put on a pair of sneak-ers because we are going for a walk. That's his way — brusque, sudden; questions are a waste of saliva. I'm sick of Heathcliff, so I follow without protest. Before we leave, my grandfather grabs the birdcage.

204

"Why are you bringing that?" I ask as I shove my heels into my tennis shoes.

He tells me we're walking the birds. Apparently this is a frequent pastime of the retirees of the city, dating back to the Qing dynasty. The logic is that birds are not supposed to stagnate in some dusty corner of the living room; they are meant to be outside, to be in constant movement, to have the sunlight of their surroundings shift and change. So old men get up every morning at dawn and hook the round wooden cages around their fingers, walking along the winding alleyways, letting their pet finches and sparrows see the cooked yams and crystallized hawthorn berries of street vendors.

We walk through the hutong, passing by the women fanning themselves while sitting on plastic milk crates, the men absorbed in games of Chinese chess. My grandfather greets the ones he knows with an inclination of his hand, causing the birds to scatter in fear every time. Somehow I can't believe that this is an enjoyable experience for them, no matter what Qing traditions dictate. They are jostled about, leaping from bar to bar. They don't pay much attention to the world outside their cage, their small black eyes gazing inward unless a passerby's sleeve happens to brush too close.

Near the mouth of the hutong my grandfather stops at a wall of one of the ancient four-walled courtyards that line the alley. He places the palm of his hand against the crumbling wall, tracing a red spray-painted character that's all angles.

"Chai," my grandfather reads. It means demolish. A hundreds-year-old building, memories slapped to its sides like plaster, is condemned and all the birds can think to do in their cage that hangs from my grandfather's finger is twitter.

Before dinner my grandfather chops up bits of lettuce and carrots for the birds as I try to memorize a Yeats poem for the literature section. Turning and turning in the widening gyre. The falcon — it was a falcon, I'm positive — the falcon cannot hear the falconer. I set the collapsible table with the dishes that my grandfather has cooked, repeating the poem under my breath.

What were the next lines? Things . . . things fall apart, the center cannot hold. As we eat I notice that my grandmother's eyes have acquired the habit of locking onto anything, with an empty persistence. She chews her small pieces of beef and beans, making bovine circles with her lower jaw, bits of spittle dangling from the corner of her mouth. But it's really her eyes that frighten me; though they share the same shape and color, the same wrinkles borne from loud laughter in the corners, they're so different from my mother's.

The center of my mother's eyes lock with fierce purpose. They stare resentfully at me, for what I can never remember, when she tells me how she struggled: struggled when the Cultural Revolution forced her family to the countryside and she had to skin frogs to survive, struggled to get into the top school in the country, struggled her way to America and, when there, struggled to make it in a land where the past is brushed away with last week's Taco Bell enchilada. I can understand my mother's resentment; after all, I am her blurry photo negative, pale and unprocessed. Her without the memories. There's so much of us within each other that aunts and uncles often mistake me for her. I'll pick up the phone and they'll start talking of some problem or some throwaway gossip before realizing that the voice on the other end of the line is not hers. They'll only notice it when they feel the absence of something within my speech, some conviction, some neat alignment of words.

In the past few weeks, three streets down, the demolition teams have destroyed an entire courtyard, spraying thousand-year-old rubble and plaster dust over the cobblestone ground. And my grandmother has been calling me by my mother's childhood nickname.

Things fall apart.

We meet other birdwalkers at the park on some days. They are usually toothless old men, faces pleasantly creased and browned, a white nappy fuzz crowning their heads. Once at the park they hang their cages in one long line against the walls of the park so the birds can socialize through the bars. Then they grab long sticks and dip them in buckets of water and practice water calligraphy upon the cement ground, creating transient brush-strokes of characters and landscapes. The dominating theme is often birds, birds with flapping wings above reeds, birds skim-ming sky and water. My grandmother used to draw calligraphy birds with fine horsehair brushes, each deft flick of her wrist translating into delicate feather and talon. But now her hands shake so much that she can't paint anymore.

According to the birdwalkers, illness can be released through the birds. Simply open the cage door and let the birds fly into the open air, taking under their wings the malignant spirits that plague you. "Bird release," one of them says as he suckles hungrily from his cigarette, "is a release of evil and worry." My grandfather has known of this superstition for quite some time already but he nods his head in thanks. I watch the

207

birdwalkers brush the ground with water, etching smooth lines of upturned wings and claws.

When we make our way back, my grandfather points to a square building opposite the mouth of the hutong. "We were going to go to that hospital," he says. "They could perform an operation on her — drill two holes on the top of the head, connect a live wire. The jolt helps with brain function. But we didn't. It cost too much and she is too proud." He says this with his charismatic unabashed candor, eyes fixed firmly ahead, even bluntly digging a thumb and forefinger into my scalp to illustrate the details of the operation. After a moment he releases his two-digit grip upon my head and says, "You were born there, you know. That hospital."

This is the sort of information that shouldn't matter to me. It's like the photographs of me my mother is intent on keeping, me with the plump cheeks and elfin chin and strange ears, me bundled up for winter, me dancing in a pink cotton dress. "For your memories," she always says, but they're not my memories. I don't remember winter in Shanghai. I don't remember my birth.

I do remember the day when my mother received a phone call in the spring of last year, around the time that my grandmother first requested my grandfather to keep two birds. I am in a conference room that smells of disinfectant, answering question number 47 of the State Trivia Bowl mythology section: Which of the following was the monstrous creature that the King of Crete enclosed within a labyrinth? It is C, Minotaur. I am positive. Janine is doubtful — she thinks Chimera — but I press the buzzer anyway. And as I shout my answer to a string of applause, the phone in our house rings three times before my

208

mother picks it up. (She has been in the shower.) I can imagine her voice, resounding with the confidence I have yet to inherit and then faltering with a low groan.

At the State Bowl we pile into David's car. The team congratulates me, Janine ruffling my hair and offering me beer. We've always envied Janine because she is the only one of us whose parents leave six-packs out in the open like that. It wasn't so much the taste of beer itself that could counteract the Friday nights spent memorizing minutiae in our rooms.

"Glad you didn't listen to me," Janine says to me as I sip from the can, licking the edge of the steel, my nose wrinkling at the shock of alcohol.

"You were great." David turns from the front seat and grins, and I feel the beer coursing up my nostrils and my ears and my fingers, the tips of which seem to glow with warmth. I say thanks, and as he leans over he spills a few drops from his can onto my turquoise flip-flops. Before I can say anything he conjures up some Kleenex and wipes my feet.

"You've got cute toes," he says, before turning around and starting the ignition.

There's really no protocol to follow when someone gets Alzheimer's. Births and deaths are simple — congratulations or condolences — little ambiguity to the natural rhythms of celebration and mourning. But there's little to offer someone whose mental faculties are being systematically chipped away like crumbling plaster and rotten wood.

The only thing we could do, my mother decided, was to play Ariadne, to offer some sort of fine golden thread for the darkness. So when David dropped me off in front of my house,

209

when I returned with my gleaming state trophy and a mouthful of Winterfresh to hide the smell of beer on my breath, my mother told me that my grandmother had Alzheimer's and asked me if I wanted to go to Beijing in the summer.

If only understanding were a light switch. If only there were something in our genetic code of bundled double helixes that could store our memories, contain them so that we could possess all the stories that we have in our blood. I've always been obsessed with memorizing but I can't remember what I never knew. And I don't know my grandmother, not really. I can't recall the first time she felt the white void of snow crunching beneath her feet or that night when she went fishing, plopping each silver fish into a bucket, sleek bodies like captured moonlight. I can't know what she's forgetting.

"Sure," I say. "I'll go to Beijing."

And so I'm in Beijing. I'm in an apartment so humid that the green wallpaper seems to stick to my skin. I'm sitting at the collapsible table, the birds chattering in the background, as my grandfather pulls out a newspaper and a dog-eared calendar. As we stab at dates, consulting the paper's weather forecast, my grandmother sinks into her black leather sofa, engrossed first in soap operas, then in shampoo commercials, then the situation in the Middle East. As the over-lipsticked announcer talks about Mahmoud Ahmadinejad, whose name I barely recognize when translated into Chinese, the three of us establish a date of release, the same date as my flight back to California.

The shoes are hideous. They're yellow and I've never liked yellow, especially not this particular shade of cheap cheddar. They've got clunky heels that I could never walk in and some sort of large, plump polka-dotted bow at their tips, too exuberantly tacky to be ironic. I slip my feet into them while sitting on the corner of the bed that I've made mine for the past month. I'm proud of the indentation of my body upon that rock-hard mattress. It's nice to leave a mark.

On the wall of the room hangs a photograph of my grandmother and grandfather in their twenties. I haven't paid much attention to it in the last few weeks, just noted that they were indeed my grandparents, probably at the beginning of their careers at the Foreign Ministry, young and smiling. But now I look at it and drink the details in. My grandfather has a hand barely raised in greeting toward the unseen picture-taker, his smile frozen in mid-laugh. My grandmother's eyes, so like my mother's, burn like an architect's might before a set of blueprints as she places a hand on her swollen stomach.

She pads softly into my room, finding me with those clownish yellow shoes upon my feet. It's one of her better days and she smiles at the shoes complacently, reveling in I-told-you-so. She tells me she bought them because they reminded her of a dress she used to have when she was young, when she went to her first dance at college and danced with a boy who would recite Tang poetry to her. "Like Po," she said. "Or was it Du Fu? I can't remember."

I've tried to memorize Tang poems with strangely wrought titles like "On the Moonlit Precipice of the Three Gorges, Thinking of Shang" before but I can't read Chinese well and so much is bent and twisted in translation. My grandmother rests her head on my shoulder as we both pant in the humidity, her head leaving a patch of sweat on my shirt, but neither of us shifts in discomfort.

"You've always been a good daughter to me," my grandmother says, holding my hand in hers. "When you were born in Germany, Fräulein Fischer next door sent over one of her cakes and told me that you were such a beautiful baby, because you were golden, golden like the sun."

I tell her I love the shoes, I don't think I'm lying. As we sit motionless in the morning humidity the fan hums and the birds continue their chirping.

On the date of release my bags are packed, waiting expectantly in the corner of the green living room. The birds are next to them. They have grown fat with days of gorging on millet. I'm worried that they won't be able to fly away; they seem to pant more than usual after a bout of fluttering. Or maybe it's just the heat.

My grandfather hooks the birdcage with his forefinger. The birds think it's just any normal day, just another walk around the hutongs and the park to sit with cigarette men and other birds, the same jostling, the same brushed sleeves. They aren't expecting liberation.

We step outside, all three of us. My grandmother walks first with her small, mincing steps, then my grandfather, birdcage in hand. I follow them both. We make our way past the apartment complex, past the mimosa trees that line the hutong and scatter pink blossoms across its sidewalks. We wind past the rubble of the destroyed courtyard and ignore the clangs of the bulldozer, ignore the spray-painted signs of condemnation and focus our eyes on the dusty center of things.

At the park we find a secluded spot underneath the junction of two willow branches. The cage is placed on the grass. The two birds are unusually quiet — perhaps they sense something missing within the rhythm of our usual walks. We are still, our breaths evaporating mid-esophagus. Then my grandfather opens the cage.

The birds rattle out with the tenacity of escaped convicts, never even daring to look back. We expect them to land in the willows but they don't. They keep flying, soaring faster and faster until we can't keep track where they are or where they're going. They are far above ground now, somewhere with a cool wind, and we three, their once captors, are losing the significance of oppression with every foot in gained altitude, turning first into dwarves and then specks and then invisible altogether. From their view the hundreds of thousands of twisting labyrinthine hutongs writhe and shimmer under the harsh sun. In a few hours I'll see the same scene from the window of an airplane but for now I cling to the wrinkled paper hands of my grandmother and grandfather, wondering if they too feel something shifting and locking into place in the pit of their stomachs.

"Isn't this better than two holes in my skull?" my grandmother says, her face tilted skyward. "Cheaper and easier on the eyes." Slowly, we make our way back.

– *Jasmine Hu*

Shells

My mother wished she had retired a year earlier. She thought she had enough patience to deal with another year's worth of reckless children and obnoxious parents, but it was only the first day of school and she was already unraveling. I hadn't been home three minutes after *my own* first day of high school when my mom — who normally didn't come home from teaching third graders until the nightly news began — opened the front door and yelled for me to get in the car.

As we pulled out of the driveway she said, "Someone stole Melville."

"A student was kidnapped!" I couldn't believe it.

"No, Melville was the red-eared slider that Coral gave me." Coral was another teacher my mom worked with. She was Cajun and played the piccolo, but I didn't think she was anything special.

"You mean someone took the class pet, a turtle?"

"You wouldn't think these kids would be dumb enough. Well, I take that back — obviously they are dumb enough. The state tests prove that." She nodded, agreeing with herself.

"Are we going to PetSmart to buy a new one?" I asked.

"No, I'm getting him back," she said. She flipped up her visor.

"Why do I have to go?" I flipped my visor down.

"You have a dentist appointment this afternoon. Remember? Jesus, you'd think one of my children would have grown up to be responsible for themselves." She referred to my brother, who ended up in summer school every year, and my forgetfulness.

"Do you know who took the turtle?" I asked.

"This smart-aleck kid named Hub who was in my class last year. It is his second year in my class and I know it was him. He always said he wanted a turtle but his daddy cooked the wild ones he found." I remembered my mom telling me she had a kid bring a deep-fried rat for lunch once. I'm pretty sure she was kidding but she said this kid chewed on the tail like jerky.

I asked her how she came to suspect Hub and she went on to tell me about Pelzer Elementary's only custodian, Renee, who'd started working there after she finished high school. She was a skinny lady with yellow hair and a black scalp. Her son was in the fourth grade, spending another year with the same batch of kids. All of the classes were so small that the students were all related in one way or another. My mom taught Renee's son the year before, so Renee considered her a friend.

My mom told me that they had been in the teachers' lounge not long after school had ended when Renee tried to casually bring up what she'd seen. Renee holstered her feather duster in her belt loop and asked my mom if she'd brought the turtle to school that day. Renee said that she'd seen Hub with his back-pack open and kids gathering around him at the bus loop. She figured all of the kids were pointing at the turtle.

That was all the proof my mom needed to look at Hub's student information sheet and copy his address onto the back of her hand. It wasn't unusual for teachers to visit students' homes in rural areas. There tended to be generational poverty, meaning there were very few working telephones and even fewer computers capable of e-mail. Most of the parents avoided PTA meetings and threw school newsletters away with the junk mail. Face-to-face communication became necessary.

Hub's house was technically behind the elementary school but we took about a thirteen-mile detour to find it. His family lived in the woods, and right in front of their house was an upside-down truck wedged between two trees. It looked like a double dare gone wrong. My mom told me not to pay attention to the threats that were spray-painted on the truck's windshield. We got out of the car and I asked her where we were. She said it was an area called Turkey Ring.

I walked through a spiderweb and was pulling sticky string out of my hair when a tall girl opened the door. The T-shirt she wore almost reached her knees, and it looked like there might have been a college logo on it, though it was too faded to tell. She slicked her bangs out of her face and spoke so fast I thought her teeth were going to talk themselves right out of her mouth, "We didn't shoot anybody's dog, my husband wasn't even home last night."

"I'm not with the police, Mrs. Capps."

"You hear gunshots last night?"

"I don't live around here. I'm Mrs. Gamble, Hub's teacher, and I need to speak to you and Hub about some trouble he's gotten in at school," my mom said.

"Well, if you're wondering, we didn't shoot the Franklins' dogs, or pig. I think it was some teenagers who go to the high school up the road."

"Mrs. Capps, Hub is in a lot of trouble and I need to have a few words with you about it."

"What have you got to say about him?" She scratched at a mole on her neck, and when it started to bleed she let her arm hang limp at her side.

"I believe he's stolen the class pet," my mom said.

"What kind of pet do you got?" Mrs. Capps asked.

My mother shifted her weight from one leg to another. Off in the distance I heard someone — an adult — say, "Get your own Popsicle."

"A turtle," my mom said.

"We got turtles in these woods. Why don't you go find one and take it to your class? Some snap, though, so watch your fingers." Hub's mama had the door barely cracked, just enough so I could tell she wasn't wearing pants. She had the prettiest feet I'd ever seen, though. There wasn't a single bulging vein.

My mom said, "Can I come inside? This really isn't something we can discuss like this."

Mrs. Capps said, "Hub's daddy isn't going to like it."

From within the house I heard a man talking over the TV and saying, "Close the door before all the moths get out."

My mom said, "Well, we'll just have to explain to him what Hub has done and then he'll understand." I was halfway inside when Mrs. Capps noticed me. She looked at my mom and stuck out her thumb in my direction.

"She your kid?" I nodded. "She can go in the back with Hub and Stripe while we talk. I'll just call them inside after we're better acquainted." Then Mrs. Capps closed the door and I was alone on the porch.

They kept furniture in their woods, arranged in a series of rooms. A semicircle of recliners was set up around a fire pit, and just beyond that was an old stove overgrown with fungus. A cluster of thick, burgundy centipedes writhed in the bottom of a watering can.

I found boxes full of Christmas tree lights stacked on top of an old toilet. I figured the Capps family were Light People. The Light People had a tradition of cocooning themselves with holiday lights on Christmas Eve and waving at passing cars. They stood on curbs in front of their houses, and if they didn't have a curb of their own they'd waddle through Turkey Ring until they found one. The participants were tangled in a ritual that their grandparents began. They were a coalition of mummies that made the streets glow. I wanted to join the Light People on the curb, drinking homemade cider, and become a part of the tradition.

The Light People gained their fame from being on the ten-o'clock news every Christmas Eve. Local television stations sent big neon-painted vans full of journalists and cameramen to interview the first-timers. For kids, it was a big deal to have their very own box of lights. It was a family's way of showing off their kids like debutantes. People came all the way from three counties over to see it for themselves. I looked up from the boxes of Christmas lights and saw a boy with a cracked magnifying glass in his hand doubled over a beetle. He came over to me and said, "All those lights in that box right there belong to me."

The boy introduced himself as Hub, not as a turtle thief, and showed me the beetle he was observing. It was copper colored with a round back and not a whole lot different than an acorn. Hub wasn't at all the delinquent I pictured.

He knew my name, probably because my mother told her students embarrassing stories about me, and Hub had already heard a year's worth of them.

"That's my sister over there. I can't remember her real name but we call her Stripe. When she was a baby I'd give her Zebra Stripe gum and it always made her stop crying." Hub pointed at the wheelbarrow his little sister hid behind. I asked Stripe if she wanted me to braid her hair. She nodded vigorously, came out from behind the wheelbarrow, and sat in front of me.

"I'm not going to braid your hair if you are going to pull it out when I'm finished," I said.

Stripe sat Indian style and pinched her toes. "I promise I won't, and I won't tell anybody you did it for me. Ask Hub, I don't tell secrets." She looked old enough to be in a stage where all she wanted to do was tell lies but she must have outgrown it early. Hub said their mama told them everything and expected it not to be repeated to anyone. I'd heard stories about dog fighting and domestic violence in these parts and hoped that wasn't what these kids were withholding.

I overlapped ribbons of Stripe's white-blond hair while she rambled. "You know, I can stay home as long as I want, Mama says I don't have to go to school."

Hub lay on his stomach and arranged twigs like Lincoln Logs. He was neat and methodical about it, never looking up. He said, "That's not true. I have to go and so do you."

"Nuh-uh!" said Stripe.

219

"Fine," said Hub. I tied a hair band around the end of Stripe's braid. When her hair was out of her face, I could see how pale her eyes were, almost unnatural, and the veins on her temples that shone bright blue. It reminded me of something I saw on TV, about how animals with white fur and blue eyes were prone to insanity. Stripe played with pots and pans on the stove, pretending to cook dinner. She definitely was an unusual little girl, but not crazy.

I watched Hub arrange twigs, and he said, "I'm building a jail for myself."

"Why?" I asked.

"I know why Mrs. Gamble is here. She's going to take me away." He punched his jail and all the sticks scattered.

"Why did you kidnap Melville?" I asked.

"Everybody was mean to him at school. All last year I saw kids bully him and I knew he'd be in for another year of it if I didn't save him." Hub would be in dilemmas like this his entire life if he kept trying to help what shouldn't be helped. I figured he was the kind of person who thought he could fix everything.

"Where is he now?"

"Gone. I let him loose in the creek back there. Dropped him into a pool of water that had big rocks to hide under. I made sure there were places to hide because he's got to take care of himself now that he's in the wild." I thought I could hear the sound of running water behind us, but over my shoulder I saw Stripe peeing on a tree. I wanted to tell Hub that there would always be people who broke the rules and he'd have to learn to pick his battles. He wouldn't understand so I told him to lie instead. I couldn't wait to see my mom's face when he denied everything.

"Hub, you're going to lie, aren't you?" I said.

He furrowed his eyebrows, like he'd never considered lying before, as if he didn't think it was an option. "You're supposed to tell the truth all the time, aren't you?"

I told him, "You need to lie or you'll get in big trouble. I know my mom. She won't let you off easy. It would just be a little white lie, a tiny fib, you can do that."

Dirt smeared across his cheeks when he tried to wipe swelling tears from his eyes. He said, "I'd probably get spanked with the principal's paddle if they knew it was me." Hub cringed as if he felt the pain already.

I said, "Okay, when they ask you if you took the turtle just lie and tomorrow at school pretend it never happened. You did the right thing when you freed Melville."

"I did save him, didn't I?"

"Of course you did," I said, or at least I hoped so. I hoped the turtle wasn't going to be captured, boiled, and eaten.

When we heard Mrs. Capps calling us inside we shook the dirt off our clothes and jogged up to the house together. The back porch led to the kitchen, which had blinding fluorescent lights and tumbleweeds of animal fur rolling across the linoleum floors. Plastic silverware filled the sink and an old pair of hiking boots sat on a butcher's block on the countertop. The pantry doors were wide open and it was obvious they wouldn't be running out of Little Debbie cakes anytime soon.

Hub led me into the living room where everybody waited. I almost sat down on the sofa next to my mom but Mrs. Capps said I couldn't because it was Lazy Legs's old seat. Hub said Lazy Legs was a pet squirrel they had that died over the summer. The rodent gained its name because its hind legs were paralyzed and Hub said it ate food out of an ashtray and drank water from an eyedropper. Hub said he'd even tried to make a scooter once, like the kind paralyzed lapdogs had, so the squirrel could be mobile. He disassembled a Hot Wheels car and attached two of the wheels to a harness that was made from a Chinese finger trap, but the wheels fell off and Lazy Legs nearly suffocated in the finger trap because they just couldn't pull him out of it. Most of Lazy Legs's fur rubbed off when they twisted him around in that harness and his hind legs swelled up because of bad circulation.

They loved him so much that they always kept that seat empty as a memorial.

Mrs. Capps had decided to end the squirrel's pain by thumping it in the head with her middle finger. So, I just leaned against the wall.

Hub's daddy never once looked me in the face, though he eyed me up and down and smirked like I was a funny memory. He drank from a plastic flask of Rock N Rye — which was a liquor my mom drank when she had strep throat, which was about once a month — and pulled Hub onto his lap. He was a tiny man, with a caved-in chest and shrunken shoulders. There were tattoos on both his forearms, though his skin was so weathered it was impossible to tell what they were. He ran his hand over Hub's buzzed head and said, "Listen, boy, your teacher says you took something from school. Did you?"

Hub looked at me, then said, "No, sir. I didn't take anything."

Mrs. Capps sat smoking by an open window, Stripe sitting at her feet.

"You better not be lying to your teacher. Are you sure you didn't take anything?"

Hub tugged on a string hanging off the bottom of his shirt and when it snapped he wound it around his finger until it turned yellow.

He said, "I swear."

My mom said, "Mrs. Renee saw you with the turtle in your backpack, Hub. There are witnesses."

His father licked his lips and put on a pair of dirty glasses. "My boy said he didn't take anything, Mrs. Gamble, and if he swears to it he's being truthful."

My mother said, "Mr. Capps, just because a person swears to something doesn't make it true. People lie every day over nothing. Of course, a little boy isn't going to want to tell the truth when he knows consequences are waiting."

"This isn't a courtroom and I don't appreciate you saying we're all a bunch of liars. He didn't take your turtle if he says so." Mr. Capps jostled his leg and Hub bobbed up and down. He blew on the Rock N Rye bottle and his breath whistled over the gap.

My mom slapped the top of her thighs, stood up, and said, "We're leaving. I'm not going to argue anymore, and Hub, when you start to feel guilty you can admit to stealing the turtle." My mom went out the front door and yelled for me to get in the car. I started to leave, but Hub tapped my arm and whispered, "Thank you."

My mother and I left Turkey Ring, and instead of going to my dentist appointment, we sought the nearest pet store. She picked out the healthiest-looking turtle and made me hold it in my lap on the way home. The next day, she would put the new turtle in the aquarium before class started and the kids would never know the difference. Some of the more observant students might comment on how the turtle seemed smaller or how the shell was a different color, but my mother would lie and say Melville hadn't changed at all.

– Wynne Hungerford

The Numb Acre

I.
I never noticed your stubble
or the pebbled groove of your spine,

but I saw your arm hairs stand up,
soft sentinels moved by the October wind,

my fingers protecting a few of them
as the breeze spun through us, to the harbor.

II.
Water hisses and screams in the kettle.
We mistake it for passion

and imagine ourselves origami:
I crane, you tiger, folding together.

III.
A weight fills the numb acre
between my breasts and my sex,

the erotic slide of your solid language
suddenly absent from my ears.

– *Virginia Pfaehler*

On Newbury Street, July

Wearing just one fluttering rag around the waist,
Jungle-Boy comes skipjerking and spinning down the sidewalk,
dodging trash cans, strollers, the people eating alfresco.
I turn to watch him, like he wants me to,
as he meets some other primates
unleashing it on the corner,
homeless, or hopeless hipsters —

The jaded kid on guitar with
hot pink shorts and black exploding curls,
the girl with laughter like splatter paint and chestnut hair,
her gilded voice (shooting hose-spray of
water over awnings breaking
into sunlit beads),
slurring bluesy vowels as Jungle-Boy
hops in her face,
about to piss on her feet or kiss her pretty knees.

Then there's the other girl, faceless,
who blends into the pigeons

like a flattened half-smoked butt or a chained up singlespeed,
the kind the skinny boys ride and ride in their quarter of the city,
all canvas shoes and cardigans.

Pigeon Girl, your friends stole the show.
All I remember
is a snitch of your vintage dress.
I see you washed up on benches in the summer,
sometimes alone, sometimes with Camus,
once with an art school man taking Polaroids.
I can't walk away from the feeling you give me —
it's like watching a plane
work across a white sky in winter
and pass behind a beige-brick building
— something like loneliness.

– Will Fesperman

Love and Loathing in the Waffle House

"Is that flannel?" The waitress reaches over the counter and gropes at my arm until she's holding only the fabric of my sleeve. She slides her fingers over it. "Ooh," she moans. She quivers and brings her hand back to the pen and pad. "You're just too sexy for me."

I must not have heard her right. "I'm sorry?"

"Too sexy. I said, 'You're just too sexy for me.' My first husband used to wear flannel."

"Oh." I put my menu down. It's midnight by now, or close to it.

"I wear flannel to bed every night. I come in the bedroom and my boyfriend says, 'Ah, shit, here she comes wearing that sack.' I know he hates it. But I just can't get enough. He don't know why."

I'm not sure if I'm being invited to respond. Probably not. "I think I'll have —"

"You know how some people talk about Christmas in July? That's what it's like for me, wearing flannel, even on a hot night like this. I used to think all that business was silly, but I think I understand it now. Some people just want to keep the feeling going, you know? Even though it's gone, and don't come back often."

I am silent now. She looks at me expectantly. Her irises are pale blue but the whites of her eyes are a veiny yellow. Porcupine hair, throaty voice, skin like peeling stucco.

She takes my order and walks away.

I used to hate this place. The first thing I remember is finding a human tooth stuck to my menu, slightly yellowed and casting a shadow over the breakfast specials. Can you imagine that? The contents of someone's mouth, a tiny little thing once kept alive by wet tissue and grazed by hot breath. I scrunched up my face and flicked it so hard that my mother looked up and asked me what was wrong.

"Nothing," I said, though I heard it faintly clicking across the tile and grout.

The bell clinks pitifully when two guys my age walk in. I recognize them. I used to go to school with them. One plays the drums. The other plays bass. They look but do not quite recognize me. They head to a booth in the corner.

That booth they picked, that's where most of the kids sat after the eighth-grade dance. Not me; there hadn't quite been room for me. Which was convenient, seeing as how I had just admitted to a year-long crush on Stephanie Morgan. I sat at the counter with the castaways and watched her pluck bits of scrambled egg from her pink and blue braces.

The hash browns were a little late that night. Our short-order cook was arrested. I was the first one to spot the men in black vests slinking around outside, signaling each other to cover the back and side doors. Finally one came in through the front, and the bell clinked, and he said, "Crystal, it's time to go," and as Crystal was dragged away, her dyed-pink bangs fell down between her eyes, eyes with that dead look that results from someone thinking, *I'll never get what I want.*

My eyes skim over the slim bodies of the musicians I recognize. Pants like a second skin, vinyl high-tops, trendy shirts with collars that plunge past pale clavicles. Hair like they just rolled out of bed. A perfected look. From across the restaurant I think, *This is what people want.* Some people are born with it, this assurance. Some people aren't.

They pry packs from their pockets and wrap their lips around cigarettes.

I could go over, ask for a smoke, and see if it jogs their memory.

I don't, though. I've never been able to smoke right. Nothing comes out on the exhale, nothing ever has. It stays in my chest, like it's trying to fill a gap. Can't be healthy.

The waitress is back now. She asks if I want more coffee. She doesn't look at me, she doesn't look down. She looks out the window while she pours. There's really nothing to see. Traffic. Her own reflection, maybe. Even without looking, she knows exactly when to stop pouring.

The waitress has been on a slippery slope ever since I reminded her of her first husband. The cook snaps at her for making him pull too much bacon. She walks tiredly over to the booth with the musicians. It takes her some time to understand their order. She apologizes. She asks them please not to get smart with her.

231

A few minutes later, she presents tickets to a handful of customers in one deft pass of the counter. She slaps down my own grease-stained slip with a sigh and keeps walking. I look over the shoulder of a nearby man. He has flipped his ticket over to reveal our server's name, printed legibly. Laura. I flip mine and find a chaotic scrawl in the same space: loops colliding with loops, letters becoming unrecognizable hills and valleys. Like the readout on a heart monitor. It's as if Laura put her pen to this paper and felt an overwhelming urge to get home, to sink into a fabric more forgiving than her black nylon apron.

For a tip, I leave everything in my pocket. A loose dollar, twelve or so coins, a movie ticket stub. I go to the cash register to pay. On the way out, I almost, but not quite, leave her the five-dollar bill she has given me for change.

I am leaving, and the bell clinks, and I am in my car, and the engine is starting. I'm on the road now. I do not like driving by myself at night. *Scared* isn't necessarily the right word. I've never wrecked before. I just don't like how my headlights gesture toward the darkness.

I put my foot to the floor, and the car kicks and presses me back into the seat. Because sometimes you do this; sometimes you want to hear the engine rev up and fill that silence.

Portals

The deal is on, yes, the deal is on, yes. Runs through closing time today, which makes it Darrel's lucky day, and that is good. Because Darrel needs luck — luck, and many other things.

The customer-service man stares down at Darrel over his thick nose, and Darrel's eyes have trouble making it all the way back to the man's, have trouble making contact. That schnoz, that gargantuan honker is in the way. This doesn't bother Darrel all that much — even if he can't see the man's eyes, he can at least look to the walls for consolation. Lining them are glossy, blown-up photographs of people with their devices pressed to their ears. All of them are young and very attractive. Most of them have their heads thrown back in a joyous cackle.

Darrel can't see the man's eyes, but he can see the teeth of the people in the photographs, and Darrel likes their teeth, trusts their teeth, takes comfort in their whiteness and straightness. No hint of decay in their mouths.

"After I've switched to your company, will I be able to keep my phone number?" Darrel strings his words together self-consciously, as if trying out a foreign language. Really, he should have been keeping up with these types of things, but Trina had always handled the phones, the bills, the insurance; with her gone, Darrel feels as though he's walking around the Grand Canyon in the dark. Perhaps he's at the bottom of the gorge, and that's why everything sounds so echoey. Or maybe he's on top of a plateau, the cliff just a few blind steps away. Who's to tell?

The man snorts at the stupidity of Darrel's question, and again Darrel isn't so much offended as scared the exhilaration will blow him away. *After all*, Darrel thinks, *the bigger the nose, the greater the air intake. Or is that the way that works?* For a few moments, Darrel imagines a microscopic version of himself riding the brisk stream of air as it flows into the man's right nostril, imagines watching the dark bristles — swaying like trees — remove imperfections from the flow, imagines following the sweet oxygen all the way down to the capillaries of the man's lungs.

Darrel imagines the gift of life, reenacted at the rate of twenty times per minute.

Noses are good. Breathing is good.

"Yes," moans the man. He clicks away at his keyboard with long, pale fingers that form harsh angles at the knuckles. The computers are arranged in a cordoned-off circle at the center of the store, with another sign swinging over them: a giant, glossy, satisfied customer confined to two dimensions.

"There are *laws* that protect your right to *keep* your cell phone *number*," the man continues. Darrel is up in years, sure, but not old enough to be addressed like the mentally handicapped. "*You* just fill out the *paperwork*, and then we'll wait for *your number* to come through the *portal*."

What in the hell is the portal? Darrel thinks. He doesn't like the sound of it. Portal, to him, means something like a miniature black hole, swirling and fuming and ominous. Distortion,

234

irrevocable transportation to another place. Someone who is there and then not.

Darrel takes his old cell phone out of his pocket, cradles it in his palm like an injured bird.

"How long will it take?" he asks.

The man stops clicking around on his computer. "*What?*" he groans. "How long will *what* take?"

"The . . . the switch. Or transfer. You know, how long before . . . how long until you are in charge? Of my phone?"

The man abandons his computer altogether and turns his entire body toward Darrel, who is momentarily intimidated by the man's khakis, his logo-emblazoned black polo, his silver pen hanging onto his breast pocket with one gleaming claw. Darrel finds the man's sharp, protruding Adam's apple off-putting. Darrel reads something in the man's face (or, at least, the disgusted twitching of his nose) — something that says, *The customers have reached a new low.*

"*Sir,*" the man drawling in the general direction of Darrel. "*Your* old phone won't work with *our* service. The *chip* isn't *compatible. You're* going to need a *new* phone. Now *you* look around the store and try to find one while *I* draw up the paperwork. *Okay?*"

Darrel says nothing.

"*Sir?* I assume you still want to take advantage of our *deal?* No registration fees for *new* customers if *you* join *before* the store closes tonight? *Discount* for the first year of your *contract?* Remember? Isn't that why you're *switching?*"

Darrel nods meekly. The man exits the round altar of computers, heads for a printer in the back. Darrel looks down at his old phone. He must have bought it, what, five years ago? Six?

235

He can barely remember. Trina was with him, the driving force behind the purchase. They needed to join the twenty-first century, she had said — the kids were always trying to call.

Darrel looks down at his phone. It's a solid, sturdy, standard-looking thing — shaped like a tiny casket — bought before they could flip or even slide open. Its plastic antenna is bent and sad-looking, its buttons are worn and gummy. The tiny screen below the earpiece is scratched from being dropped and chewed on by the cat. Sometimes it lights up, sometimes it doesn't. Even when it does, displaying the time, date, and number he dials is the extent of its ability — blocky black letters on a dim green background.

It is nothing like the phones Darrel sees as he makes a half-hearted lap around the cellular store. There are phones with $100 price tags, phones with $200 price tags, phones with $500 price tags. They take pictures, they record videos, they play music and have games and can get on the Internet. Some of them have little keyboards. Some of them have no buttons at all but large screens instead.

I need a phone, Darrel thinks. *Not a tiny television.*

A girl in a similar polo as the man asks if Darrel needs any help, and Darrel laughs dejectedly and says, "Yes, I need help affording them." (Why hadn't they planned better? Where had the money gone?) The girl nods somewhat assuredly and escorts him to the back corner of the store, to a shelf full of phones that look basic in a way not unlike his own.

"You pay for these as you use them," says the girl.

"What about the reception? As good as my old one?" asks Darrel. Darrel had seen his children performing borderline-surgical procedures on the fancy phones they bought with leftover scholarship money, but not his — never a problem, not in all those years. He could always hear, clear as day, his son complaining about the job market, his daughter complaining about her boyfriend. He could hear Trina's sweet voice, and could keep track of her even when he couldn't see her — the shuffling of papers on the kitchen table as she looked for a receipt, the opening and closing of cabinet doors as she looked for a prescription.

"Depends on the towers in your area," says the girl. She hands him a ratty-looking box. "There's a test phone in here," she says. "You can use it tonight, make sure you're satisfied with the reception. Bring it back tomorrow."

Darrel thanks the girl. He tells her he has to sign a contract tonight, but he'll run outside and use the test phone if he has time. "One more question," he says. "Say I'd like to keep the voicemail greeting I have now. How would I go about making sure I still have it?"

The girl looks confused. "You can't just rerecord it?"

Darrel searches for his words carefully, then settles for full disclosure. "Sentimental value," he says under his breath.

"Oh," the girl frowns. "Well, we certainly can't get your own service provider to send it to us. Things just aren't open like that. It took enough bloodshed to get the portal up and running. A world where two competing companies share more customer info would make our jobs a lot easier, but it just doesn't work out that way." Here the girl laughs. "Two companies who share voicemail systems! Can you imagine?" She slaps Darrel playfully on the arm.

Darrel is petrified. "What about the chip?" he asks. "Can't you take it off the chip?"

237

The girl frowns slightly. "Your voicemail greeting isn't saved on your chip," she says. "It's saved in some server at the headquarters of your old service provider, millions of miles away. You could maybe pay some sort of specialist to rip it from somewhere," she hesitates, "but —"

"But I don't have that kind of money," Darrel finishes for her. She nods sympathetically.

"Hey," she smiles. "Just think of the deal you're getting! It's a new day."

A woman sits at the counter next to Darrel screaming as he tries to fill out his paperwork. She wears an unbecoming pink velour tracksuit and tennis shoes. Her eyes are red and puffy from angry sobs. She's yelling about something — her contract? They won't let her out of her contract. Her cries are shrill; her blond hair is crazed — parts of it appear curly, parts of it appear straight, parts of it are pinned down, and others bounce freely with her ranting.

It occurs to Darrel that the fight between the woman and the man, from far off, would look like a battle between a blond mop and a giant nose.

How is he supposed to finish his paperwork here, with this ruckus? How can he remember his social security number with the woman screaming about trust and loyalty and fair business practice, about the money she doesn't have, about the money nobody has?

The woman asks to speak to the manager. The man informs her that he is the manager.

The woman would still like for him to get someone on the phone. The man, after snorting and groaning a bit, leaves to do so.

The woman covers her face with her hands and turns to Darrel. She says she knows she looks like a mess and apologizes. Then she drops her hands and weeps, not angry this time but helpless, and a few tears splatter onto the dark, plastic counter.

Between sobs, she tells Darrel that "sometimes it's just us versus them."

Almost immediately, Darrel is scared to stay in the cell phone store — scared that the woman's hysteria will enter and fester in him through osmosis. He sets the clipboard down on the counter and turns to leave. He takes his old phone and his test phone with him.

"I need to go eat dinner," Darrel tells the man, who has returned to the counter and is holding a receiver out to the woman. She grabs it with a sticky hand, brings it slowly to her ear, as if she expects the words to fall on her like axes.

"The *deal*!" the man calls after Darrel. "Store *closes* soon! Don't *forget* about *the deal*!"

"I won't. I'll be back," Darrel tells him, but he isn't so sure.

There's a hole-in-the-wall Mexican restaurant down the street that Trina found on her drive home one night and insisted they try. They had gone here at least once every two weeks ever since.

The waitress asks Darrel where Trina is, and Darrel says she's in bed, not feeling well.

The waitress suggests he order a carryout, bring some chips and salsa home to Trina. "They're to die for," says the waitress.

"I know," smiles Darrel.

He orders his quesadilla and chimichangas. He eats them.

He orders a flan. Not his favorite dessert, but Trina always loved it, right down to the caramel sauce left at the bottom of the saucer.

The way the whipped cream blooms out of the flan reminds him of the baby's breath in Trina's casket spray.

The way the whipped cream disappears into the portal of his mouth reminds him of the way Trina sank into the portal dug in the ground.

The whipped cream is not coming back.

Darrel takes out his test phone and calls his old phone.

His old phone rings too happily, clashes with the music in the Mexican restaurant. The voicemail kicks in. Trina's voice.

"Hello, you've reached Darrel and Trina's cell phone —"

I've reached you? I'll never reach you again. I reach and reach and reach and feel nothing. I am walking blind in the Grand Canyon, and you are a star in the dark sky, and the light that reaches me is an image of the way you were then, and I won't feel you blink out until years after the fact, and this rift in time, this portal that sucks away all of our minutes and hours, it kills me.

"— please leave us a message after the tone —"

If I speak into this, store a recording for you in a server millions of miles away, will you hear it? Where is your answering service? How is your reception up there? Down there? Can you hear me at all? All that time spent together and now it's the chips that will rob me of the last part of you, the chips and so much else will separate us, the chips and millions of miles and people smiling in posters, the people who aren't really customers at all but models who don't know the misery they're smiling at with approval. Why are they smiling? Why are they laughing at the clouds? Do

240

they look up and see you? Are they talking to you and are you talking back and are you paying-as-you-go? Can I?

"— and we'll get back to you as soon as possible."

Get back, get back, get back.

The tone sounds, and echoes through Darrel's head in a deafening way that could last forever, but it's gone again before he can miss it, and Darrel hears nothing.

– Jake Ross

No Straight Lines in Curved Space

This is how it goes:

I work the graveyard shift at a 24-hour Walgreens. For eight hours every night, my universe shrinks into that 6,000-square-foot fluorescent temple. Ten minutes into the shift, the grumbling of automobiles is my only line to the world outside. Thirty minutes later, the cash register becomes the center of my existence. I don't hear the cars anymore. Time slows to a tortured crawl, and the clock becomes the bane of my existence. My life implodes into a rush of sickly faces and bloodshot eyes and "thank you, come again."

All of the customers past 2 A.M. are zombies. Once, a woman held two cartons of ice cream — one chocolate, one vanilla — in her hands until her forearms swam in cool syrup. Her green eyes, dulled by the steady monochrome fluorescents in Aisle 4, had the glassy look of the consideration of the dead. She left without buying anything. I mopped up the mess with neither resentment nor pity.

This is how it goes:

Three hours into the shift, time loses all meaning, and I lose all traces of humanity. I am C-3PO, human-cyborg relations.

I am the dead, going through the motions of life. Sorry, sir, we only have plastic, and fuck you, R2-D2.

Mostly frat boys and unhappy working-class husbands come on midnight runs for cigarettes and milk and Red Bull. I don't care. I don't know. Sometimes it's something different. But all I do is ring it up, and the crash of the cash register ricochets in my skull until finally I don't think anymore. Kids in their parents' cars buy Marlboros with fake IDs — they always pay with change. Limp dollar bills and a thousand pounds of silver clatter gracelessly into the appropriate plastic tubs. There's a little dish for loose pennies. A single piece of copper has been rusting there contentedly for the past few eternities.

This is how it goes:

On the graveyard shift, autobiography becomes fluid. Some nights, my name is Sarah; some nights, my name is Carrie. My name tag reads "Lisa" and my ID says I was born in 1982, but none of that matters. My identity disappears along with time. This is the Bermuda Triangle.

A small man sits at the electronics booth. His name is Pablo, and he gets paid five dollars an hour. Pablo is a thin, nervous man who constantly checks his fly. He jumps when the door chimes.

Sally is older. The late nights eat away her time between middle age and menopause. She mops the floor with harsh black hands. Pablo is fucking her. They go through the "Employees Only Please" door thirty seconds apart. They don't talk to me because I'm white.

Sometimes I wake myself from the daze and look at the clock. The numbers leave bitter déjà vu behind. The fans cycle stale air endlessly. I slip back into the blur. This nothing place is holy. Curiosity is replaced by comfort. Undertones of malaise permeate my dream state in waves, but it's better than being alive.

This is how it goes:

It was a dark and stormy night. I use cliché because my memory holds no emotion. Thunder crashed and the windows wept. The noise was enough to drown out the cash register, and the monotone ventilation was completely lost. It was a dark and stormy night, but we were lit up like some fluorescent lollipop purgatory. Sally and Pablo had disappeared into the stockroom again. Maybe it was 4:30. Slow night. I was unable to deafen myself to the storm. I heard the windows shudder in their frames. I heard my heart beat in my chest, as if it were still pumping blood to my brain. All night, I tried to get caught in my temporal slipstream. I felt like a person again, and how strange the sensation! Perhaps it was the collective unconscious preparing me for the bizarre intersection of fate. I don't believe in stuff like that.

I heard the gentle bump of tires against concrete from the parking lot. A haggard transvestite wobbled through on five-inch heels.

"Two packs of Chesterfields, darling."

Blush like scarlet fever jumped from his cheekbones. His eyes fluttered glitter onto the counter, and his lips were painted coral. He removed one of his pumps to dote on a blister, then slipped his foot back into the satin-lined puddle.

"God, it's really coming down, isn't it?" I said, stooping down for the cigarettes.

"Oh, yes, my wig aches when it rains like this."

He winked at me, and I let out a surprised bray of laughter. The graveyard shift does not invoke laughter.

"Have a nice night, ma'am," I said as the door chimed again. I still had a smile on my face when the other unusual stranger came in.

This time, I heard tires screech and the smack of a car's nose against the wall. A man in a shirt and tie ran in, cradling his hands against his chest. He sang a strangled mantra: "Oh Christ oh Christ oh Christ." When he passed by the front cash register, I saw that there was blood on his hands and splashed across his shirt and pinstripe pants. I let out a kind of choked gasp and sat heavily back onto the stool behind the counter. I kept wide eyes on this rain-battered man as he cleared out of the liquor aisle with an armful of clinking bottles. As he came closer, I saw smeared coral lipstick on his palms and glitter swiped across his sweaty forehead. He was crying.

"All of this, all of this, all of this," he muttered. His breath already spoke of alcohol.

"Um." My mouth gaped open and shut stupidly. I noticed it had stopped raining.

The man reached for his wallet, balancing the liquor precariously with his one arm and his chin. Somewhere, blocks away, a police siren started up, then another. He screamed and the bottles crashed into a flood of broken glass and alcohol. I jumped. The terror in his eyes grew. He lives a nightmare, I thought. He lives in life. With each anguished breath he took, he shattered my listless paradigm. I shrank from him and everything he represented.

The sirens raced toward us.

"Oh Christ!" he moaned.

Pablo and Sally ventured out of the stockroom, holding hands. They looked like children.

245

I started to cry.

The drunken man ran out of the door, skating on broken glass. The door chimed. Pablo checked his fly.

Presently, I became deaf again. I shrank into a fluorescent spotlight, feeling the tears I had not shed drying on my cheeks.

There were no more customers that night. By dawn, everything had receded into that foggy, hallucinatory existence. At 7:30 I walked, with a clean line, into the world. The door chimed on my way out.

This is how it goes.

– Lillian Selonick

As Thin of Substance as the Air?

She sweeps by sweetly, a demure smile on her face, her brown hair folding at her shoulders. In her quiet glance I see everything I desire reflected back at me. I have barely spoken to her and yet I have learned to love her gentle, throaty voice. My imagination has taken her innocent smile, rather attractive features, apparent intelligence, and, most important of all, her taciturn nature, and conjured the perfect person, my internal complement. Her friends seem pretentious, even obnoxious, and yet on some near-unconscious level I have decided that she is somehow different. Clearly I have caught my imagination and questioned it just before letting it run away with me, but despite logic I have been unable to quell the fluttering in my stomach that I feel with such intensity at this very moment as she passes. Even though I realize that I am awake, I cannot help but pursue the creations of my imagination, characters from dreams that are probably nothing more than aspects of myself, and even though I realize that I am superimposing eidetic images of my own invention on a quiet girl who has betrayed very few of her thoughts, I cannot help but allow my fantasies to seize me, on the off chance that I will encounter someone resembling the person I have created, an affirmation of the existence of the mind out of which I peer curiously.

I meet her eyes for a brief moment and then allow mine to fall to the floor. I am too shy to be looked at, too unsure of what she'll see. In one moment I swear that she is smiling at me and in the next I curse myself for thinking it, for wanting something that isn't there. She takes her seat. She is wearing corduroy again. The teacher calls on her to read her sonnet. She meekly whispers a soft string of words. "That was beautiful, Lacy," says Ms. Hardy, beaming at her. I am called on next. I don't have anything. Last night I became lost in complexity and eloquence eluded me. "A writer has but one lifetime, Aidan," jokes Ms. Hardy. "Just get it in next time." I return her smile weakly because I know that one night will never be long enough. Failed poets often make the best writers of prose because their writing comes compellingly close to re-creating the reality of human experience that you feel an almost spiritual communion with their words. The blank page before them demands definition, demands that they bare their soul rather than trade the truthful conflict of their poetry for romantic delusions, for shameless lies. When I sit down to write, my thoughts inevitably drift to Lacy and then all understanding becomes obscured by the familiar ache of concupiscence. The bell rings and the class rushes to leave. She thoughtfully finishes a sentence and slips her notebook into her bag. As she slings the strap over her shoulder and blithely walks toward the door, I want desperately to make myself known to her.

"Hey," I call out too softly to be heard. It's too late . . . she has walked away before I can tell her how much I liked her poem.

248

I don't go straight home after school. Instead I take the long route to the park by the bay. I watch the pelicans floating in the breeze, falling from time to time into a graceful dive to catch a fish below. My mind defies the calm, returning to the words I wrote last night, to all that they are unable to express. I tried to write my poem about Lacy, but none of it made sense. It was an absurd assortment of abstractions that refused every word I wrote. I have felt this way before. I have wanted so badly to see an ideal realized that I convinced myself of its existence, only to see the beautiful illusion shattered, because it was never anything more than an image in a mirror. Still I struggle with these abstractions with the desperate hope that they will unfold into meaning. Still I find myself trying to translate the truth of all my sensitivity because it has always seemed possessed of such profoundness.

A hand on my shoulder disrupts my thought suddenly and I jump in response. "Relax," says Michael, laughing, "I'm not trying to steal your wallet." He runs his hand through his greasy blond hair with a sly, almost mocking grin stretched across his face. "I saw you sitting here all alone and I thought I'd bring you a surprise."

I know what it is before he takes it out, and I know that even after having gone a few months without it, I won't refuse.

"I was just about to find myself a little spot to light this up, and then I saw you sitting over here and decided to make your day," he says as he sits beside me, looks around and, seeing no one, lights his joint.

He passes it to me and exhales. I take a deep drag and hold it in. When I first started smoking, I decided that there couldn't possibly be anything wrong with the gentle relief the pleasure allowed me. It felt as though I had found all the comfort, all the understanding that seemed to have been forgotten by the world around me. Slowly, subtly, it wove itself into my psyche. It became the only thing that I believed in, and I clung to it the way I had always clung to ideals. The more I smoked, the more I found the world inside my head to be irreconcilable with the one around me and tried desperately to escape it. The illusion fell apart, and just like all of the other illusions my mind had conjured, it left me all the more alone, all the more lost. In my withdrawal I retreated to the familiar safety of introspection. I began to read voraciously. I went to the library every day and pored over novels, books on philosophy and poetry. I savored the wondrous beauty of reality. It was months before I smoked again. Even though my will to discover meaning has kept me from returning fully, I still have these moments of uncertainty. I pass the joint to Michael.

"I heard you dropped out," I say to Michael.

"Yeah, that place wasn't doing shit for me. I moved out of my house too. I've got my own apartment now. All I do is chill and smoke."

He flashes me that same sly grin and I catch his eye as he passes me the joint. I remember catching his eye just like this a long time ago, when we were younger, before we had passed joints between us. I remember seeing his eyes fill with light like two blue stained-glass windows. Now, as he quickly looks away, I see nothing of that light. I want to say something meaningful to him, to reason with him, but no words come to me. My body begins to flood with pleasure and feel heavy as I pass him the joint. A moment later he flicks the roach to the ground, says that he really should be going and begins to walk away. I sit on my bench until the water rises and turns a deep orange color.

Lacy's eyes, light brown like her hair, seem to glimmer with receptivity whenever I work up the nerve to say something to her. She smiles at my jokes, even those I tell to whomever happens to be sitting beside me in class in hopes that she will overhear. I think of nothing else as I make my way home, catching myself for a moment before continuing my reverie: I must accept that it is more likely than not that she too is an illusion. How dangerous it is to hope, to allow myself even to consider the possibility that I have perceived the truth of who she is intuitively. It occurs to me that she would probably be repulsed by everything I've done today: my pathetic, longing call, my smoking, my whole preoccupation with her. More often than not, when this happens to me, when I build someone up in my mind and finally ask them out, full of expectation, they sense my delusion and are repelled by all the conflict within me. They see the way I look at them, my eyes filled with supplicating light, and somehow they know it's not them I love, but something I have projected onto them, something I've been looking for all of my life in one form or another. Sometimes they touch my arm, bat their eyelashes, tell me how important I've become to them, and then when the moment of expectation comes, the illusion is shattered and for all I know I imagined the whole thing. But when I look into Lacy's eyes I cannot believe that she would be repulsed because they seem full of such understanding. I suppose that's easy to believe when you want it to be true, and when the person has yet to say anything to contradict your image of them.

251

The screen door bounces against its frame three times before it finally clicks shut behind me. There is a plate of chicken and rice on the table. Mom must be going out again. Several dresses are laid out on the sofa with a few pairs of heels on the floor below them. She emerges from the bathroom, curlers in hair, lipstick in hand. She smiles, kisses me on the cheek, and continues changing frantically. She asks about my day and complains when I offer limited responses. I sit on the couch and avoid her eyes. A car pulls up outside just as she slips her heels on. I kiss her good night, glad that she finished readying herself in time, relieving me of an awkward encounter with her date. "Well, I'll be back by eleven. Your dinner is on the table. Love you."

I take my stuff into the bedroom, which is divided in two by a sheet hanging from the ceiling. When we moved in she insisted that I take the bedroom, arguing that I was going to need a quiet place to study. She said that she would be comfortable enough with a room divider in the living room. Her eyes used to fill with tears when I brought home straight As. She would go on about how I was going to have a wonderful job, be a good man, marry the perfect girl, have children, and be happy. She has always given me more credit than I deserve. While I liked to see her as happy as she was when she was fantasizing about my future, there was something about those tears that filled me with a terrible anxiety. In the year I stopped caring about those stupid letters on a piece of paper, because I decided that they had no meaning, I stopped showing her my grades and she didn't say a word. She preferred to pretend that nothing had changed. She caught me smoking that year and she wept disconsolately, shrieking, completely unwilling to listen to my feeble attempts to explain. When I looked at her, I was overwhelmed by that same terrible anxiety and promised I would stop. And then it was over. She looked tired the next day, but she smiled at me, preferring to pretend that the whole thing had been some sort of bad dream.

She goes out several times a week, trying to find someone who will love her. The hair dye she uses to keep the gray from showing and the creams she uses to hide her wrinkles sit on her nightstand. She cannot help but believe in love. She cannot help but believe that if she is a good person, then there is no conceivable reason why life should not bring her love. And even though the truth of her life seems to contradict her philosophy, even though it seems likely that her belief is an awful form of self-deception, she cannot question any of it because losing faith in love would mean losing faith in life. "Finding a man will make it all better," she tells herself. She lives for that moment that will confirm that her many years of unwavering faith in love were not wasted. I think of what it must have been like when she was twenty, pregnant and in college, when my father left her, and I can't feel anything but pity for her. I came up with the idea of sharing the bedroom. You have to pass through her side to get to mine. She gets the closet and I get a quiet place to study.

I lie down on my bed for a while and then move to the living room to do the same on the couch. I can't imagine bringing Lacy here, sitting with her on this ratty secondhand furniture in front of this TV that doesn't get any channels. Maybe she's like me and doesn't like TV anyway. I eat and then grab my notebook in hopes of producing a poem. I turn Lacy's words around inside my head.

The assignment was to write a sonnet and Ms. Hardy said that if we were moved to write something romantic, as we have been reading *Romeo and Juliet*, all the better. Before Juliet, Romeo loved Rosaline. If you could ask Romeo whether or not his feelings for Juliet were true love, he would tell you yes; but if you could ask Shakespeare, he would tell you that both wanted love so badly that they imagined themselves in the other. Both were lucky — debatably, not so lucky — to have found someone just as deluded as themselves. No one intelligent enough to craft Romeo's emphatic vows of love would be as ignorant of his condition as he. I have never known what to tell a girl and have always made a fool out of myself. "It is the east and Juliet is the sun," whispers an idealistic cynic from above. I have no one to whisper brilliant lines in my ear. There is only my own internal monologue.

My lower lip gently draws Lacy's further into the kiss. I am aware that we are somewhere in school, but the intensely pleasurable tension that fills my body dims that awareness. My hands run up the arch of her back, pulling her toward me. I feel a tremble escape my control. It flows from my body into hers like an electrical current. My eyes open suddenly. The sharp sound of a lock clicking into place and a key being drawn from it wake me. Mom must be leaving for work. I am still on the couch. I realize I didn't finish any of my homework. There is a quilt wrapped around me. How strange, how incredibly absurd it is to be having such tender dreams about someone who is essentially a stranger! My alarm clock beeps loudly in my room and I get up to shut it off. Breakfast is on the table: scrambled eggs, fruit, and tea.

I shower, dress, eat, and walk to school. I don't pay much attention in my first period. When I get to Ms. Hardy's class I walk quickly to the back of the room. She doesn't ask me for my poem. Lacy walks in and I imagine her merging with her dream counterpart that so willingly embraced me. She takes a seat in the row to the left of mine a few seats up. Ms. Hardy begins class, but I continue to stare at Lacy. "I hope everyone brought their books today. . . ." Lacy turns around suddenly, looking directly at me as though she had felt my eyes on her. I turn awkwardly to look at Ms. Hardy, who begins to read from the scene with Mercutio's famous rant about Queen Mab and dreams:

True, I talk of dreams,
    Which are the children of an idle brain, Begot of
nothing but vain fantasy; Which is as thin of substance
as the air . . .

She stops there. "Some critics have argued that it is in these lines that Shakespeare comes fully to the surface, using Mercutio to express his belief that all that comes to pass between Romeo and Juliet is nothing more than the playing out of 'vain fantasy.' After having read this play, what do you think? Do you think it is through Mercutio that Shakespeare speaks to us?" She looks around for someone to call on. My heart sinks as her eyes come to rest on me. "Aidan, what do you think?"

I look at my desk for a moment, wanting to disappear. Sentences start to form themselves and I begin to speak. "No, I don't agree with that. Mercutio is the defiant, vulgar, witty, colorful character that he is because he believes that dreams are 'as

255

thin of substance as the air.' On a deeper level, his wit is his attempt to create meaning within the meaningless dream that is reality . . . he makes puns even as he is dying as a last act of defiance against the madness of meaninglessness. Shakespeare kills Mercutio to show us that he is as flawed in his philosophy as Romeo, because believing that the world holds no meaning is just as emotional of a response to life as blindly believing that it is full of meaning."

Ms. Hardy beams at me the way she beamed at Lacy the day before. I don't listen much for the rest of the class. I am not nearly as certain as Romeo and Mercutio. I look at Lacy. I cannot feel love, or anything for that matter, without questioning it. The bell rings and I resolve to defy all of my uncertainty and speak with her because even though I can never hope to receive a definite answer, it is the only way to test the nature of dreams. I move toward her as she makes her way to the door. I have no idea what I will say, but I feel as though Fate is forcing me in her direction.

"Aidan," Ms. Hardy calls, motioning me to her desk. Lacy walks away, again. . . . Ms. Hardy tells me that my grades have been slipping due to my failure to turn in assignments. "Do not squander your intelligence," she says. I apologize and tell her that I have had a lot on my mind. She offers me her ear should I ever want to speak to her.

I walk to the park after school. How ironic it is that every moment demands that we react, and yet we are deprived of the meaning of the interaction. I sit on the seawall and watch the undulating flow beneath me. The light plays upon the water's surface, shimmering brilliantly as it merges with its own reflection. I remember an experiment I read about that proves that electrons are both waves and particles. They are only particles when they come into contact with a conscious observer. The rest of the time they are waves of possibility, potential matter. Some quantum physicists assert that because the manifestation of the material world is dependent on a conscious observer, consciousness is more fundamental than matter. Others disagree that it is consciousness exactly that is collapsing electrons into physical reality, but it seems that no matter what you call it, some essential aspect of the observer is more fundamental than matter. But what do I know? I'm not very good at math. I read a book by a physicist that said that quantum mechanics is suggesting what Buddhism has been professing for thousands of years: that the divide between what is within and what is without is an illusion. He meditates for hours to detach himself from this illusion of isolation for a momentary glimpse of reality as it is on the deepest level of truth: consciousness permeated by a sea of infinite possibilities. I'll probably never be able to do the calculations, but is not poetry a system of symbols as well? Einstein dreamt of writing an equation to talk to God, of seeing his symbols reveal all the meaning he had been searching for his whole life.

I get home and find immense vulnerability and complexity spilling from me. I struggle with the structure, but after an hour or so I look down at the page, riddled with markings and crossed-out lines, and see my finished sonnet scribbled in the corner.

Before I know it, I am in front of the class, preparing to read my poem. I look over at Lacy and delight in her apparent receptivity, imagined or not. Perhaps after I read, I will find that no one understood a word I wrote — it has happened before — but I will continue to try to translate these abstractions because I can't deny the feeling that they hold some sort of profound meaning and I know nothing beyond what I feel. When I finish reading I look directly into Lacy's eyes, she looks back smiling, and I know that today I will catch her before she walks out the door.

– *Matthew Llarena*

Eve

I don't remember being that single, bloody rib.

The stark white bones sprouting like bald, jointed trees. Breasts,
flabby knolls erupting from muscle striped like plowed fields.

Adam giggling in the corner, I'm sure, adjusting his single,
    well-positioned leaf,
startled at the sight of something so strange and different,
at me.

I started remembering at the time of the skin rippling
over everything,
from head downwards, toes upwards, meeting to connect at
    the bottom of the pelvic
bone, then a nauseating shuddering and rolling like
a boulder about to topple off a cliff, teetering at the tip, then —
"Good enough," God said,
and my skin went zipping together, inwards instead of out.

There was a hole.

Where Adam had a summit, I had
nothing. Raw, unfinished, air.
I asked Adam why. In his innocence,
there was only the vague sense that his leaf might be getting a
    bit tighter,
so I left.

I sat in the garden,
surrounded by so much beauty it was
commonplace, flowers as big as my head blooming
    beside me,
the pollen coating my skin like gold,
and I would wonder.

The animals Adam and I had named
Refused to answer my questions, or maybe they just
Didn't know.

The snake and I compared our bodies,
Looking for a similar
Incompleteness on her smooth underbelly,
Finding none.

I was alone. God had finished everyone else.

And then, the next time I visited the snake and her tree,
she told me
I could know why. I could know almost
as much as God knew.

"Eat this," she said, handing me a fig. I took a small, scared bite,
finding, even as I chewed, that it had needed to be done.
I tasted something pungent and strange,

Then I knew.

I expected a rift in the earth, thunder at least,
but all was silent as I looked down and saw what I had to be
    ashamed of.
Calling over Adam, I told him, "Eat, and get that thing away
    from me."
Flowers wilted under our feet as we took our last steps
out of the garden. Our sorrows multiplied under God's icy glare.

He was the master of the silent treatment.

With each step away, I felt a twinge
between my legs.

With each step,
a drop of blood,
leaving a trail
we could never follow back.

– Elise Lockwood

Laughing at Bullets

It's morning, I'm in Nigeria, and our bodyguard, Wednesday, is shooting in the air again. I know that's a strange name for a man, but think of Wednesday as our John Doe and you'll see how some Nigerians name their children after days of the week. The best I could do that Christmas was go to my parents' homeland. They bought flights and bolted every lock on our house when we left. So I'm on a porch in Nigeria that morning, dreaming of my American home, though I wouldn't even have a key inside.

Flashing between laughs, Wednesday's teeth seem painted, whitewashed each morning with some toothbrush. He lowers his machine gun. My father had always told me not to be scared, that the bullets would never reach me, and this look-alike soldier was just having fun. Wednesday dressed in army fatigues each day, as if a uniform made him some sort of trained soldier. This was my fourth trip back to Nigeria, where the air is always thick with diesel smoke. Even that morning the stench tickled my nose, though there weren't many cars out. Wednesday didn't seem to notice, inhaling like this was clean air and he wouldn't want it any other way.

If we're talking about desires then, I'll admit I never wanted Wednesday's security. But after a while, I stopped telling my family that. They always handed me the same mantra: *You've never lived here. You couldn't understand.* And maybe that's true. But ten years earlier, the first time I came to Nigeria, there was a gun battle outside our Greyhound bus. *Cut the head-lights*, a man yelled from behind me. The driver turned off the engine entirely, and night enveloped us. The gunshots sounded cheap, like they'd come from some Western my father can never tear himself from. This is what we heard for minutes: the pop and bang of ammunition. A mother cradling her fright-ened child, whispering some joke so he laughed just a little. Another pop. Another bang. A little laughter. A scream from outside, then silence. I don't even know how we ended up on that road. Men and motorcycles sped away, passing without acknowledgment.

So yes, I understand danger. But I see machine guns and think Vietnam, not street battles, not men like Wednesday, who are paid to protect the people who can afford him.

I should have expected the next round of shots. Wednesday had counted down from ten. But I was halfway listening, and forgot to cover my ears and muffle the sound. I regret that. Because the blast of a machine gun is ruthless, it's a punch in the gut that leaves you dazed, and then laughs at you.

When the shots rang, I dropped down on the porch where we stood, the way I assume soldiers on some battlefield do as soon as bullets fly. This may as well have been a war zone. Shell casings rolled down the concrete, stopping only to bump into me or lodge in cracks of the pavement. Wednesday pulled me up, laughing.

"You could kill someone with that," I said. The porch bordered a market. Below us an old man in only gym shorts pushed a cart along. Its wheels creaked like hinges needing oil.

Wednesday said, "I'm keeping all the bad men away. Do you want to shoot?" I examined the gun's body, the barrel that seemed longer than my arm, the Nigerian flag painted on the shell magazine. I said no, and Wednesday laughed again. The sort of hysterical cackling that I've only seen in movies, where the character actually ends up in a deep sob. Wednesday stepped a foot back to keep his balance and pointed the machine gun up. It was heavy. He wavered. Again the countdown. I plugged my ears and backed away. Shells sprinkled the ground like gold coins.

That afternoon, I found a fruit vendor by a diesel fuel shop, and expected some tropical blend of bananas and mangos and guava to fill me up. But something else did, one I couldn't sniff out just yet, one I can't help but remember. Behind the shop, a black cloud rose higher and higher, painting the afternoon with that kind of smoke you only get from burning gas. I would've asked about it myself, but knew the woman keeping shop wouldn't know English any more than I knew her language. I asked Wednesday instead and he translated, the machine gun held so tightly his chest seemed to embrace it. You'd think at least the young shopkeeper would notice fire behind her, but she didn't or maybe didn't want to. Maybe since there's so much heat in Nigeria, she couldn't even tell the difference. This marketplace seemed thirsty. Palm trees straddled the dusty roads, a much-needed shade, but no one escapes the dust, dust that climbs up your legs and grits your fingernails.

The young woman spoke, then turned to a box of mangos, feeling each for firmness.

"The Bakassi boys burned a man who stole today," Wednesday said. I'd heard of the Bakassi, whom some called vigilantes and others a saving grace. They went through cities and fought crime with machetes and assault weapons.

"So they burned him?" I asked.

So many faces around me, and I wondered how no one else questioned. A woman balanced water on her head as a toddler trailed behind. Two little boys danced in only underwear. A vendor yelled "Rosaries for sale," while draping picture frames from his arms like wooden bangles. And I heard laughter everywhere, cackling, saw men and women and children throw their heads back in uproar. So many teeth. So many smiles. As if everyone knew some joke I hadn't been let in on. Smoke rose in the close distance, black and unrelenting.

There was no track or sidewalk safe enough. So I ran along my uncle's cobblestone driveway, on a night so quiet I wouldn't have noticed the push of a passing wind had it been there. In Nigeria, heat blazes even when the sun has abandoned its sky.

Up, then down again, my legs pumped past the gatekeeper who looked drowsy as usual. I've never known a kinder man, but he wasn't good at his job, always forgetting to lock the gate. A man and a teenage girl ran into the driveway. She had a nose like him — broad and bent upward. I couldn't say whether their eyes shared any resemblance. His left one was punched bloody and swollen, his right bloodshot from crying. "Lock the gate," the man screamed and dropped to the ground in front of me, trying to catch his breath and keep his composure. The girl

265

pulled at his tattered V-neck, "Daddy, get up." He said robbers came to his house, then he put his fingers against his temple and said they put the gun right here.

"Who are you? Get out of here." Wednesday ran up, yelling. This was the first time all day he hadn't carried his gun. His arms bare, I finally saw them, and their thick veins running down the sides like swollen rivers.

"I'm his friend," the man said, pointing to my uncle's balcony. The front lights were on, though no one was home. Wednesday grabbed the man's torn collar. "Robbers. They came to my house and put a gun right here." He demonstrated again. The girl sobbed harder.

I stood quietly and tried to empathize, understand maybe, but there was no way I could even look at the man's bloody face without getting sick. You know I could've used some laughter right then. I mean some gut-wrenching comedy. The kind Wednesday couldn't help but dish out that morning on the porch. The kind that erupted from the bellies of those marketplace people and filled the streets. Laughter growing by the moment, pregnant, leaving its offspring in the throats of those people. I'm convinced of one thing now: They laugh to muffle the pang of bullets, to be carried above Nigeria's violence. And what else could do that better than a mere chuckle, the sweetest sound I've ever heard.

– *Uchechi Kalu*

266

Birthright

A while after my mother disappeared, my father devoted him-self to science. This was part of his strategy of exploring, rather than experiencing, grief. But he didn't know much about it and came up with insane, pseudoscientific ideas better suited to a medieval alchemist's lab than to our home, which was caught between woods and early '90s suburbs in the South. When, after four years, my mother had not returned, he decided she must have died, and he became obsessed with his theory of rein-carnation. He tried to explain this to me.

"Richard, look at it this way," he said. "It's not that when we die we return as another being. Our essence is absorbed by what is most important to us." This was how my father always talked. He didn't have much formal education, and nothing seemed to scare him more than the idea that people might assume he was unintelligent. To drive the point home, he wasted no opportu-nity to show off the vocabulary he'd picked up just by reading the newspaper every morning. "My lexicon has not suffered for my education," he would often say.

At eleven, his idea made no sense to me. At twenty-three, it still seems silly, but I can see the logic in it. Even more than that, I can guess why it was so important to him. If my mother had died, then whoever was closest to her would have taken on her characteristics — and, if he could find some of her in himself, that would mean she died caring for him. I think this is what he was driving at.

Still, it struck me as nonsense. I was eleven, and I went to a Baptist school (my mother's doing); new ideas of spirituality were beyond my concern. "I don't understand," I told him.

He said that was okay, I didn't have to understand. "I'll prove it to you," he said, excited, I thought, by his own ingenuity, "with science!"

Standing with my father in the pet store, I could smell the animals' food, wood shavings, and the stale scent of urine wafting from open cages. "Do we have to stay here?" I asked him. I hated the place. I thought the animals stared when I turned my back.

"Only long enough to pick out a couple rabbits," he said.

An employee approached us. "Can I help you?" she said.

"Those rabbits," my father said, pointing. "Do they like each other?" She asked what he meant. "Are they solitary, or will they bond?"

"I guess they'll bond."

"About how much food do they need?"

She ran down the list of procedures. Pellets, water, lettuce. At my age, I wondered why she didn't say anything about carrots.

"And what would happen if I didn't feed them?" She looked confused, so he clarified himself. "How long would they take to starve?"

"A couple weeks," she said, then composed herself. "But, sir, I can't sell you an animal if you're not going to care for it."

My father laughed. "Just a joke," he said and bought two.

"What should we call them?" my father asked as we drove home with the rabbits.

"I don't know," I said. I wanted nothing to do with this. Ever since my mother disappeared, I'd put up with his increasingly erratic behavior. If we weren't sitting in the woods trying to hear what the trees had to say, we were playing chess without pieces (to strengthen our memories) or looking for acrostic messages in the *Beaufort Gazette*. I was just becoming old enough to resent him.

"Well, at least come up with something!" he said. "Come on, I'm trying to get you to be useful. That's a real virtue in life."

I figured I'd do what he wanted, so he'd stop nagging me. "Call them Jacob and Esau."

"That's a great idea," he said. "You really don't know what good names those are for these rabbits. I'm very pleased with your creativity." He was quiet for a little while, then said, "You know, your mother would be proud."

I turned away from him, toward the window.

My father's idea? — starve Esau. The name I'd chosen, he told me, was a bit of unintentional gallows humor. Since the famous Esau had sold his birthright for food, our Esau would die for lack of it.

"You're going to kill a rabbit?"

"No, Richard. I'm going to sacrifice it. For science."

"Please don't kill the rabbit."

"Don't cry. You'll scare Jacob and Esau."

He explained to me that this was the best way to objectively test his theory of reincarnation. He would continue feeding Jacob as was considered appropriate for a rabbit. Then, when Esau died, he would allow Jacob to eat as much as he wanted. If Jacob developed a ravenous appetite, we'd know he had absorbed Esau's soul.

"Do rabbits have souls?" I asked.

"Don't ask stupid questions," my father said. "I'm trying to teach you about the natural world. There are people who get paid a lot of money to come up with ideas as good as this one. And sometimes, for the sake of progress, animals have to give their souls to science. This is collectivity. Us and the animals — we're in this together."

When my father fed Jacob, he would take Esau out of the cage and put him on the living room floor, so I could play with him. At first, he would jump around, a little afraid of me, but fairly active nonetheless. After a week, though, he wasn't doing so well. He'd walk tentatively across the floor, and he usually tried to stay close to a wall or the furniture. I watched him sniff around, probably looking for food. I even considered feeding him, but I knew my father would keep an eye out for mutiny. In matters of science, as in those concerning my mother, I was expected to defer to him.

"Richard, are you taking notes?" my father asked me. "You should really consider keeping a diary about this. I would if I was any good at writing. If people start to really believe in reincarnation, we'll be remembered as scientific trailblazers. A diary might be worth a lot one day. It would be like the inheritance I could never give you."

I tried to tune him out and play with Esau. I decided if the rabbit tried to bite me, I wouldn't defend myself. It was hungry and needed my flesh more than I did.

I changed the topic. "I'm really sore," I told my father.

"Well, have you done anything strenuous?"

"No."

"Maybe you're having a growth spurt," he said. "Man, I really do wish I had time to write a diary about this. Something whiz-bang and exciting. But you know I am a slave to my responsibility. I don't have time to spend frivolously; it's all I can do to find time for Jacob and Esau and science. If I had the opportunity today for an education like yours, I wouldn't squander it."

My fifth-grade teacher said I didn't seem my usual self. "Are you sick?" she asked. "Because you can go home if you're sick."

"No," I said. "I don't want to go home. My dad's rabbit is dying." This didn't seem to satisfy her, so I added, "Also, I'm having a growth spurt."

She gave back our most recent religious tests. I'd nearly failed, because I couldn't keep Elijah and Elisha straight. There I was at the top of the paper: Richard Murray, Jr., 75 percent. My father was a very tall man. When I got a low grade, I tried to appreciate the duality — that I was, for now, only three-fourths of him. But I would have to dispose of this paper before going home. After class, I went to the dumpster behind the school, balled up the paper with my name, and threw it away.

＊　　＊　　＊

271

Then Esau died. I wasn't surprised, but I was a little upset — I'd never been party to something's death before. My father spent every spare moment that week watching Jacob. Jacob didn't seem to eat any more than usual. But unfortunately, I'd been very hungry that week, probably because of the growth spurt. I'd spent nearly as much time with Esau as Jacob had — if I ate a lot, I knew what my father would think. I decided I was going to have to fast.

"Don't you want something to eat?" he asked me that night at the table. I shook my head. He looked concerned. "Are you sure?" I nodded. He pondered it for a moment, then said, "Did watching Esau die hurt your appetite?" I shrugged. "Well, you know, Richard," he said, "sometimes things die, and it isn't anybody's fault."

My fast did cause trouble at school. Two days in, as I handed in my homework, my teacher asked me why I was so sluggish. I told her I hadn't slept well the night before.

"Did you forget to say your prayers?" she asked.

"Probably," I said.

The homework had been to write one paragraph on any Biblical event. I chose God's gift of manna and pheasants to the Israelites when they wandered in the desert. Manna and pheasants was a really good present to give hungry people, I had written, which is why Moses was punished when he struck the stone for water. He was only supposed to ask permission, but that wasn't good enough for Moses. No way! He just had to smack it, so then he couldn't go into the Promised Land of Milk and Honey, and, if I had been an Israelite, I wouldn't have let him eat any of my pheasants.

I didn't get a spectacular grade for that assignment either.

✻   ✻   ✻

I broke my fast after four days. By that time, I was so hungry that I ate all the food my father made for dinner, and I still wanted more. My father was pleased.

"I knew it!" he said. "You played with Esau so much, you were more important to him than Jacob. Took a while, though — I guess there's a latency period." Then he got excited. "You know what this means, right, Richard? We're going to be world-famous scientists."

He spent most of the night pondering his discoveries. He didn't talk about it again until that Saturday, when he told me he was going to the public library to research "past advances in the science of reincarnation."

"Also," he said, "I've been thinking about the results and their implications for our situation. Since I don't seem to have become any more like your mother used to be, and neither have you, then if she died, she must have died happy. Really something to think about, huh?" Then he left.

I was furious. I had never been furious before — when my mother disappeared, I was too young to really grasp the idea of fury. But I was just old enough at eleven to understand that he'd starved the rabbit over her. Even then, I knew she wasn't coming back, whether she was dead or not. I didn't know why she left, and I didn't expect to learn; it was enough to know she was gone. I decided something had to be done.

Without any reminders of my mother, I thought, my father might have a better chance of forgetting about her. So I gathered all the photographs of her in the house, and I cut them into long strips with a pair of scissors. By the time I was done, I had what looked like a pile of glossy confetti on the floor, which I swept into the trash.

273

"So why'd you do it?"

"I don't know."

"You know, she's your mother. Not just my wife."

"I know."

"Your mother."

I think my father was too exhausted to be angry. But I could tell he was upset that he didn't have the pictures anymore. Which was why he started taking art classes at the community college — so he could draw her picture before the memory faded.

"We start off just drawing with pens and pencils," he told me, "but if we master that pretty fast, we might move on to charcoal and paint before too long."

"Charcoal, huh?"

"You know," he said, "I always thought charcoal was just for barbecue, but apparently it's also used for making art."

"That's really interesting, Dad."

"I know, isn't it? Also," and his eyes sparkled at this, "this is a little controversial in a small town of this nature, but, if our class shows especially high potential, we may work with nude models." Then he started laughing, and I realized he was joking, trying to ease the tension between us. I snickered a little, to appease him.

I played on the floor with Jacob while my father sketched at the kitchen table. Jacob hopped around, occasionally approaching me, but more often checking out the room for himself. He hadn't spent nearly as much time outside the cage as Esau had — but that seemed to me a fair trade-off for continued life. At the moment, he was sniffing one of the legs on the table.

"How's that rabbit doing?" my father asked.

"He's okay," I said. "I don't like him as much as Esau."

"That's because Esau was selfless, Richard. He knew what he had to do, and he did it. Jacob's lived a comparably sheltered life." He said he had to use the bathroom and stood up and left. While he was gone, I looked at the picture he was drawing.

On the page, shaky lines made a deformed circle of a head, with little ovals for eyes and a lopsided mouth. Still, I could tell it was my mother represented by the thin lines of the lead on paper — my mother as I might have seen her had I just awoken some afternoon, my eyes not yet adjusted to the light.

When my father came back to the room, I said, "Dad, I'm sorry I ruined all the pictures of Mom."

He looked at me, completely quiet, his eyes blank, and nodded to himself. Then he sat back down to the table and continued putting the final touches on his picture.

"I'm not going to take any more art classes," he told me. "It's too expensive. And I've already gotten what I wanted out of it."

The next day at school, we had our weekly art class. Our regular teacher took us to the art teacher's room, and we stayed there for forty-five minutes, learning to draw scenes from the Bible. The teacher often praised my patience and my ability to draw mostly straight lines in crayon.

"What Bible story would you like to draw today?" she asked us.

"Jacob and Esau," I said, before anyone in class could pre-empt me.

"That's not a very interesting story," she said. "Wouldn't you rather do Jacob wrestling with the angel?"

"No," I said. "Jacob and Esau."

"All right, Jacob and Esau," she said. "Let's see what we can do with this."

She turned to the blackboard and drew Esau — a man with long, shaggy hair, dressed in animal fur — standing in the foreground facing backward. In the background, facing Esau, she drew Jacob, fair skinned, clean shaven, stirring a pot on what looked like an electric stove. I thought of Esau saying, "Behold, I am at the point to die: and what profit shall this birthright do to me?" and I thought of Jacob, later, kneeling before his blind father in deception. I thought of their mother, Rebekah, how she must have internalized over so many years that the elder would serve the younger. And I thought of their father, Isaac, tied to a pyre, as his own father raised a sacrificial knife.

"All right, class," our teacher said when she was done. "See if you can draw that."

I looked at the picture. It was simple, and it was uninteresting. But I knew, looking at it, I could not possibly draw Jacob and Esau any way the class might comprehend. Still, this was class — I had to do something. I lifted my pencil. I held it to the page, and I began to draw. I tried not to think of my father. I tried not to think of my mother, maybe reincarnated in my pencil's graphite tube, the image I created, or the sequence that had led me to create it.

– *Allen Butt*

Stargazing

"Somewhere, something incredible is waiting to be known."
– Carl Sagan

It's 9 A.M., a Saturday morning, and my mother would like to do some laundry. When she comes through the kitchen, however, and into the laundry room, the washing machine is full, though there are no clothes inside. Instead, there is me, curled carefully inside the washer, my seven- or eight-year-old body fitting easily inside. Over the glass window I have taped a picture of outer space cut from a magazine. The clipping is curling up at the edges.

Earth, a swirl of ocean and land, of heartbreak and miracle invisible from such heights, hovers far away, in the bright space I am pretending to inhabit. Within the washer, I expand this damp, dark corner into bright, sharp-edged outer space, where I am no one — it is only me, floating in this emptiness, and perhaps I, too, am ethereal, as planets might be imagined, or stars, bits of crushed ice, dust, gas. Perhaps I, too, have no substance. But simultaneously, I am someone — the only solid thing for thousands of miles, a whole universe of insubstantiality — fields of ghostly stars and asteroids, broken pieces of worlds, light spiraling out into nothingness, but still I exist, boldly whole. Only I exist. Here, gravity means nothing. Less than nothing — less than, at this age, love, cleanliness, the art of good manners.

My mother, her hands full of soiled shirts, rags, and undergarments, kicks lamely at the window of the washer. "What are you doing in there?" she asks.

"Nothing," I say.

"Hurry up. My hands are full." Her voice is thin with impatience. I press my hands against the glass and kick, rolling my way out of the rubbery lips of the washing machine to escape back into the sunny glare, the electricity of the summer afternoon. After my disappearance, my mother simply crouches in front of the machine to fill it with clothing. When I returned to the laundry room, the magazine clipping had been peeled from the glass.

We never mention the incident again, but still I wonder what my mother thought, finding me in the recesses of the washer. Did she think me a strange child, maladjusted, that this was another of my strange ideas? Or was she even a little proud of my interest in space — pleased by my apparent interest in the sciences, a field that, in her eyes, granted me a promising future? If it was the latter, she would, in time, be sorely disappointed. My mother liked books, but saw no future in writing them. Pursuing such a career was naïve and impractical when other, more sensible paths could be chosen — a doctor, an engineer, or at the very least, a lawyer. During those years, however, my mother's wishes were temporarily granted in a small way: I wanted to be an astronaut.

I wanted both the anonymity and eminence that outer space promised. I wanted the blackness, the sharp pinpoints of light that, even from a spaceship, were too far away to comprehend. Besides, I almost wanted to preserve their distance, their smallness and delicateness, as they were. Transformed, they would be unconquerably large.

I always find it strange that while space became a long-term obsession, the rest of the world — or at least the Western Hemisphere — became disturbingly uninterested in space. In the late '90s, people everywhere tried to reinvent space, to rekindle dying interest. There were new television series about space, new space missions planned to Mars and Saturn, and new planetarium programs. Nothing worked. As Nicholas Wapshott wrote in the *London Times*, "Ask a seven-year-old boy what he wants to be when he grows up and 'an astronaut' will not be on the list." No one else shared my dream. The space obsession haunting the past four decades as a result of the space race had disappeared: in the '90s, space was out. Public interest could not be revived. As alleged in a 1997 article on Mars, curiosity about space had been lost for the first time since the discovery of the universe. As early as the 1600s, astronomers such as Galileo, Kepler, and Huygens began telescopically monitoring space, studying it intensely. Since then, it had been a subject of great public interest. In the twentieth century, people watched with great enthusiasm the takeoffs of ships speeding into oblivion, have seen in their television sets the Earth itself, insignificant in cold, airless space. The foreign nature of emptiness intrigued the masses. As Fred Langa of *Byte* magazine reminds us, "At the dawn of the era of artificial satellites, it was not unusual to see neighbors clustered on darkened street corners, necks bent upward, trying to catch a glimpse of some newly launched Sputnik or Explorer or Echo."

Somewhere in the late stages of elementary school, my class embarks on a trip to the city planetarium. From the outside, it doesn't look like much: a square, dark-bricked building with a cracked parking lot where the bus drops us off. Inside, there are four or five rows of seats, all on one level, and in the middle of the dome squats a giant projector, already lit up and ready to go, though the lights are still on. Soon, when we settle down and the noise level is down to a loud whispering, a woman stands near the projector, ready to talk to us. After her primary chatter about the majesty of the stars, she settles in to talk about the myths of the constellations. While she describes each, I have trouble seeing the pictures in the stars. None of them seem to form patterns.

"Andromeda was a princess in Greece. Her father gave her to a sea monster who wanted to eat her, but Perseus saved her in the nick of time. He decided to be her husband. Then, the Greek gods put pictures of them up in the sky as a representation of their bravery." She indicates the connect-the-dots picture of Andromeda in the "sky" above us. Many of my peers seem confused by this explanation. I myself do not understand why Andromeda's bravery was celebrated, considering that she did nothing to stop the sea monster from eating her. I raise my hand, waving it frantically in front of the projector in order to be seen in the darkness.

"Yes?"

"So if we do something brave, will we get put up in the stars? By the Greek people?" I am thrilled at the prospect of seeing a picture of myself in the sky, no matter how hard it is to connect the dots. She looks embarrassed, and clears her throat.

"No. Only . . ." This woman seems put off by my question. "Only famous people get put in the sky," she says. "Not regular people." I tell her I do not think that is fair.

"Well, that's the way things are," she says, and continues her lecture on to Canis Major.

As upset as I am by the favoritism displayed by the Greek people who put pictures in the sky, whom I would not learn more about until middle school, I decide I can deal with that. Perhaps, I think, if I grow up to be an astronaut and discover a new planet, as I often imagine doing, I, too, could be considered famous enough to be made into a constellation. This became my goal for the next several years. I became obsessed with the idea of heading into space — of seeing the crystallized rings of Saturn, the craters of the moon, the impact of an asteroid — for myself.

No one quite agrees on the reason for the recently evolved disinterest in outer space. Langa concurs with popular belief: There hasn't been much interest in space since the Cold War because of a lack of motivation. There are no Russians to race to the finish, and there is no moon to dream of. It has become a reality, no longer a hope or a promise but a cold, hard fact: been there, done that. The things that we have not seen already are unreachable. We can launch a mission to Mars, but people cannot journey there. This does not interest us. As for other places — even more distant places, which we cannot see even in our telescopes — those are rendered that much more impossible by our limited technology. We can't even dream of venturing to these places that we cannot see a glimmer of. The otherworldliness of this suggestion is relegated to movies, to fiction. Reality cannot encompass such dreams.

But others find different reasons. Wapshott dismisses the newly budding space station, blaming it for the recent disinterest. People aren't interested in a space station built for observation. What matters to the American people is forward motion — the escape to another world, another galaxy. And, more importantly, the search for extraterrestrial life.

Which leads us to another reason interest in space might be waning: a lack of interest in the kind of "life" that may or may not be out there. Before Kennedy's mission to put man on the moon, people thought of extraterrestrial life as sentient. Green men? Huge robots? They could be anywhere. If we exist, why can't every planet be so lucky to be populated too? The voice of reason had not yet been established, and people expected that if other life existed, it would be big. With recent observations, however, it has become evident that if life does exist elsewhere, it probably isn't much more than bacteria. This is not the stuff of fantasy — worlds the size of toothbrush bristles do not count, in the public's eye, as extraterrestrial life.

As time passed, I began to realize that an astronaut, perhaps, was not the best profession for me. I excelled at reading and writing at school, did well in English and history courses, but was a disaster at algebra. Nor did I enjoy earth science or chemistry. To be an engineer, a pilot, or for that matter, anything useful aboard a spaceship, I would have to be proficient in these fields. I found I enjoyed writing more than any of these things, and enrolled in an arts and humanities–based magnet in high school instead of applying for the science and math magnet at the rival school. Both my parents and my desire to be an astronaut seemed to counteract my talents, the inner workings of my brain. Periodically, I fretted about this.

One of these times was on a trip to Disney World on the eve of my youngest brother's seventh birthday. We stood in line, waiting to get on Space Mountain, and the building that housed it was full of space paraphernalia. The walls were covered with screens displaying asteroids, Saturn, Venus, and Jupiter flying through space. I quickly became transfixed by the possibilities they embodied, was reminded of a trip to space camp years before, when I was given the role of a pilot during the simulation. I remembered the pride I felt, even though I knew it wasn't real. It was still where I belonged. I felt a sudden burst of melancholy.

"I wish I could still be an astronaut."

My father did not turn from the space-covered walls when I spoke. "You can still be one if you major in a science field in college," he answered, unperturbed. On other occasions he seemed more engaged in my future, but now seemed tired of hearing my worries voiced.

"But I like writing, not science," I said, biting my lip. My father shrugged.

"Write grants for NASA." This idea had not occurred to me, but it still did not seem a feasible one. Always on the sidelines, I would have no chance to go into space. I decided I could think about this later. I would find a way to be an astronaut, if that was still what I wanted.

"Do you think it's stupid to still want to be an astronaut in high school?"

My father did not answer. I turned back to the starry walls to watch an asteroid career through space.

There are other possibilities for the current disinterest in space. One reason often cited is that the reality of space exploration becomes uninteresting beside the romanticized, fictionalized accounts Hollywood has provided in the movies, an idea Langa finds comical because of the irony: all of Hollywood's space films depend on technology that is largely the result of the space program's findings. It can be said, however, that much of what we have not yet discovered can be found on the TV screen: planets we cannot dream of traveling to have been colonized in the movies. It is true that we may be more interested in these dreams than the reality we cannot yet reach, may never be able to reach. Perhaps we will never achieve the kind of technology needed to move beyond the Milky Way — the kind of technology people see in the movies.

Perhaps the most interesting reason cited for a deflation of interest in outer space is a very different idea: that the sight of Earth from space scared the American public. Paul Hoffman of *Discover* magazine says, "From the vantage point of space it was clear that Earth's atmosphere was a thin shell, like the skin of an onion, and not a boundless layer that could suffer whatever abuse — whatever pollutants — we foisted on it." Rumors of global warming and air pollution became cold, hard fear. We discovered how small we are, how fleeting our planet could be. Buzz Aldrin himself observed that the Earth looked so small, he could erase it from the universe with only his thumb. According to some, it is this viewpoint that drove Americans from space. They did not want to be reminded of the damage they were causing every day. The vulnerability of our planet was much too frightening; it was better for them not to see such things, but to simply go about their days thinning out our atmosphere spared the guilt they might have felt otherwise. Better to glance upward and see a reassuringly opaque blue sky. Better not to see our thin shell.

The night was strangely warm for Cedar Mountain. Usually, the days were unbearably hot, and the nights were chilly enough to require a sweatshirt, enough to make you want to huddle together, to collapse your arms inside your shirt to stop goose bumps from forming. Tonight, though, we wandered from our cabins in shorts and bare feet, feeling summer, with the grass alive beneath our toes. Our counselor led us to the dock, where we curled on yoga mats to watch the sky. The wood felt young and splintery; the dock had just been built the previous spring. The sky was distantly black, unmarred by fog, clouds, light pollution. A silver-dollar moon hung in the middle.

A sudden streak of orange exploded in the corner of my eye — a firefly, I thought briefly, but no — a shooting star, like a rocket, shot across the sky. It seemed four-dimensional, perhaps, speeding not only through space, but through time, shooting through hours like sheets of glass, changing the course of history in a burst of starshine. It was my first shooting star, and I was twelve years old. Gasps erupted around me as the other girls spotted the same phenomenon. My counselor, Erin, had a conflicted look on her face; one of joy, and of fear. I did not understand this.

I thought about where the star might have landed. I wondered what they are made of, once they strike the atmosphere.

Did they land whole, five-pointed, like sizzling starfish? I guess I must have known that wasn't true, but still, I assumed a shooting star was just that: a star. I later learned that they have nothing to do with stars; they are simply meteoroids burning up as they fall through Earth's atmosphere. If a broken piece survives, it crashes somewhere, becoming slag, a melted rock from space. Despite the romanticism of the fictionalized "falling star," the meteorite is, perhaps, even more amazing — a piece of a broken world, a fractured life, falling to Earth.

– *Victoria Cole*

PUSH
YOU ARE HERE.
www.thisispush.com
Meet the authors.
Read the books.
Tell us what you want to see.
Submit your own words.
Read the words of others.
this is PUSH.
PUSHWEB

this is teen

Want to find more **books, authors, and readers to connect with?**

Interact with friends and favorite authors, participate in weekly author Q&As, check out event listings, try the book finder, and more!

**Join the new social experience at
www.facebook.com/thisisteen**